A Whiskey Jack
in a
Murder of Crows

Sam Knight

Print Edition 2014
Knight Writing Press
KnightWritingPress@gmail.com

Cover design by Lance Card

Author Bio Photo by Stacey Vowel

First Publication January 2014

ISBN-10: 1628690186
ISBN-13: 978-1-62869-018-7

DEDICATION

To my wife, who actually liked my story.

ACKNOWLEDGMENTS

Without the love and support of my family—my children who let me ignore them for hours at a time to write, my wife who supports me in my follies, and my parents and grandparents who taught me to love to read and who have always supported me in everything—this book would never have existed.

Thank you, David Boop, for pulling me into your writer's group and showing me how things really work.

Thank you, Peter Wacks, for the right words of encouragement at the right time. They made all the difference.

Tony and Renee Allen, and Kris Sams. Thank you for being great beta readers, idea founts, and moral support.

Christopher Salas, without you, I would have just spun in the wind and likely never published. Thank you.

Thanks to Tonya, John, and Fantastic Journeys Publishing for being supportive and lending a guiding hand.

And a special thank you to Keith J. Olexa for editing the heck out of this story, and to Jessyca Hogue for finding my mistakes.

I have also had some helping hands along the way, people who have offered support, encouragement, and instruction. If you are on this list, I have a reason for putting you here that was important to me, even if you don't know what it is. Thank you.

Mario Acevedo
Quincy J. Allen
Kevin J. Anderson
J. A. Campbell
Guy Anthony DeMarco
Betsy Dornbusch
Alan and Rebecca Lickiss
Rebecca Moesta
Pam Nihiser
Phyllis Parrington
Katheryn Renta
Samantha Shu
Stacey Vowell
David and Diann Wacks

There are always more names I could add, and I am sure I have missed some. If I have missed you, I am sorry. Please know that I am grateful.

A Whiskey Jack in a Murder of Crows

ONE

The deer's back appeared broken and her eyes were wide and filmy. Her tongue stuck out of the side of her mouth, ringed with dried foam and blood. Jack Tabor imagined the small doe died of thirst mere inches from the water gently lapping next to her head. Had she dragged herself all the way here, inching her life away as she tried to escape the pain of her injuries?

How long does it take to die? The question rippled through his mind, unbidden, as it had so often since he had been lying in his own pool of blood, six months ago.

Limping along the side of the road this morning should have been good therapy, if only the walk could have quieted his mind as well.

He grimaced with each step, teeth gritting slightly. Six months ago, he had thought he would never walk again, thought the hand holding the cane would never work again, so he didn't begrudge the pain. He was old friends with the pain.

He forced himself to walk on past the doe.

Although this was his first view of Rainbow Lake in the daylight, the first time he had walked this road along the shore, the rubber tip of his cane was already beginning to show signs of wear from the gravel chewing at it every time he put his weight down.

The sun coming over the green manicured mountains of Rainbow County reflected off the lake and made him squint. Neat rows of grapevines, the hallmark of California's wine country, latticed the sides of the mountains surrounding the lake. The tidy green rows were sullied by the rundown houses and trailer parks lining the valley highway.

He could feel the dead eyes of the doe behind him trying to get his attention.

How long does it take to die?
The sound of popping gravel caught his attention. He looked up to see an old Ford truck driving towards him. The driver raised two fingers off the steering wheel in greeting as he passed. Jack nodded back solemnly. So far, the people out here seemed nice. Maybe he could get used to a small town. Maybe he would even want to stay here—as much as he would want to stay anywhere.

He tried to admire the sunlight playing on the fog bank floating in the center of the lake like a misty island. Even the stillness of the water and the birds lazily circling the mist couldn't calm his soul.

How long does it take to die?
He turned around and headed back to his uncle's farm. Once these thoughts started, they cascaded uncontrollably.

He avoided looking at the doe again, as he walked by, but the doe's eyes were calling to him, pleading.

He felt his knees buckle as he looked into her pleading eyes once again. He couldn't pull his gaze away. They were so much like *her* eyes; pleading.

His hand shook violently on the cane.

Please, Daddy, help me...

TWO

Toni looked up just in time to see the man topple over. "Damn!" she muttered to herself. *Another damn drunk or meth-head.*

She hurried into her open garage and grabbed the folded up wheelchair her mother had used for so long. She popped the wheelchair open with the easy expertise of long practice and hurried down the driveway as fast as her old legs would let her. Although she had her cellphone in her pocket, she never would have called 911. Too many of the people around here would resent the involvement of the authorities more than no help at all.

When she reached him, his face was ashen and his eyes were glazed. Toni kneeled carefully next to him. Ignoring the gravel that stabbed into her kneecaps, she was mindful of the pain in her old back and hips.

His face was clammy to her touch and she worried for a moment if he had overdosed on something.

This man was clean-shaven, well groomed, and wearing clean clothes. He was not the typical person who walked up and down the roads around this lake with a thumb sticking out for a ride. Likely, he was a tourist, but he was a long walk from the nearest resort. Although he looked young, in his thirties, she thought maybe he had suffered a heart attack.

He was breathing and that meant his heart was still working, so she tried talking gently to him, as she had her mother so many times for so many years

"There, there. You're going to be all right. I'm right here to help." She stroked his dark hair gently and tried to soothe him and call him back to this world. She lifted his head up and brushed some of the gravel off his face.

3

His eyes fluttered and he gasped deeply as if he had been under water. Color began returning to his cheeks. "There you go." She smiled down at him. His brown eyes met hers and then began searching, trying to figure out where he was and what had happened. "You're going to be all right. You just had a bad spell there for a minute." She crooned softly to him.

He tried to say something, but his voice was dry and choked in his throat. He licked his lips, looking up into Toni's face anxiously.

"I saw you fall, but that's about all I can say. Too much exertion, maybe? You have a heart condition?" she asked him gently.

He took a couple of deep breaths and realized where he was and what had happened. His ears started to burn a bright red.

"No. No. I'm okay," he smiled weakly at her. "No heart conditions. Not yet, anyway. I just fainted."

Toni chuckled lightly. "You usually faint?"

"No. Maybe. I didn't used to." He started to raise himself up. Toni put her hands under his head and helped him.

"I'm okay, now. Thank you," he said trying to step away from her.

"Maybe you should just take a minute and make sure." She used her sleeve to knock gravel and goat-head stickers from the back of his shirt, and then tried to guide him into the wheelchair as he stumbled slightly.

"Really, I'm fine," he protested, leaning heavily on his cane.

"Let's just take it one minute at a time, shall we?" Toni suggested. "The chair is already here, might as well make use of it to catch your breath."

He swooned again. Toni expertly caught him and sat him into the wheelchair. When his eyes came back into focus, he tried to stand up again, but she gently held him in place and laid his cane across his lap.

"Give it a minute. Did you hit your head when you fell?" She started pushing the chair back towards her house while he tested the back of his head with his fingers.

The sun was up and shining on them now. Their long shadows stretched out before them, leading the way.

"I don't think so," he answered finally, dropping his hands. "I'm all right. Let me up."

4

Toni ignored him. "Where are you visiting from?"

"I just moved here. Got in last night." His voice was still shaky and hoarse.

"Welcome to Hell." She didn't sound like she was joking. She pushed him into her empty garage and absently kicked the wheel brake into place.

"I've been to Hell," he answered after a long moment, "and this isn't it. Not by a far cry."

Toni snorted. "You just got in yesterday. You're still blinded by the paving stones made out of good intentions."

"Could be," he nodded.

She walked around to the front of the wheelchair and looked hard at him. "Post-traumatic stress disorder?" she finally asked.

His eyes met hers and he slowly nodded his head.

"Come on, I'll buy you a drink."

Using his cane, he rose up out of the wheelchair. "What makes you think I drink?"

"Never met anyone with PTSD who didn't at least want one. Come to think of it, I never met anyone with PTSD who didn't drink."

"Maybe today's the day."

"Is it?"

He stood up to his full height, a head taller than the woman. "Not yet. Maybe you'll meet someone like that later. Whatcha buying?"

"Depends on what you like. I got it all."

THREE

Jack leaned heavily on his cane as he followed the old woman across her backyard. She had a grandmother's figure and waddled as she headed toward a larger building thirty yards distant. As they drew near, Jack realized the building was a bar. The building faced the highway that paralleled the small county road he had been walking.

The bar didn't look like much from the outside. White paint was peeling away in places, showing the building had once been blue and possibly peach colored in the past. A large, splintery indentation, from where a car had hit the building, needed repair.

As he rounded the corner, he spotted the sign at the edge of the parking lot: Bubba's Bar. He grunted in amusement. The place certainly looked like a Bubba's Bar.

Across the highway, at the base of the green mountains, sat a trailer park full of permanently parked mobile homes. Each had a satellite dish pointed towards the southern sky, and was separated by a scraggly oak tree. Broken cars, broken chairs, and broken dreams littered the area.

A lean dog charged aggressively out into the middle of the highway to bark at Jack and the old lady. Two or three unseen dogs somewhere in the poverty encampment took up the baying. Gruff cursing came from one of the trailers. Intended to quiet the noise, Jack found it more offensive than the dogs.

Shaking his head, Jack followed the woman through a side door into the bar. The door led into a rundown kitchen area that failed to brighten as the florescent lights flickered to life.

"Pardon the mess. I gave myself the day off." The old woman waved one hand nonchalantly and continued through a swinging door. The tip of Jack's cane squelched and slipped on something greasy. Pushing open the door with his elbow so he didn't have to touch the smears, he followed her into the bar proper.

The rich redwood walls and long, polished walnut bar surprised him after the bleak kitchen. The room was warm and welcoming; this place had seen a lot of laughter. Dim faux storm lanterns hung from the ceiling, their orange colored bulbs casting ruddy reflections on the dark woods of tables and the floor. The morning light filtered through old single-paned windows like rays from heaven.

Jack eased himself onto a stool and leaned his cane up against the bar as the woman lifted the bar's pass-through countertop and shuffled through towards the alcohols.

"What'll it be?" she asked as she flicked on a switch, illuminating rows of bottles stacked in front of the bar mirror.

"Whiskey." Jack whispered harshly. He swallowed to clear his throat.

"That's a little vague." She grabbed a bottle of Crown Royale and poured the amber liquid into a glass big enough to be a bowl. She stopped just short of overflowing the glass. "What's your name?" she asked as she filled a second one the same way.

"Jack."

She turned around and thunked one of the glasses onto the bar in front of him, carelessly sloshing the contents. Turning back, she picked up the second glass for herself.

"To your health." She drained half the glass and sat it next to his. She reached down behind the bar and came up with a pack of cigarettes and a Zippo. She gave him a sideways look over the lighter as she lit up with its distinctive metallic clink-and-grind noise. Her grandmotherly face shone in the light of the flame and her eyes twinkled brightly, daring him to say something. "Not business hours. Goddamn no-smoking laws don't apply yet. Don't gimme any shit. I just scraped your ass off the middle of the street."

Jack picked up his glass and toasted her in return. "To *your* health." He drained half of the glass and set it next to hers.

"Need a refill?"

Jack chuckled at her. "It's a long walk back, and I'm not too steady to begin with."

"Good man." She came around the bar and sat on the stool next to him. She flipped ashes in the general direction of a trashcan at the end of the bar and picked up her glass again. "I hate to see someone who has problems with their liquor."

She sipped from her glass as she watched him. "Let's see. You just moved here, huh? Welfare?" She blew smoke out of the side of her mouth.

"What makes you say that?"

"People come here for one of five reasons." She began ticking the reasons off on the liver-spotted hand holding the cigarette, starting with her pinky. "Fishing vacation; but you said you moved here." She held up her ring finger. "To retire; but you're too young for that unless you are really rich," she looked him up and down and nodded at his cane, "and you don't strike me as that lucky."

Jack smiled.

"To invest in a winery and get rich, but you don't strike me as that lucky, either. Or that stupid. No one ever seems to pull that one off."

She took a long drag of the cigarette and blew it out up into the air.

"To get healed, which you certainly seem to qualify for, but the 'healing springs' resort burned down over fifty years ago." She waved the hand with the glass in it through the air. "And last, but most common, because welfare money goes a lot further in this county than any other in California, and welfare money in California is generally better than anywhere else."

She took another long drag, emptied her drink in a quick gulp, and put the butt out in the bottom of the glass. "So I picked welfare. I know you didn't move out here to follow a job, 'cause there ain't any."

"Maybe I'm a vet and living off my disability."

"Maybe that don't pay shit and the closest VA is four hours away in San Francisco. Vets don't live here unless they came from here."

Jack nodded solemnly but didn't say anything.

Toni got up and went around the counter, grabbed the bottle of Crown and a new glass. She filled her new glass halfway. "More whiskey, Jack?"

Jack shook his head and picked up his still half-full glass.

"Whiskey Jack. I like the sound of that. Fits you. Just like the little bird, come flying in out of nowhere, all friendly-like, share a little of whatever I got, then fly away again. I used to love those birds when I was a kid."

"My grandpa called those camp robbers."

"Ain't stealing if it was given to you."

Jack looked around the room and spotted what appeared to be the original 'Bubba's Bar' sign on a far wall. "I assume that you are not Bubba."

"It's my bar, but Bubba's been dead for, oh eighty years now. He was my grandma's second husband. Her first husband owned a lumber mill and thousands of acres of land, hence all the nice wood here. But Bubba was a Southern boy with little taste for work, and he whittled it all down to this bar. Thought it would be the biggest thing ever with the repeal of Prohibition. Then he drank hisself to death and left my grandma to run it with a three-year old daughter."

Jack wasn't sure how to respond, so he let the silence hang in the air.

"You don't talk much, do you, Whiskey Jack? Well, my name's Toni, and I've spent my whole life behind this bar. I know everyone who's fucked everyone in this God-forsaken county for damn near sixty years, so when I tell you welcome to Hell, you better believe me. I know this county. The people here are either trying to leave, can't leave, or waiting to die."

"I'm sorry you feel that way." Jack cleared his throat nervously and downed the rest of his drink, concerned his welcome was wearing thin.

"Don't be. It ain't all bad. Can't be, or they wouldn't have named it Rainbow Valley. Rainbow Lake, Rainbow County, Rainbow City. Fucking rainbows everywhere. At least the Board of Tourism makes money selling bumper stickers to all those people who come up from San Francisco for the Rainbow fucking Festival."

Jack laughed. "I didn't realize it was that kind of a festival."

"Wasn't. Up until around 1980 or so. Then San Francisco went ape shit over rainbows. Now it's a goddamn fuck-fest every year. I remember when it was just a county fair and the only Rainbows were the girls from the Masonic Lodge. You a Mason?"

"No." He made to stand.

"You need help getting back? I could arrange a ride for you."

"That is very kind of you, Toni. You have been very helpful and generous, but I think I can make it back on my own."

Toni watched him carefully get up and balance himself with his cane. "You never did say why you moved here. You gonna?"

Jack stopped and looked at her with a bemused smile. "You're pretty forward, aren't you?"

"And you're pretty judgmental, for someone who's had four fingers of whiskey before the cock finishes crowing."

Jack nodded. "That I am. It's a bad habit I'm trying to break. I apologize for my lack of reciprocation of your hospitality."

"Big words confuse me." She pulled out another cigarette and pointedly turned back to face the bar.

Jack hesitated for a moment, then moved back to the barstool and sat again. "My uncle passed away. He left me his place out here, and I've got no place better to be."

"I'm sorry to hear about your uncle."

"Thank you."

Toni took a long pull off her cigarette and stared at herself in the mirror behind the bar. Jack got the impression she had won that staring contest before.

"You Bobby Ratchet's nephew?" she asked.

"That's right. You knew him?"

Toni leaned her head back and blew another long pillar of smoke up into the air before turning to look at Jack.

"I caught the family resemblance. I hope you brought boots with you, Whiskey Jack, 'cause I'm afraid you just stepped into a big ol' steaming pile of shit."

Toni went around the backside of the bar again. This time she brought the bottle of Crown back with her. Instead of filling her glass though, she filled Jack's.

"Don't worry. I'll get you a ride. Meanwhile, we have a little talking to do, and you're gonna want this." She pushed the glass towards him. "Even if it's just to look at. Unless you smoke?" She offered her pack of cigarettes to him.

He waved them away. "No thanks. I don't."

"You may change your mind here in about two minutes." She sat the pack on the bar. "First, let me say I'm sorry about your family." Her demeanor softened. "Bobby told me about the shooting, or at least what he knew of it."

At the mention of it, Jack's chest tightened and he fought to remain in control, to keep the feelings from overwhelming him again. *How long does it take to die?*

11

If Toni noticed Jack's reaction, she didn't show it. "He came in pretty shook up after he heard about your wife and little girl. Needed a beer to calm his nerves. He already had his flight reservation to go see you in the hospital, but he couldn't get one soon enough to suit him." She didn't look at Jack. Her eyes flitted along the rows of bottles lit by the lights behind the bar. "That was the last time I saw him."

She lit another cigarette and pointedly crushed out the shorter one before turning to look at Jack.

"I liked your uncle. He was good people. That's why I feel I have to tell you this." Her eyes flicked around the room as if she was making sure they were alone. She lowered her voice to a whisper. "I'm pretty sure Bobby was murdered."

"My uncle died of a heart attack." Jack said levelly.

She ignored his glance.

"Yeah, that's what everyone heard. But listen to me for a minute. Bobby lived here for what? A year and a half?" She rubbed at her nose absently.

"Less, I think."

"He didn't have no one else around here. And you were his only family. He talked about you all the time." She glanced at him, gauging his reaction.

Jack nodded.

"Bobby took to walking down here most nights and having a beer and dinner. Needless to say, I got to know him a bit. I ain't exactly shy, in case you didn't notice. After a while, we started having pretty good talks about things, and he opened up about some things that were bothering him. I guess he got the land from a brother-in-law?"

Jack nodded. "He was the last relative of his sister's husband, by relation or marriage."

"And you're Bobby's last relative?" She grunted to herself, "You're the end of the line. I'd watch my back real careful, if I was you."

Jack grimaced, "I try."

"Two weeks before he died, Bobby told me he thought his brother-in-law had been murdered. I just kinda rolled my eyes at him."

"But you believe it now?"

She waved a hand dismissively. "He said someone had been

messing around on his property. People around here always mess around on other people's properties. If not to steal something, then to find a quiet place to get high, or get laid. It's a typical thing here, but Bobby insisted this was different.

"He claimed it was like someone was watching him, or looking for something. He couldn't prove anything. Said it was little things like three or four cigarette butts under a tree, or the barn door lock being on backwards. I figured he was just getting old. It was just him rattling around that huge farm, after all." She took a last drag off her cigarette and added it to the growing pile in the glass. It hissed as the remaining liquid put out the ember.

Toni sighed deeply, steeling herself. She eyed Jack, as if reassuring herself she should confide in him, before she continued. "I had a friend, Judy, who worked at the funeral home." She picked up her other glass and sipped her whiskey. "Rainbow fucking Funeral Home," she muttered.

"I had introduced Judy to Bobby a while back, so when his body came through she recognized him right off. And she's seen enough to know that things weren't right."

"What kind of things?"

"Things like someone who has money getting the quick and quiet cremation service usually reserved for transients and indigents." She paused and looked at him askew. "Things like bruises around his throat. Scrapes and cuts on his face."

Jack stared at her for a moment. "They said they found him out on the property where he'd had a heart attack and fallen into a pile of rocks. All of the bruises and scrapes could easily have come from that."

"They could. And that's what everyone was told they were from. The officials didn't agree with Judy that the bruises had the shape of a shirt cuff and buttons. Just like as if someone had put him in a choke hold." She eyed Jack hard, her mouth a grim line. "And the police didn't agree that a hole in the back of Bobby's skull the size of your fist was unusual!" Her voice quieted. "But they weren't here the day before Bobby died. When Bobby told me he thought he figured out who was watchin' him and why."

Jack shuddered. "Did he say who?"

Toni shook her head. "Didn't say why, neither. Just said he didn't want to point no fingers 'til he could prove it."

They sat in silence for a long moment as she finished her

cigarette. "That was the day before he found out the death of your wife and daughter. He had a rough day, that day. It showed on his face. He was a haunted man and he didn't want to talk much, I suppose. I reckon I was one of the last ones to see him alive. Spent a good bit of time wondering if there was anything I could have done. At least I did, 'til Judy ..."

"Judy seen a lot of dead people over the years, and she told me she was positive what happened to him. Made me wish I'd believed him more, wonder if I could have helped. But I only kinda believed her, you know? Figured she maybe had a little thing for Bobby. Maybe she was seeing somethin' that wasn't there. Then Judy turned up dead." She dropped her eyes to the floor. "Now I figure the only thing I might've done is delay his murder or get kilt myself.

"If only I woulda listened to them. They needed my help, and I didn't listen ..." Toni's voice trailed off into her thoughts.

Daddy?

His daughter's words came again.

How long does it take to die?

Jack's vision blurred. His wife. His daughter. And now his uncle?

Jack swooned on the stool. Toni caught him by the arm and balanced him so he wouldn't fall. "Damn it." She muttered.

14

FOUR

Jack waved a final thank you to the battered car as it turned around. Two quick honks floated back to him as it headed back to the highway. Jack watched the departing car for a moment. He leaned on the cane to steady himself and took a deep breath of the fresh air.

The old porch floorboards creaked under his weight as he looked out into the walnut orchard surrounding the old three-story Victorian style house. The thick foliage of the trees cast deep shadows, making the orchard a cavernous, immaculately groomed forest.

Jack had spent several hours on the phone months ago arranging caretakers for the property. They had been expensive, but from the look of things they had earned their pay.

Jack could see why his uncle had moved here when he inherited the property. It was a dream-come-true for anyone who had ever wanted to be a farmer. His uncle had been doing most of the work himself, using the equipment he had inherited with the farm, but sitting in a car was still difficult for Jack; trying to stay on a tractor would be laughable at best.

Jack was feeling better now. The second glass of whiskey had worked its way through his system and he couldn't feel its effects anymore. When he was still giddy from the whiskey, he had promised Toni he would come back for dinner, but he was beginning to regret it.

The long talk with her had been less than therapeutic. He needed to quiet himself, to regain control of his emotions and his life. He felt foolish for letting her story get to him, for letting his emotions and fears get the better of him. Why would anyone murder his uncle? He had been told there was no break-in and nothing was stolen. There was no possible reason. It had been a heart attack and that was that. Surely, Judy's death was coincidental and Toni was reading too much into it. People die all the time, and drowning while kayaking alone on the lake at sunrise, as Judy had, was not unheard of.

He looked back to the house. The old wooden porch swing called invitingly to his stiff body. It would be nice to sit there, look out into the orchard for a while, and recompose himself.

Taking a deep breath, he stepped off the porch and down into the driveway. He knew if he stopped pushing his body, stopped using it and started sitting on the porch to watch the world go by, he would lose all he had regained. He would be relegated to official porch sitter and world watcher. That was *not* why he had survived.

He balanced himself and took his weight off his cane. He stretched his arms wide, arched his back as best as he could, and stretched his whole body. He woke up all the muscles, willing everything to work again.

He looked up at the blue sky above the green of the trees, awed by the contrast. There was not a cloud in the sky.

"Señor Tabor?"

Jack jumped. Recovering his balance, he turned to face the speaker.

"Si?" Jack easily fell into speaking Spanish. "Señor Torres?" He asked, assuming this was the man he had put in charge of the property's upkeep.

"It is nice to finally meet you." The stocky man spoke in English. He held out a calloused and sun-browned hand to Jack, who shook it firmly. "I was surprised when I got the message that you would be arriving, I was under the impression that ... Well, that you wouldn't be traveling much."

"You had the right impression." Jack smiled and cocked his head. "I thought you didn't speak English." He had spoken with Miguel Torres on the phone more than once while confined to a hospital bed. The fact that the conversations had been in Spanish hadn't bothered Jack. After years of working with the criminal justice system, Spanish had become a second language to him.

"I thought you didn't speak English!" Miguel laughed. "You always spoke Spanish when you called me."

"Everyone who recommended you spoke Spanish, so I just assumed. You have done a wonderful job here." Jack gestured wide with his arm.

"Not me. This old man just struts and yells at the boys to keep his place in the hen house. Can I show you around?"

"Please."

Miguel walked slowly as he led Jack to the barn, enjoying the conversation rather than making sure Jack could keep up. Jack was impressed with the size of the farm, and found the irony of the name, The Gardner's Patch, amusing. Miguel pointed out that the buildings on the far side of the highway were all part of the ranch. Uncle Bobby had clearly been out of his league to try to run the place by himself. Jack said as much to Miguel.

Miguel nodded slowly as he opened up a doublewide door on one of the three barns on the lakeside of the highway. "One man can run this place, but it is hard work. He would have had to take care of everything himself until harvest season and then scramble like hell to find enough workers to help him. Workers he could trust. That is the hardest part around here."

He walked over to an army green ATV that looked like a golf cart with six wheels and offered Jack the keys.

Jack waved them off. "I think I'll just sightsee today." He moved to the passenger side and carefully worked himself in one leg at a time, stuffing his cane between the seats.

"Did you know the Gardners? The people who owned the land before my uncle?"

"Sure. Most everyone in Rainbow County knew them. Jim Gardner was a major presence locally. Up until twenty years ago this was still a very small rural area, everyone knew everyone. I remember when they used to have the Rainbow Festival here. They did that for, oh, five or six years. Some kind of argument over the county fairgrounds, if I remember right." Miguel started the vehicle and grabbed the two levers it had in place of a steering wheel. The ATV lurched forward, and they were out of the garage and into the sun.

"In fact, I remember coming here one Easter when I was just married. They had hidden plastic eggs with money in them all through the orchard." He waved toward the trees. "They weren't walnut trees back then, they were apple. One of the kids found an egg with fifty dollars in it. That was a lot of money back then." He looked at Jack.

"The Gardners did a lot for this county. You'll find their name all over it: the park, the senior center, the fairgrounds, the streets." He pulled one lever back and pushed the other forward to turn onto a well-worn dirt road that circled the orchard.

"What happened to them?" Jack asked over the sound of crunching gravel.

"I heard his wife died from a stroke or something, long time in the hospital, that kind of thing. He died a couple of years back. Tractor accident." They reached the end of the orchard and the road ended into the main highway.

"Hold on." Miguel said as he got out and opened an aluminum gate attached to the rickety barbed wire fence running along the highway. He got back in and drove through before getting out again and shutting the gate behind him. He repeated the whole ritual with the gate on the other side of the highway.

"Too many people pull into open roads to allow the gates to be left open, this limits our liability," he explained. "*Your* liability." He nodded at Jack. "Plus, about five years ago there was a rash of walnut tree thefts."

Jack laughed, enjoying the ride, the sun, and the company. It had been a long time since he had really enjoyed anything.

"I'm serious," Miguel told him. "The bottom of the walnut trees, the burl, is very valuable. It is used for making veneer. Someone stole a bunch of trees in the middle of the night from various orchards."

"Really?"

Miguel nodded his head. "The gates won't stop someone like that, of course, but it stops them from driving in and scouting it out during the day."

Jack shook his head in disbelief. "That's just not right. I imagine people get really upset when their *trees* get stolen. I mean it took years to grow it big enough to produce fruit and then …" Jack's voice faded.

"Yeah, pretty messed up. Most farmers roll with it, though. It's the water thing that really pisses them off."

"What water thing?"

Miguel deftly avoided a rock as he answered. "A hundred years ago, the neighboring county bought the water rights to the lake. Really screwed a lot of farmers but the county officials were kind of in on it at the time and lined their pockets pretty well, so they didn't care. As a result, most of the farmers around here have to buy their water from the other county, even though it is already right here and upstream from the ones who own it."

Jack's eyebrows furrowed. "I seem to remember that California law grants riparian rights to the land owner adjacent to a body of water."

Miguel laughed. "It does. But those people lining their pockets a hundred years ago knew what they were doing! The law says that the water can only go the parcel that is adjacent to the water, and that it can only go to the smallest parcel that *ever* existed, not the one that currently exists. So if you buy a bunch of land and consolidate it into one parcel, you can't suddenly water all of that land with the water, you're still stuck only being able to water the small one. And these guys who bought the water rights to the lake went around most of the lake and bought up very small strips of land. Only a very few already established farms with smart owners, like this one, didn't get permanently screwed."

"So all of the farms around here have to buy their water?"

"Most of them, yeah. Unless they have springs up on the mountains, like this one."

"So this one has both? I guess this one is a pretty lucky one to have!"

They scooted around a cluster of buildings as large as a city block and Miguel pointed out where the old fruit drier was housed and where the walnuts and almonds used to be air dried. "Modernization has changed all of that now. Now we just sell the nuts and fruit and let the companies worry about what to do with them." He glanced at Jack, "I'm glad, actually. Less work for us, and we don't have to update all the equipment all of the time. I hear that the almonds all have to be pasteurized now." He shook his head. "Too damn many laws about too damn many stupid things to keep up with."

Jack pondered the idea that there might be more to the whole farming thing than he had ever imagined as they followed the dirt road. It twisted and turned its way up the side of a small mountain covered in dried grass, scrub oak, and occasional oak trees.

"What kind of tree is that with the red peeling bark?" Jack

asked over the sound of the gravel and the motor.

Miguel followed Jack's outstretched finger. "Madrone. The Indians used to chew the berries or make tea out of them or something. Tastes like hell. Don't ever try it. Makes pretty good firewood though."

At a switchback, Jack could see out over the lake and back down to the house and barns where they had started. The sun was bright and hot, making the blue water and the green trees below seem like a beckoning oasis surrounded by the brown mountains. The farm below sprawled around the contour of the lake, the highway splitting it in two. He really could not imagine his uncle trying to take care of it all alone.

"Did the Gardners have any children?" Jack asked.

Miguel pushed and pulled levers to steer around another switchback. "Three. I went to school with the youngest. William. Billy, we called him. He died up here a bit further." He nodded up the hill. "Slipped and fell a hundred feet off the rocks, broke his neck. His sister, Charlotte, died in a car accident when she was seventeen. Rumor went around that it was drugs and alcohol. And the oldest, James Jr., was killed in 'Nam."

Jack let that hang in the air for a while. The ATV topped a hill that overlooked a smaller valley filled with row after row of grape vines. Miguel stopped to take in the view. Jack whistled.

"How big is this place?" Jack knew it was over ten thousand acres, but knowing that and being in it were two very different things.

"Big. This is the real moneymaker here. Looks to be a good harvest coming in, too." He waved an arm expansively at the neatly groomed rows. "These are all dry-grown. That means we don't water them. It makes for a much smaller grape, but a much more intense flavor. In the past, Mr. Gardner actually had wineries bidding on his harvest. If I had to guess, I would say this is where the majority of his wealth came from.

"In recent years, lots of people have planted vineyards so the supply has gone way up and the price way down, but I am sure we will be able to find a buyer for these." Miguel drove down to the nearest plants and stopped. He reached out and gently caressed a small cluster of purple grapes in his large calloused hand.

"These will be ready for harvest in a couple of weeks. I need to get my act together and find a buyer." He gave Jack a 'you know how it is' look.

"What if we don't find one?"

"Then there is no point in wasting the time and money to pick the grapes."

Jack thought momentarily. "Can we make our own wine?"

Miguel hesitated for a moment before answering. "Of course. But without permits and licensing, we couldn't sell it. Not to mention we would need a winemaker to blend the wine and make it drinkable." He pulled off his straw cowboy hat and anxiously ran his fingers through his hair.

Jack waited a moment and then pressed Miguel. "What's on your mind?"

Miguel shut off the motor. They both gazed out at the yellowed mountains around the valley for a long moment before Miguel spoke. "My son has been begging me to ask to you about something ever since you hired me. My son, he ... My son went to school to be a vintner, and this," he again waved his arm expansively, "is a winemaker's dream. My son would like to ask you if he could make your wine."

"Thanks for the tour." Jack grunted as he wormed his way out of the seat of the ATV. The inside of the garage was hot and smelled of exhaust.

"We just scratched the surface. I still haven't gone all the way around the property myself." Miguel slipped out of his seat with ease. "I sent a team of guys around to check the fences when you first hired me on, but to be honest they didn't bother with the old property line fence, just the ones around the highway. And the vineyard to keep the deer out. They'll eat the hell out of a grape vine. And roses." He came around and offered Jack a hand, which was gratefully accepted.

"When I was a kid, I remember a fantastic rose garden behind the main house over there. There are still a few bushes, but nothing like it was. I am sure the deer ate them all."

"What about that huge pumpkin patch? I didn't see any fence around that. Deer don't like those?" Jack brushed dust off his pants and stood up straight, stretching his sore back.

21

"You noticed the pumpkins, huh?" Miguel looked a little sheepish.

"They were hard to miss. That is the biggest pumpkin patch I have ever seen."

"I, uh …" Miguel took off his hat again and rubbed the back of his neck nervously. "I really didn't expect to see you come out here this year—or ever, to be honest."

Jack nodded in understanding. He had still been an invalid in a hospital bed when he hired Miguel to keep up the farm.

"When I was a kid they had a harvest festival out here in the fall and I was hoping to do that this year." Miguel toed at the dirt boyishly.

Jack reached out and gently slapped Miguel's shoulder. "When I hired you and told you to run this place as you saw fit, I meant it. I thought that you understood that was why your salary is a percentage of profits."

Miguel looked up gratefully from where his boot had worn a small trench in the dust. He nodded, "I know. I just felt like I might have been overstepping my bounds planning a festival on the property, especially with you living here now."

Jack smiled. "There's nothing I'd like more than to see a bunch of kids out here picking pumpkins for Halloween. Can we afford to give them away? How much did it cost to grow them?"

Miguel laughed. "If we sell about half of them to the local market we can give the rest away for free and still come out ahead."

Visions of a harvest festival full of kids filled Jack's imagination. His family would love it.

Jack's stomach knotted and he felt sick. His family *would have* loved it. He took a deep breath and tried to push the queasiness away.

"Are you okay, Señor Tabor?" asked Miguel.

Jack waved him off.

"Call me Jack. I'm fine. I just …" He took a deep breath and blew out as much of the pain as would go. He smiled weakly and retrieved his cane from the ATV. "I just move a little slow these days. Hey," Jack changed the subject. "Any of your guys reported seeing anyone doing anything on the property?"

"You mean like stealing walnut trees?" Miguel smiled again.

"No," Jack chuckled. He was thinking of what Toni had said.

"There's always something out here. Someone smoking weed,

shooting up, getting drunk. It's a hazard of being just off the highway on the edge of a little town. The cops like to use the driveway to sit and wait for speeders. I kind of like that. Keeps the riff raff away."

Jack nodded. That matched what Toni had said about the people out here. He looked out across the farm buildings. "Which of these is the winery your son is going to help us start up?"

FIVE

The old wood floor creaked under Jack's weight as he put his empty suitcase into the closet and shut the door. Each step had its own unique sound as the floorboards shifted and sprung. Jack listened closely to each step he took, enjoying the sound. It was as if the house was glad to have his company and was happily chatting absentmindedly to him.

He turned around and admired the room he had chosen. It was one of the smaller bedrooms. The single-sized bed was framed by a nightstand and a small wooden chair. The light streaming through the thin, yellowish curtains shone upon an antique wooden dresser. An oval-shaped rug, an expensive indulgence once intended to be the centerpiece of the room, covered the floor at the foot of the bed. A basic room, to be sure, but comfortable and unimposing.

His midnight arrival and the pain from traveling all day had not been conducive to exploring the house. He had slept on the couch his first night in the house, rather than braving the stairs, a good decision, it seemed, now that he had discovered none of the upstairs lights worked.

The only thing he had done upon his arrival was find a place to hang the spy-camera clock his attorney had given him with the insistence he used it. He felt silly setting up a spy camera, but his attorney's paranoid advice had saved his life twice already. Not that a camera would save his life, but at least it could reveal his killer should the next attempt be successful.

Leif Postumaus was his lawyer's name, a name which, when said aloud, became 'leave posthumous'. Leif's colleagues often joked that he should have become a criminal defense lawyer rather than a civil law attorney. The smile he presented when this occurred was a practiced one.

Jack had been leery when Leif approached him to bring civil suit against the city of Arroyo after the murder of his wife and daughter, but he was grateful for the offer of representation on condition of payment only in the event of a successful resolution. After the death of his family, weeks in the hospital, and so many surgeries he couldn't argue the accuracy of any bill, Jack had been beyond broke. Leif had seen through the propaganda intended to make Jack the patsy during the media frenzy, and he had taken Jack under his wing. That was when people had started following Jack, parking outside his house, bribing his doctors, bugging his house— and shooting at him.

Jack grabbed his cane and headed for the stairs. He had changed into lighter clothes. The day had heated up considerably since his tour with Miguel. He carefully made his way down the stairs and outside to search for the electrical panel.

A cursory inspection of the outside revealed no familiar metal box to check for tripped circuit breakers but did lead him into a second walk around the house for the sole purpose of counting doors. He found seven. He shook his head as he made it back to the front porch. *Who could possibly need seven doors to the outside of their house?*

He went back inside to search for the electrical panel and to check the doors to the outside, to attempt to fathom their purposes. His initial thought that this was a Victorian style house was long gone. The house was a maze of rooms and hallways, and he found himself accidentally wandering into rooms he had already seen.

The house looked big on the outside, but seemed even bigger on the inside. The ground floor alone had six rooms, and each had its own door to the outside with the kitchen carrying the extra door, giving it two. He stood in the center of the kitchen and stared at the two doors. They were on adjoining outside walls no more than ten feet apart. *Just in case you couldn't bring yourself to walk around that corner of the house*, he decided with a raised eyebrow.

He gave up on finding the electrical box and went looking for a phonebook to call an electrician.

Dusk crept up on Jack as he poked around his new home, and by the time he started thinking about eating dinner, it was too late to do anything but keep his promise and head back to Toni's—make that 'Bubba's'—Bar. Disliking the idea of walking home in the dark, he decided to drive his rental car, instead. He would just have to make sure he stayed away from her whiskey.

Carefully folding himself into the little blue Prius, Jack slid his cane into the passenger seat and pushed the button that turned on the electric car. The dash lit up, and he took a moment to mark his location on the GPS system as 'home'.

He turned off the temperature control and rolled down his window. The night was welcoming after the warm temperatures of the afternoon, and the electric car was quiet enough he could hear the cacophony of frogs by the lake. It seemed silly taking the car for a three-minute drive somewhere, but the fifteen to twenty minute walk back in the dark didn't seem prudent after his fainting spells this morning.

He parked right in front of the bar, regretting his choice of parking spaces when he noticed he had parked where the building had been hit before. He decided to leave the car parked where it was.

Jack climbed up the three worn wooden steps. Less than five minutes from doorstep to doorstep, he thought. The openness of the orchard and the highway made it seem a lot further away. Or the speed of modern transportation made it seem closer.

He grabbed the tarnished brass door handle and pulled. The bar felt warm and welcoming. As he entered, a couple of people glanced his way, but they occupied only three of the twelve tables and only two more men were seated at the bar.

A big clock above the bar said it was nearly nine o'clock. He hadn't realized it was so late. The late sunset of the summer day had thrown him off. Deciding he had fallen off the barstool enough for one day already, he headed for the table closest to the bar and seated himself.

Toni came out of the kitchen looking just as she had when he had left her twelve hours ago. Maybe a bit greasier, he thought glancing at the smears on the apron she wore. She spotted him and smiled. She looked like a grandmother baking cookies, but Jack was sure she could hold her own against any drunk who had ever passed through the doors of her establishment. She came straight to his table. "Glad to see you back. I was afraid I scared you off."

"And miss out on this great hometown cooking I've been hearing about?"

She snorted. "You ain't heard nothin' of the sort. I don't know why I didn't see the resemblance to your uncle sooner. Same quirky smile, same mischievous eyes. You boys would be two peas in a pod."

"I thought you pegged me pretty quick."

"That was an edjumacated guess. Now I'm seein' the obvious." She reached into an apron pocket, pulled out a paper napkin and a fork, and put them on the table in front of him. "You want the hot food or the cold food?"

"What do you recommend?"

"The hot food is better'n last night's, and, as the cold food is made from last night's hot, I'd go with the hot if I was you."

"Sold."

"Cuppa Joe?"

"No thanks. I never touch the stuff. Can I have a soda pop?"

Toni laughed. "Soda pop! I ain't heard that in years! Next you'll be askin' me for an orange Coke."

"No thanks. I like mine brown and full of caffeine."

"One carbonated coffee full of syrup comin' up!" She laughed at him and headed back to the kitchen, pausing to scoop some trash off the corner of a table as she went.

Jack glanced around the bar and noted the people. Most were dressed in well-worn casual clothing and appeared to be in various states of dishevelment or maybe just didn't care about their appearance. He couldn't help but notice one woman's teeth were mostly rotted and black. Meth, he thought, and pulled his attention away, afraid of projecting his disgust. He had worked with criminals for too long not to judge some things instantly, whether or not he wanted to.

He was using the corner of his napkin to clean some sort of smudge off his table when the uniformed woman walked in. Starched to razor edges, her drab green and tan uniform meticulously maintained and fit well enough to have been custom tailored. Even the bulky green denim jacket she wore couldn't hide her classic figure.

Jack noticed the Fish and Game Warden's sharp blue eyes

28

assessing the room as she entered, quickly taking in the patrons before she had finished crossing the threshold. Jack wouldn't have noticed it if years of entering rooms filled with convicted felons hadn't conditioned him to do the same thing. He didn't know anything about game wardens, but he knew a cop personality when he saw one.

In a gesture of propriety, she took off her hat, tucking it in the crook of her arm, revealing her jet-black hair pulled back into a tight braid. The way she held her hat left her quick access to the weapon holstered on her hip.

Jack turned his attention back to the other patrons in the bar. Most had noticed the game warden enter.

One of the two men sitting at the bar had suddenly become very interested in his beer. Jack glanced back at the warden. She had noticed it too. She smirked, betraying the personality Jack suspected had been there.

She made a beeline for the patron.

"How's fishing, Charlie?" she asked in a firm, yet friendly tone.

The reply was brusque, with barely a glance in her direction. "I'll let you know in five months."

Jack shook his head as he watched the conversation play out. The only fishing going on here was the warden trying to see if she could catch these guys up to something. Before his family had been killed, Jack would have done much the same thing with the inmates he had dealt with at the halfway house, but now it irritated him to watch it.

"Who's your friend? I don't think we've met." She nodded towards the man sitting next to Charlie who was also unnaturally fascinated by his own beer.

Charlie just shook his head and refused to meet her gaze. The man next to him took a drink of his beer with a shaky hand.

"Don't be like that Charlie. There's no reason why we can't all be friends. I caught you fair and square, you know that."

Charlie sighed heavily and twisted sideways, supporting himself with his elbow on the bar, to look at the warden and the man sitting next to him. "Merle, this here is California Fish and Game Warden Archer Durante. Warden Durante, this is my *not* fishin' buddy, Merle."

"Nice to meet you, Merle, you can call me Archer. All of my friends do." She smiled at him in a way that was warm, yet predatory at the same time.

Jack grunted in disgust. The warden's eyes flicked to him then back to Merle.

"Awful nice of you to help Charlie find ways to pass the time until he can get a fishing license again, Merle. Worthwhile friends are hard to come by."

The sentence hung in silence for a moment. Everyone in the bar had been listening in on the conversation.

"Well, you boys enjoy your beer. Drink responsibly. It was a pleasure, Merle. I'm sure we'll be seeing each other around." She nodded her head towards Charlie in farewell. "Charlie."

Jack renewed his interest in the smudge as the warden turned back to face the rest of the bar. The idea of talking to an officer, any officer, made him feel ill. He'd had enough of police to full a hundred lifetimes. He sighed as he realized her gaze had fallen upon him and he sensed her approach.

"May I join you?" Her voice was softer than it had been with Charlie and Merle, but still, it wasn't a question.

Jack looked up and feigned a smile. "Uh, sure." He gestured to a chair.

She placed her hat at the edge of the table and seated herself with her back to Charlie and Merle. Her eyes kept looking past his shoulder, and Jack realized she was watching their reflections in the windows. "What can I do for you, Warden Durante?" Jack kept his tone pleasant and even.

"Please, call me Archer."

"Of course, all your friends do." Jack's smile faded.

As she contemplated him, the practiced smile left her face too. "You smell like a cop."

Jack had been accused of being an officer before. Something about the habits picked up after working around criminals for too long, he suspected. Once upon a time, that hadn't bothered him, but since police officers had gunned down his family in cold blood, he didn't like the comparison.

"So do you," he replied coldly.

"But there is something not right about you. Want to tell me what it is?"

"Not really. Why don't *you* tell *me* what's not right about me?"

She didn't like his answer.

Jack tensed. In the last six months, he had faced down more

than his share of cops. He would be damned before he let a Game Warden walk into a random bar and try to intimidate him.

Toni came out of the kitchen before the warden could say anything else.

"Oh! Good! You've already met!" Toni sat the food down in front of Jack. "I was really hoping you'd come in tonight, Archer. I wanted to introduce you two." She hugged the warden and Jack tried not to smirk as Archer fought back the embarrassment beginning to show in her eyes.

"We've only started introductions, Toni." Jack smiled wanly up at his hostess and then offered a hand out to the warden. "My name is Jack Tabor."

Archer hesitated and then warily shook his hand.

"Call him 'Whiskey Jack'. He's just moved into the Gardner's Patch," Toni interjected. "He's Bobby Ratchet's nephew."

A flicker of recognition flitted across Warden Durante's face. "I was sorry to hear about your uncle. He seemed a good man. I liked him."

Jack nodded quietly in response.

"Whiskey Jack is good people," Toni stated matter-of-factly as she patted him on the shoulder. "I can tell." She turned back to the warden. "Are you eating in or out tonight?"

Archer eyed Jack and then his plate of food. "Both, I think, Toni. I'm going to have a late night tonight, but I'd like to get to know Jack here a little bit better before I go. How about a hot one now and a cold one for the road?"

Toni nodded. "Coffee?"

"Can you bring me one of those big ones? So I can take it with me when I go?"

"Sure thing, Green Cheeks." Toni turned and headed for the kitchen. Warden Archer Durante looked as though she might blush.

Jack raised an eyebrow at her. "Green Cheeks?"

"Don't go there ... Jack," she warned him. Her emphasis on his name showed she was willing to ignore Toni's nicknames if he would.

"Wouldn't dream of it." Jack smiled, his first genuine one since the warden had entered the bar.

"Okay." Archer leaned in a little. "Here's what I think. You watch the room like a cop, but you *really* didn't want to talk to me.

You don't seem to approve of me. That's what set off the alarm in my head. I think I understand now. I remember the news reports about your family being killed by police officers. I'd forgotten you were in law enforcement. You're a cop, but you hate cops."

"I'm not a cop," Jack bristled.

"You were a cop."

Jack breathed slowly, trying to control himself. She seemed callous for someone who knew what had happened to his family. Her questioning was likely nothing more than it had been with Charlie and Merle—fishing. Nonetheless, it grated on him.

"I worked in corrections."

"Almost a cop then."

"Yes, like you, almost a cop."

Warden Durante paled. "Not like me. I *am* a cop. Just a cop of a different color."

"A green cop?" Jack's voice had more sneer to it than he intended, but she was pissing him off.

"Something like that," she said icily. Jack had obviously hit a nerve.

Jack felt his ears start to burn. He had to get control of himself. He slowly pushed his chair back a couple of inches from the table and leaned back, taking a deep breath. He had to salvage this. No point in making the police here hate him, too. Police tend to cause a lot of problems when they don't like someone.

"I'm sorry, Warden Durante. Yes. My family was killed by police officers. No. I am not over it." He paused briefly to look into her eyes to show his sincerity. "I don't blame you. I don't know anything about you. I don't even really know what your job is. I've never met a Fish and Game Warden before." He ended with another deep breath to try to relax the tension he felt winding in his gut and chest.

Warden Archer Durante had leaned back in her chair during Jack's apology and, after watching the window reflection of Charlie and Merle quietly slipping out the back door, she seemed to relax slightly.

"Someone's been in therapy." She commented glibly.

"A lot of it." Jack assured her.

"Apology accepted. Please also accept my apology. I felt I was only doing my job by attempting to learn more about a situation that appeared … unusual."

"Understood, and accepted." Jack smiled back flatly.

Toni came back with a plate of food matching Jack's and a brown paper bag he presumed held the 'cold' dinner.

"Glad to see you two are finally playing nice," she stated cheerfully.

They both glanced up at her, surprised.

"What?" she asked. "You think I don't know what goes on in my bar? By the way, don't back up without looking under your tires." She jerked a thumb over her shoulder at the empty barstools. "Charlie Tuna and Pearly Merle took their beer bottles with 'em."

SIX

Y ou sure you don't mind?" Jack asked as he carefully pulled himself up into the front seat of Warden Durante's green pickup truck. The sun hadn't come up yet and the light from inside the truck spotlighted Jack in his driveway.

"Of course not. There couldn't possibly be any liability involved in intentionally taking a crippled man, who is known to file civil suits against the state, into a potentially dangerous situation."

Jack froze just as he was about to seat himself. Archer flashed him a smile. "Get in, Gimpy," she teased him. "It's your property. If you wanted, you could just get in the car and follow me up there anyway. This is no different than if I gave you a ride-along."

Jack buckled up and smiled back, amused that she felt she could be away with calling him Gimpy. They had warmed towards each other, with Toni's mediation. She wasn't quite the over-the-top-cop he had thought, and he wasn't the criminal she had suspected.

"Is your shirt on inside-out?"

Jack looked down and flushed. "Sorry. The lights in the house aren't all working. I've got an electrician coming out to look into it."

"If you say so, Wrong Way." She shook her head at him with mock exasperation.

"Is that Riegels or Corrigan?" he asked.

She raised her eyebrows at him questioningly.

"Wrong Way the football player or Wrong Way the pilot?" he tried to clarify.

"Wrong Way the Gimp." She sneered at him good-naturedly as she shut her door and the light went out.

The truck's headlights lit up the dirt road ahead as they crossed the highway to the gate Miguel had taken Jack through the day

35

before. Archer stopped at the gate and Jack started to get out to open it.

"Stay in the truck, Gimpy. You're too slow," she called as she was halfway to the gate.

Archer checked her GPS as she drove the truck over up the top of a rise. The sun wouldn't be up for an hour yet, but she had wanted to get an early start. Most bad guys liked to sleep late, unless they were hunters, and she had a feeling she was going to find a poaching camp today. It was fortuitous to have met Jack at this time, as he now owned the property she wanted to inspect. Not that Fish and Game Wardens needed permission, but friendly relations were always a good thing.

She spotted a natural gap in some madrone trees and parked the truck in it, wincing slightly at the screech of scraping paint. She wanted the truck to have as much camouflage as possible when the sun came up.

She glanced at Jack as she dug out her satellite photo of the area. He hadn't spoken or even glanced at her since the gate. Perhaps she shouldn't have teased him.

"Where do you get a satellite photo like that?" Jack asked quietly.

Archer snapped out of her self-reflection. She had been staring at the photo without seeing it. "Off of the internet," she answered. "I'm sorry I called you a Gimp."

Jack chuckled. "No worries." He seemed to study the photo in her hands for a moment.

"You and I seem to apologize to each other quite a bit," he blurted. He faced her. "Tell you what ..." he paused and she glanced at him. "I'm pretty new around here, and I could use a good friend or two. I'd like to just skip the get to know you crap and call you my friend."

She raised her eyebrows and then furrowed them at him. *Here it comes,* she thought.

"Not like that! Look, I'd like to think I am a pretty good judge of character, and, apparently, based on our initial meeting last night, so do you. Uh ... think that you are a good judge of character." He frowned at himself. "Anyway, I hereby declare that I consider you a friend. You no longer have to apologize unless I tell you that you hurt my feelings. And as a friend you hereby earn the right to be told when you have hurt my feelings." He held her bemused gaze for a moment before turning away to look back out the windshield into the madrone trees. He held his voice in a mock weak monotone, "If you reject the position of friend, my feelings will be hurt."

Archer laughed. That wasn't what she had thought was going to happen. He hadn't struck her as someone with a dramatic flair to his sense of humor. "Okay. But I can't promise full reciprocation."

"I'll take what I can get."

She eyed him for a second, and then laughed. "For the record, my first duty in the position of your friend is to declare that you are a dork."

He gave her a cheesy grin and didn't deny it.

She laughed again and turned her attention back to the photo. She studied it just long enough to get her bearings, then pulled out a portable GPS and marked a couple of points on it. She folded the photo and stuck it in a pocket, grabbed an extra clip for her gun and put it in another pocket on the side of her leg before turning to look at Jack. "You know, I thought you were the strong quiet type until you wussed out on me like that."

"I thought you were the smart over-achiever until you settled for being my friend," he retorted.

"Wow. That had hidden meanings. Which one did you mean?" Her eyebrows arched at him again.

"The one that means I'm too slow-witted to toss witty retorts."

"Got that right."

"See how much easier it is now that we're friends?"

She threw him a quick smile and he returned it with another grin.

"Are you really going to be okay here for the next couple of hours?" she asked seriously.

"Yeah. I've been fantasizing about watching the sun come up in the mountains for a long time now. It's kind of a Zen thing."

"Are you Buddhist?"

"No." He smiled at her. "But that doesn't mean I think they've got it wrong either. I'm just looking for my own inner peace. Is it all right if I walk down the road a little ways?"

"You tell me. It's your land."

"Yeah, that part is still pretty surreal."

Archer got out of the truck and shut the door gently with a quiet click. Jack followed suit.

"Which way are you going?" he asked.

"North." She pointed at the top of the mountain in front of them, clearly visible against the brightening sky. "I'm hoping to get a good vantage there to look down into the valley on that side there. Get a good look at what's in this photo before I go stomping in there."

"You really think poachers would set up a permanent camp?"

"They do it all the time."

"And you're really going in there all by yourself?"

"I do it all the time."

"One cop, all by yourself, walking into a camp full of who knows how many people who are all breaking the law, who all are armed, and who all know you are a cop?"

"Yep."

"No backup?"

"Cell phones don't work here."

"No dispatch?"

"Line of sight radio doesn't work here either."

Jack looked her straight in the face. "Archer?"

"Yeah?"

"You got balls."

"Could be worse."

"Really?"

"Sure. The photo could have shown a pot farm. Those can be bad news." She winked at him. "See you in a couple of hours. There's some water in the cooler if you need it."

⁂

Jack settled into the sunlight as the sun's rays finally moved low enough down the mountain he could reach them. He found an old stump where a tree had been felled to widen the road's clearance, and tried to make himself comfortable. He examined the rubber tip of his cane and decided he would need to get something sturdier if he was going to stay in Rainbow County. He had walked about a half of a mile down the road and found a place where the mountains parted just enough for him to glimpse Rainbow Lake's dark waters.

Small birds flitted all around. Some sang, most just squawked. He spied a large, black shape at the top of a dead tree that turned out to be a turkey vulture slowly spreading its wings to warm itself in the sun. Down the road, some squirrels, the same color as the dirt in the road, scurried back and forth, often stopping to wrestle each other.

A loud shot echoed across the mountains. The birds silenced. A second shot and a third followed. The squirrels disappeared and the turkey vulture took flight. Two more shots filled the world around him.

Jack felt panic rise up in him. Tightness pulled across his chest and gut and his hands shook. That had to be Archer. *Was she in trouble? What could he do to help? Not a damn thing. God. Not again.* The nightmares threatened to come up to the surface and take control. His body shook with fear and weakness as his breathing became ragged.

No, no no nononono! He was mentally screaming at himself. He couldn't give in, couldn't lose control. Not again, not ever. *Get up! Get up!* He willed himself to his feet, forced himself to stand. He would never be trapped a prisoner of his own fear in his body again. He dug deep for rage, for pain, for anything that would help motivate him and slowly, awkwardly, he reclaimed control of his body and started moving in the direction the sound of the gunshots had come from.

He grimaced as the memory of being shot caused his six-month old scars to ache. Each one became a burning ember on his skin as he pushed himself into a limping jog back to the truck. The morning no longer seemed vibrant and alive. Instead, the dirt road resembled a desert with the vegetation along the sides dried out and dying. The world was empty to his ears straining for any sounds that might hint at what had happened. *How long had it been since the last shot?* He had stopped wearing a watch months ago, when time had no longer mattered to him. *Maybe fifteen minutes had passed. Maybe it was twenty.*

He made it back to the truck out of breath and with shaky legs not used to being pushed so hard. *How long had it been since Archer had struck out on her own? An hour?* He glanced at the sun up in the sky. He didn't know. The only thing he knew was that he had to do something.

He opened up the truck and pulled the shotgun from its holder between the seats. He checked to see if it was loaded and then chambered a round, mumbling to himself the whole time. *I hate guns. Oh how I hate guns.*

He leaned on his cane for a moment, then, coming to a quiet decision he stuck his cane between the seats, quietly clicked the door shut, shouldered the shotgun, and started slowly off up the mountain in the direction he had seen Warden Archer Durante go. The brush that had seemed so sparse and dead a few minutes ago was now thick and hard to penetrate. He picked his way carefully, slowly. *No point in breaking my neck,* he thought, *I can't help anyone then.* He had made it maybe a hundred yards up the mountainside when he first heard the sound of voices drifting up from below.

His heart raced. He was definitely hearing a man's voice. That couldn't be good. He listened carefully, but it was hard to hear over the sound of his own racing heart. He was pretty sure he was hearing two voices, neither of which sounded female. It sounded like they were approaching from down below, where Archer had said she had wanted to eventually end up.

Had she gone down there already? Or had she still been up here? Perhaps someone had spotted her and they had shot at her through a scoped rifle? His mind raced with possibilities while his stomach churned with fear and worry. He had to go back down there to find out. Wherever Archer had ended up, those voices would have to know, one way or the other.

He carefully picked his way back to the truck, trying hard to be silent, to not scatter loose dirt and rocks down the slope and give himself away. He caught a glimpse of the truck through the trees and brush, but he couldn't see anyone. He leaned against a tree to catch his breath and listen.

The voices were getting closer, but they weren't there yet. He could beat them to the truck, if he tried. *Did he want to? Was there an advantage to that?* He started back down the mountain fearful they would reach the truck and leave before he could get there.

He arrived at the truck limping painfully, panting hard, and trying not to be loud about it. The voices were close. He dashed behind the truck for cover. When he wasn't trembling quite so much, he took the safety off the shotgun and waited. He made out a few curse words, but the rest sounded like jumbled muttering and complaining, not a real conversation.

When two men stepped out into the road, Jack moved out from behind the truck, shotgun in hand, and shouted. "Hands up!" He edged close enough he was sure he could make a shot count.

"What the hell?" said the bigger man in a drab green jumpsuit, slowly raising his hands.

"Who the hell are you?" demanded the smaller wiry man. The shotgun didn't seem to impress him.

"I'm the guy who owns this land. Where is Warden Durante?"

"I'm right here, Jack." Archer herded yet a third man into the road. "Lower the shotgun would you? Big Mike and Little Mike wouldn't hurt a flea, would you boys?"

The two men looked at each other and grinned. "Not unless it was on a bear!" sported Big Mike.

SEVEN

Gallbladders?" Toni asked as she came around the bar. "That's what she said." Jack raised his glass of whiskey to his lips and took a small sip. Toni had insisted on giving it to him after Archer had dropped him off at Bubba's Bar.

Apparently, when Jack had gone to use the little boy's room during dinner the night before, Toni had informed Warden Durante about Jack's 'weak constitution'. So, being such a good friend, Archer insisted Jack stay where Toni could keep an eye on him until she got back from booking her suspects. She had ignored his protests and declared she would be back in a little while to check on him and take him home. Then she followed it up with a warning that she would arrest him if he wasn't here when she got back.

"What the hell would anyone want a bear's gallbladder for?" Toni wiped her hands on her apron. A few of Toni's customers were trying hard to look like they weren't eavesdropping. The smell of coffee, fried bacon, and eggs saturated the room.

"Archer said they sell them on the Asian black market for a couple of thousand dollars each. They're supposed to be some kind of ancient remedy." Jack gave a look of sympathetic bemusement and arched his eyebrows at her. "I don't know. What do you do with a gallbladder? Smoke it? Make tea? Gallbladder broth?"

Toni wrinkled her nose in disgust. "Probably shove it up their asses," she mumbled as she glanced around to see if her customers needed anything. "So why the hell did she threaten to arrest you?"

"She's pissed I touched her shotgun."

Toni raised her eyebrows at him. "Dummer'n you look." She shook her head, as if disappointed with a child. "Buy you breakfast? I got bacon, eggs, and toast; burnt bacon, eggs, and

43

toast; or I can get you an orange juice to mix with your whiskey."

By the time Archer came back, Jack was seriously considering sneaking out of Bubba's and walking home the next time Toni went into the kitchen. He had eaten his burnt bacon and not quite cooked eggs and washed them down with his whiskey and orange juice without complaint, but he had been sitting on a hard chair or a bar stool for almost two hours and his body was starting to hurt pretty badly.

Archer met Jack's eyes as she crossed the room to the booth he was sitting in, her hand unconsciously resting on the gun on her hip. Her expression was unreadable but he could tell by her swagger she wasn't happy.

"So, you doing all right after trying to play hero?" she asked.

"Fine." Swirling the last of the orange pulp around in the bottom of his tumbler, he drank it and sat it on the table with a thunk that echoed through the bar.

Archer waited, allowing the silence to work on him, but finally gave in first.

"What kind of work did you say you used to do?"

Jack kept his eyes on his empty glass. "Corrections."

"Care to elaborate?"

"Community Corrections."

She nodded. "A parole officer?"

"Kind of."

"Not very forthcoming are you?"

Jack sat up straight and met her gaze. "You tried to pull my file," he said.

Archer looked away.

"I have been interrogated by the best," Jack smiled grimly, "so unless you intend to shove bamboo under my finger nails, you're not going to get much from me without being polite." He met her eyes. "Very polite."

Archer stiffened. She started to say something but Jack talked right over her.

"Look, Warden Durante. I know you want to rip me a new one for touching your shotgun. I know you were just showing solidarity in front of those guys you arrested by not letting into me right there on the spot, but I did what I thought was right at the time." His face hardened. "And if I had it to do over again I damn would!" He stopped to let his words sink in.

Archer remained impassive as she spoke. "I thought we already decided to be friends."

Jack met her gaze uncompromisingly. "I thought so, too."

"Then call me Archer."

Jack took a quiet breath and nodded at her. "All right, Archer."

"It took a bit of nerve for you to take that shotgun. You went a long way up that mountainside in some seriously poor terrain at some considerable risk to yourself—especially in light of your current physical condition."

"I'm working on that condition."

She nodded at him thoughtfully. "I did try to pull your file. And I was told it was none of my damned business, which did piss me off." She pursed her lips. "I just wanted to find out what kind of training you'd had.

"I'm sorry I tried to pull your file. You proved yourself to be a better friend in the span of a couple of hours than most people prove in a lifetime. I was just trying to find out if it was real, or if it was training."

Jack's eyebrows drew together in confusion. "What's the difference?"

"If you were a cop and did that every day for the last ten years, then you were still just doing your job. If you were a civilian and had never done anything like that before in your life ..." She waved off the thought.

"I ask you again, what's the difference?"

It was her turn to be confused.

"Is a soldier less brave on the last day of his tour of duty than he was on his first? Is a firefighter more of a hero the first time he pulls someone from a burning building or the fifth time? Is a police officer braver the first time out on patrol or the one last night? Or you for that matter, were you less brave this morning than you were on your first bust?"

Archer didn't say anything.

"I think" Jack answered for her, "you were just as brave as ever, perhaps even more so now that you really know what you are getting yourself into. But you are more experienced now, which gives you more confidence in your ability to control the situation. You know, you make it look easy now. That doesn't make it any less brave."

She smiled at him, a warm, friendly smile. "A wonderful soliloquy. Thank you, I enjoyed it immensely. It completely failed to answer my question, but made me feel so much better about myself and the world around me." There was more to this man than met the eye, she decided. Much more.

"What question?"

"About what kind of training you've had."

"Do you need an answer?"

"I don't *need* one."

"If I told you I have never carried a badge, never served in the military, and never had any weapons training outside of a hunter's safety class and the Discovery Channel, would that answer your question?"

"Yes, that would answer it. Are you telling me the truth?"

"Archer?"

"Yes, Jack?"

"Are you flirting with me?"

Archer felt a lone butterfly in her stomach and she quickly suppressed it with her confident smile. "I prefer to think of this as friendly banter."

"I take it back. I'm no longer sure I could handle being interrogated by you."

Archer stood up to leave. She leveled her gaze at him and then cocked a bewitching smile. "No one can."

EIGHT

A lmost got it …" the electrician grunted.

Jack was trying hard not make a joke about the electrician having a 'plumber's crack' and trying even harder to not stare as it continually moved back and forth in front of his field of view. The electrician was using an insulated hook to fish for the electrical wire inside the wall, and he was having limited success.

"Damn! Someone tore this up but good!" He grunted again then cried out happily. "Got it! I got it!" He leaned back on his haunches then sat crossed legged, pulling the electrical cord from the wall as he sat.

"All right! This should fix the problem." He held up the end of the wires and the new outlet for Jack to see.

"What could have done that?" He examined the ruined wiring. "Rats? A raccoon?"

"Naw." The electrician, whose shirt said his name was Danny, tapped the wall with the back of his hand. "There's no room for raccoons to squeeze in up here. This was pulled out somewhere between here," he pointed at the hole where the socket would go, "and there." He pointed up to the light fixture on the ceiling.

"Probably someone pulled out the old antenna wiring from the wall and snagged this while doing it." He screwed the wiring into the back of the socket. "They'd have been better off just cutting it and leaving it in the wall. Antenna wire ain't got no current, so it couldn't have hurt nothin'."

"Well I appreciate you coming out and taking care of this for me. I never could have figured it out." Jack hadn't even thought about television since he had arrived. Come to think of it, he hadn't checked his e-mail either. He wondered if his lawyer had been trying to get in contact with him. His cell phone did not get reception here, so he had turned it off, intending to check messages later.

"You wouldn't happen to know if there are any Wi-Fi places around here I could use to check e-mails, would you?" Jack asked.

"Not that I know of. Pretty hard to get internet in a lot of places out here. I'd call the computer store, if I was you. They'd know." The electrician finished screwing the faceplate to the wall. "I gotta go back downstairs and flip the breaker on to make sure this works."

"Do you know the name of the computer store?"

Danny gave Jack an 'are you kidding me?' look. "I'd guess Rainbow computers." He gave Jack a smile that was more like a wince and headed out of the room.

Yeah, I knew that, thought Jack.

The courthouse was old and musty smelling. The building looked fairly new on the outside, maybe twenty years old. But stepping through the front doors transported Jack back at least seventy years. The tiling and paint color schemes were drab turquoises left over from the 1960's, and the walls were faded wood from an era even longer gone. Jack wondered if they had recycled parts of the original courthouse.

He checked the directory and then entered a slow, creaky elevator to the third floor. As the yellowed floor numbers slowly lit up, Jack wondered if he could have walked the stairs faster, even with his need of a cane. The bell announcing his arrival sounded sickly and clunked instead of rang. The doors grated and opened jerkily as he stepped out. He decided he would take the stairs on his way back down.

He glanced at the sign that said Planning Department and headed over to the counter. A couple of people rustled around cubicle desks covered with old books and papers. One of them, a short balding man with a big bushy mustache, came over.

"What can I do you for?" he asked with a lopsided smile. Jack smiled back, but mostly at the sight of the man's hair. It was sticking up on the right side, as though he had just gotten out of bed.

"I'm here to get some information about opening a winery."

The man's eyebrows arched up. "Oh, gonna buy some land, plant some grapes, and make your wine? It's the dream life!" His smile was both knowing and dubious.

"Actually, I've already got the land and the grapes—and someone to make it for me. I was thinking more along the lines of licensing and zoning problems."

"Oh." The man sounded surprised. "Where is your property?"

Jack gave the address and watched as the man looked it up in a big book from the shelves behind him. He dropped the book with a thump on the counter and began flipping through the pages. Some were yellowed, smudged and obviously old. Others looked newer. The one he stopped at looked brand new.

"Here it is." The man turned the book sideways so they could both see it. "Is this the right one?"

Jack examined the parcel outlines on the paper. "Honestly, this means nothing to me. I have no idea."

The man reached over and started typing on the computer. A satellite photo of the land popped up. The layout was not as Jack had pictured it in his mind, and it was much bigger than it had seemed when he had been riding around with Miguel.

"Ah! The old Gardner's Patch!"

"Yeah, that's it."

"Nice piece of property," the man nodded in approval.

Jack explained what he was hoping to do as they looked at the plat map of the property and compared it to the bird's eye view image.

"So you wouldn't be needing to add any structures to the property then?" The man asked looking at all of the buildings on the lakeside of the highway.

"I don't think so. I think this one is where we would make it, and this one," he pointed to the computer screen, "would be the tasting room."

"Well," he turned back to the book on the counter, "it looks like they just recently updated your plat maps, so they shouldn't need to re-look at them." He glanced up at Jack. "That should save some time and money.

"And you are already zoned for this, so I don't see why you would have any problems." By the look on the man's face, Jack suspected this was one of the few pipedreams to walk through here that actually had a chance of coming true.

The man provided Jack with the names and numbers of the departments he should go to next.

"Can I get copies of both of those?" Jack asked pointing to the map and the photo.

"Yeah, but I gotta charge you for them."

"That's okay."

Jack waited while the photo printed out and the man took the book to the copy machine. He eyed a couple of public notices on the wall. One was to prevent the spread of zebra mussels in the lake, another about burning yard waste. The man came back and handed Jack the copies.

"Thank you." Jack shook the man's hand and turned to leave. He stopped and looked back. "Where are the stairs?"

Jack sat in the CyberRainbow Café waiting for his computer to boot up so he could check his e-mail. It was nothing like a café. Nor was it anything like a rainbow.

It was a unit in a strip mall that had been connected to the Rainbow Computer store's unit by knocking a hole in the wall between them.

The hole was too big to be a door and too small to make the rooms feel associated. The tables were the long folding kind. Homemade cubical dividers had been placed on them to give the semblance of privacy, but they were short enough to still see if someone was looking at porn. The floors were cheap linoleum with speckled and splotched pre-dirtied pattern. The walls were institution green.

It reminded Jack of a school cafeteria, but instead of 'Got Milk?' posters, there were computer generated 'cyber-babes' and pixilated demons being blown to 'giblets'. The room stank of burnt coffee. The pot was in the furthest corner, away from all electronic equipment. It was a steel kettle large enough to supply a virtual army. A stained piece of paper taped to the wall said cups were for sale at the main counter for five dollars each, unlimited refills.

Jack suspected that the whole point of the place was for people to get together to play online games and that his quick use of the

Wi-Fi, so common in the big cities, was practically unheard of in this little town.

He saw only one message on his e-mail from his lawyer, saying nothing was new. He turned off his laptop and looked around the room. He had driven almost fifteen miles to get here and spent five dollars to get the daily pass code to the Wi-Fi to get one message that didn't say anything.

He didn't want to do this again. He packed up his laptop, picked up his cane and limped back up to the counter.

In contrast to the appearance of Rainbow Computers, the man behind the counter was well groomed and clean. His name was Mitch. It said so on the rainbow shaped and colored nametag on his shirt. Mitch smiled at Jack expectantly.

"I just moved here," said Jack, smiling back in spite of himself. "How do I get internet set up at my house?"

"We just started our own DSL so we might be able to set you up. Are you here in Rainbow?"

"No. I am around the lake south of Paradise Falls, just off the highway. I'm in the old Gardner's place. The Gardner's Patch, I think they called it. Does that help?"

Mitch frowned. "Our DSL doesn't reach out there, but cable does and I am pretty sure we …" He tapped away at the keyboard in front of him for a few seconds. "Yeah, here it is. You should be all ready to go. We did a service call out there about eight months ago and set up a Wi-Fi network surveillance system. There has to be internet out there or we couldn't have set that up."

"A surveillance system?"

"Yeah. A real nice one, too. Eight cameras, high resolution color in the day, night vision, and remote internet access. It had it all."

"Why would someone need a system like that?"

"I don't know. To see what's going on around the place?"

Jack hadn't seen anything that looked like a surveillance system at the house.

"Are you sure that was at the Gardner's Patch?"

"Yeah. That's where we installed it." Mitch glanced at the computer and read the address off to Jack.

Jack frowned. A surveillance system, at his uncle's? "Does your computer say who ordered it?" Jack asked.

Mitch reached for the keyboard, but stopped. "I'm not sure if that's privileged information or not."

"Could you find out? I'd really like to know."

"The owner will be in tomorrow."

"Thanks, Mitch. I'll call tomorrow."

Jack followed the cable guy around the perimeter of the house for a second time, watching the man shake his head and mumble to himself.

"I guess the last guy was pretty pissed at his cable bill to do all of this. See there?" He pointed up towards the second story roof. "Right there under the soffit? Where the paint don't quite match? That's where the cable would have gone into the house."

The man stopped and turned to look back towards the power pole by the driveway. With his fists on his hips, he walked to the pole and looked up shaking his head some more.

"They took the wire out all the way back to the highway," he said, pointing further out to the next pole. "Why the hell would they do that?" His hands went up in exasperation. "*How* the hell did they do that? I'm going to have to come back with a bucket truck to get up there, and I'm going to need seven, eight hundred feet of cable?"

He walked back to Jack. "I'm sorry. They told me this was just a simple reconnect of existing service. I can't promise anything. I have no idea what they are going to say to this. We don't usually remove cable line once it has been installed. They might be charging you for it."

"Rainbow Computers, this is Mitch."

"Hi, Mitch," said Jack. "I was in yesterday. I asked you about the surveillance system you guys did at the Gardner's Patch." Jack absently pulled on the springy coiled cord of the old phone as he spoke. He stared at a slightly mismatched patch in the wall where he suspected a cable outlet had been.

"Yeah, I remember. I spoke with the owner. He said he didn't care if you knew who ordered something. Let me look it up for you again." Jack could hear Mitch's fingers tapping on the keyboard.

"Here it is. Robert Ratchet."

Jack's chest tightened. *Why had his uncle felt he needed this? Was Toni right? Was he murdered? She was apparently right about his paranoia.*

"Are you still there?" Mitch finally asked.

"Yes." Jack's voice was dry. *What the hell had happened? Where was the surveillance system now? Who tore out all of the cable?*

Jack had a thought. Perhaps his uncle had told the person installing the system why he had needed it. "I, uh, had the cable guy out, and he ran into a problem with the internet thing. I was hoping that whoever was out here before might be familiar with what was going on and would be able to help me."

"Hold on, I'll look up who installed it." Mitch's voice was tinny in Jack's ears.

Jack could hear the sound of keyboard keys tapping gently.

"I can send someone out to help you figure out the problem, but I can't send out the original guy who worked on it." Mitch sounded strange.

"Are you sure?" Jack asked. "I would really like to talk to him about the surveillance system he installed."

"Yeah, I'm sure. He's dead."

≈ ≈ ≈ ≈ ≈
≈ ≈ ≈ ≈ ≈

"So you guys didn't take the cable down?" Jack asked, as the cable guy climbed up into the bucket on the back of the service truck.

The cable guy shook his head and tested the bucket's controls. "I can't say we didn't. I've only been out here for six months, but I've never heard of the cable being taken out after it was installed. They just leave it in case the next person wants it."

He took off his hard hat and scratched at his thinning hair. "This is a pretty rural area. I'm pretty much a one-man show out here, so I suppose if someone really wanted it out, and paid to take it out, we might. But who would pay to take a cable down? It's not like it was in the way. The power and phone lines run right there with it.

"And see that up there?" He pointed to a loose line dangling in the wind. "We never do that. Someone just cut that and left it."

53

"You've only been here six months?" Jack asked.

"Yeah!" The man yelled down as the bucket began noisily lifting him up into the air.

"Do you suppose the guy who was here before you would know what happened?" Jack had to yell over the noise.

The cable guy shook his head as he reached the top of the pole. The bucket and the noise stopped. "If he did, he won't tell us. He drove off a cliff a few months before they sent me out here. Took his rig, his laptop, and damn near all his files for the last six months with him. I doubt if I will ever straighten the whole mess out. Billing has been a bitch!"

NINE

Jack hated dreams. He didn't have to die to go to Hell. Hell touched him in his dreams, and there was not a damn thing he could do about it.

Jack was dreaming now, and he knew it, but he couldn't stop it. He couldn't control it, couldn't ignore it. Hell was reaching out to touch him again, to drag him back to that horrible day six months ago as it had so many times before, as it would continue to do at its own whim, for as long as it chose to amuse itself with him. Therapy, counseling, time, and overexposure to this dream had done nothing to inure him to it, nothing to desensitize him. That was the nature of Hell: eternal, unending, suffering.

There were two Jacks in this dream. There were always two Jacks. One was as an unwilling theater patron, watching the show from a distance; apart, uninvolved, and unable to look away or even close his eyes. The other was a marionette, forced to participate, having no control over either himself or the play.

His wife was here. She always was, at first. So was his daughter. They wore matching dark green dresses with light green shawls draped over their shoulders, wide red bows tied around their waists, and green pillbox hats with red felt poinsettias on them. Jamie was obviously enamored with her outfit and loved looking just like her mother. Wendy had her hat cocked slightly to the side, giving her a rakish appearance that her daughter had no hope of imitating. They giggled quietly to each other, pretending their furred hand muffs were puppets while they waited for him.

The snow swirled lazily outside his office window; a clean Christmas Promise of high spirits. He could feel the cool draft from the window on his face as he tried to get his Grinch tie straight. Wendy came over to him and fixed the tie, smiling at his helplessness. "Thanks for coming with us." She murmured a kiss into his ear.

"We're going to miss the elephant party!" Jamie was bouncing up and down in her fur-topped snow boots.

"We are not going to miss it!" Wendy assured Jamie, rolling her eyes and glancing back at Jack, who was putting his jacket on. "She has been like this since you left last night. I can't believe you told her there would be white elephants there. She won't believe me that you were teasing."

Jack grinned at her. "Thanks for coming to pick me up." He was tired from working the night shift and half the morning shift, but his girls were re-energizing him. It had been difficult to cover the graveyard shifts on the weekend before Christmas, so he had taken it himself. It hadn't been a big deal, the halfway house was mostly empty on a weekend anyway, but it was a holiday weekend, and most of the inmates stayed out of trouble to make sure they would get to be home for Christmas.

If it was empty last night, it was downright deserted tonight. The inmates who didn't have the privilege of an over-night pass home had all been up at first light to sign out this morning. Out of nearly seventy inmates, only two were left in the facility. They were stuck due to regulations. Having only arrived on Friday, they were still on the three-day in-processing hold, and none too happy about it.

"Almost ready," he assured his pleading daughter as he finished putting away his things and locking his desk. "Okay. I need to go back up to the front desk, and then we can go." Marionette Jack followed the two of them out of his office in a wistful trance, peacefully oblivious while distant Observer Jack struggled to scream warnings, do something, anything …

Wendy and Jamie followed him through the dingy halls, walking on gray stained carpets that smelled like a men's locker room with too much deodorizer that hadn't worked. The droopy tired, green-and-red tinsel garland along the walls couldn't compete with the institutional feel of the facility. A young Hispanic man began walking alongside them, followed by a middle-aged black man who smiled pleasantly at Jamie when she waved at him. "Merry Christmas, Little John!"

"Merry Christmas, Little Jamie!" Little John was neither a large nor a small man as his name might imply. His surname was

Littlejohn, which he pronounced 'loohan', but no one else did. He was an amiable fellow and didn't mind.

"Do you like my dress?" Jamie swished her skirt as she walked.

"Very nice!" Little John beamed. "Puts me right in the holiday spirit." He had been sentenced to be a resident of the facility many times, and had watched her grow since she was born.

Wendy smiled familiarly at Little John. As a drug, alcohol, and career counselor she had held many classes and sessions in this facility and had spent untold hours in his presence.

The Hispanic teenager couldn't contain himself any longer and did a sideways dance step to look at Jack while walking.

"Come *on*! Mr. Tabor, please! I ain't been home for seven months! I told my moms I'd be home for Christmas, and they're having their party tonight!" His tattoo-covered arms swung wildly back and forth in emphasis as he bounced on the toes of his floppy high-top sneakers.

Jack shook his head without looking at the anxious teen. "And you will be home for Christmas, if you stay out of trouble, but you are still on intake and I can't bend that rule and let you go early, Alfonso. I'm sorry."

"Man! Don't call me that! I *told* you, everyone calls me *Sancho*!"

Jack smiled understandingly at him. "We don't use gang names …"

"It's not a gang name!"

"… or derogatory slang names for people here."

"It's not derogatory!" Alfonso's voice rose several octaves as he argued and gesticulated, still dancing sideways.

"I know it means 'the man your wife is having sex with'. Most people would consider it offensive."

"*I don't!*"

Jamie ignored the conversation. She was used to the outspoken and overacted antics of the inmates around her parents, so she continued her conversation with Little John as though there was nothing else going on. "I thought you weren't coming back again this time."

A sad smile crossed Little John's prematurely wrinkled face. "I thought so, too."

"Drugs?" Jamie asked matter-of-factly, as if it was old hat and she had seen it many times before, which she had.

"Jamie!" Wendy failed to stifle a laugh while trying to sound scolding. "That was inappropriate!"

"You're too smart for your own good, Little Jamie!" Little John winked at her.

"Well, I'm glad you're back. I missed you."

Wendy glanced from her daughter to the inmate, wondering at the innocence of her child. "Sorry ..." She gave Little John a sad smile.

"I missed you, too, Sweetheart." Little John smiled back at Jamie and then grinned at Wendy. "Out of the mouth of babes ... At least she don't think I'm one of the bangers."

They arrived at the front desk where a grey-haired black man, looking for all the world like Sidney Poitier in *To Sir, with Love*. He barely acknowledged the presence of any of them.

"Chuck, I know they are still on intake hold, but since it's almost Christmas and there is no one else here, I'm going to let Alfonso and Little John have visitors." Jack picked up the logbook and scribbled his final entry as he spoke. Chuck barely nodded his head to show he had heard.

"Aww!" Alfonso dipped his head in disappointment and disgust.

"Hey man," Little John slapped Alfonso on the shoulder in a friendly gesture. "It's better than a poke in the nose. Tell your mom to bring some of that Christmas ham you was talkin' about! And your sister!"

Alfonso slapped Little John's hand away. "You stay away from my sister, old man!" He turned back to Jack. "I can't call her. I ain't got no money for the phone."

"Go use the one in the back office." Jack pointed to the doorway behind Chuck's desk. "Five minutes, no more!" he called to Alfonso's retreating back as the teen skipped into the room. "And stay out of Laura's desk!"

Jack handed the logbook back to Chuck. "You got any money, Little John?"

"Naw, man. They picked me up out of the gutter and I ain't been able to get hold of my girl since."

Jack fished a couple of twenty-dollar bills out of his pocket and handed them to Chuck. "Why don't you and Little John get something delivered?"

Chuck perked up considerably and looked at Little John. "Chinese okay?"

"Make sure you get something for Alfonso, too. Just in case his family doesn't come."

"It's *Sancho*!" Alfonso yelled out of the office door. Chuck and Jack shared a smirk. Chuck loved to razz inmates about their names, especially when they hated them.

Something hit the metal side door of the building hard, rattling the glass and making them all turn their heads to see. An obscenity muffled through the locked door as someone hit or kicked at it, trying to open it. Wendy quickly put her hands over Jamie's ears, although she knew Jamie had heard it all floating around in these hallways.

"It's locked! Go around!" Chuck's voice bellowed down the hall and the banging on the door stopped. Chuck shook his gray head and muttered to himself. "They never learn. Lock it at the same time every single day, and they never learn."

"Sorry." Jack smiled at his girls and gave them a good-natured 'what do you expect' shrug of his shoulders. "Let's get out of here and go to a party."

"Yeah! Yeah! Yeah! Yeah!" Jamie jumped up and down and clapped.

"See you later." Jack waved over his shoulder at Chuck as they headed down the hallway to the main entrance. Wendy slipped her arm into his, and Jamie danced along beside them. Jack the Marionette smiled at her enthusiasm. He was glad to be off work, glad to be with his family, and he was starting to feel the holiday spirit move him.

Jack the Observer wept silently. The end of the world was at hand, yet again.

TEN

A cacophony of squawks, croaks, and caws assaulted Archer's ears as she walked through the green walnut orchard. She had developed a quiet, practiced ease of movement through her time spent alone in the California forest that brought her to Jack's side without disturbing him. Large ravens swooped and dove through the trees, their cries echoing through the trees and filling the day with life and noise. Jack sat quietly on a cement bench placed under a giant California bay tree. He watched the birds circling and playing around him with a relaxed interest.

"It's called a murder of crows." Jack spoke softly without turning around to look at Archer. His whisper startled her. She hadn't thought he knew she was there.

"Actually, they're ravens." She moved up to stand even with his bench, keeping her voice low. "Crows are smaller."

"They're still crows. All ravens are crows, but not all crows are ravens. Crows are a family."

"Aren't you Mister Smarty-Pants."

She stood silently and watched the birds for a while. They began to quiet and settle into the trees.

Archer looked down at Jack.

"Miguel told me he thought he saw you come out here. I hope I'm not interrupting."

Jack pursed his lips and shook his head, continuing to watch the birds as they took roost in the trees.

"Toni said she hadn't seen you for a couple of days, and she was kind of worried." Archer waited but Jack didn't say anything. "I was kind of worried, too." She glanced at him out of the corner of her eye to see if that elicited any response, but his face was impassive.

61

She waited a few moments longer. She wasn't used to being ignored. "Are you mad at me?" she asked, frowning slightly.

That worked. Jack turned his attention away from the crows and met her gaze, a surprised look upon his face. "Am I mad at you?" Jack looked around and chuckled nervously. "Way to make me feel like I'm back in high school."

Archer blushed, but Jack didn't seem to notice. He blinked a few times as though he had just awoken and rubbed his face with his hands. He picked up his cane from where it had been resting on the bench and moved it to the other side of him, making room on the bench for Archer.

"No. I'm not mad." He gestured for her to sit. "In fact I had completely forgotten about our little adventure." If Jack noticed the look of incredulity on Archer's face, he ignored it. "I have just had a lot on my mind the last couple of days. Been keeping busy, you know."

The ravens fell silent, as if to listen to his hushed words. He gestured again for her to sit and she settled onto the bench next to him.

"Anything you want to talk about?"

He nodded his head slightly. "I've been thinking about what Toni said—about my uncle being murdered." He was silent for a long moment. "I think she might be right."

Archer began to ask a question, but was interrupted by a loud hoarse croaking from the top of one of the walnut trees. *KAW! KAW! KAW!* She glanced over at the giant raven sitting atop the tree and was surprised when the other ravens seemed to answer in chorus. She forgot her question as the big raven called out a raspy cry and the other ravens fell silent. A lone raven fluttered down to the ground near the center of the clearing.

"Oh my God …" Archer barely breathed.

Jack whispered back. "What is it? Are you all right?"

She nodded slightly, never taking her eyes off the raven on the ground. It slowly walked to the center of the clearing, head hung low, like a condemned prisoner. Several of the ravens in the trees made a small strange crackling sounds and ruffled their feathers, all intently watching the one on the ground.

"What …?" Jack whispered again, but Archer placed a silencing hand on his arm.

The large raven croaked again, this time with a series of broken caws and muttering squawks. The bird's voice was parched and gravelly. As it spoke, the bird on the ground cocked its head sideways to look up at it.

"It's like they're talking!" Jack whispered. Archer's hand tightened on his arm and he fell silent again.

At the top of the tree, the bird spread its long black wings wide for a moment then opened and closed them rapidly before falling still. The motions were imitated by a second bird in an adjacent tree, followed by a third and a fourth. As the fourth bird fell still, the raven on the ground dipped its head and the cacophony of croaks and caws returned. Dozens of ravens began fluttering their wings and hopping around in the trees.

One crow swooped down from the trees, coming in from behind the bird on the ground and blindsided it. The bird on the ground tumbled but flapped its wings to right itself just as another hit it from behind again. Feathers came loose as a third, and then a fourth, took turns at the grounded raven. Each time the raven fluttered valiantly to right itself, but made no attempt to escape.

"They're killing it!" said Jack. Archer still gripped his arm.

"It's called a council of crows," Archer whispered. "I thought it was a myth."

"Looks real enough." Jack picked up his cane and headed for the raven on the ground as more swooped towards it.

"What are you doing?" Archer hissed after him.

Jack ignored her and hurried towards the wounded bird. He limped quickly over, waving his cane around at the swooping corvids. The others squawked in confusion and circled briefly before dispersing. In a moment, the ravens were all gone from sight with only an occasional distant croak to show they had been there. A strange crackling sound came from above and Jack looked up at the big raven that had led the council.

The black beak glinted dully in the sunlight as the bird cocked its head and eyed Jack. It clicked its beak together a few times before making the crackling sound again. Jack looked back defiantly, and Archer felt as though she was watching him being judged. The raven suddenly spread its black wings, and flew into the sky with a loud cry. *KAW! KAW! KAW!*

Jack watched it for a moment and then it was gone. He looked down at the raven by his feet. It was dazed and injured, still trying to stand. Archer arrived at his side just as he knelt to pick it up.

"Stop!" she warned him. "It could be diseased!"

Jack gathered the inky black bird anyway. "It looked perfectly fine before they attacked it." He gently tucked the raven into the crook of his elbow.

"Jack! You shouldn't have interfered!"

Jack gave her an indifferent look and headed for the house, cradling the raven in one arm, limping on his cane with the other. Archer watched him walk away, peeved that she had been so casually dismissed.

She stood alone in the green, shady orchard and waited for him to turn back to her. He didn't. He moved away from her, showing no signs of slowing or of concern that she was not following. Archer put her hands on her hips and started to make a "Humph!" sound when she suddenly felt childish and awkward again. She dropped her hands off her hips and gestured exasperatedly at his back.

Heaving a big sigh, she followed him.

"Seriously, Jack, you should have let nature run its course," she chastised as she caught up.

Jack glanced down at his charge, then back to Archer. He smiled at her, but it was a grim, smile. "There is no 'natural order' of things." He opened the screen door. "There is the way things might have been if you weren't there, and how it is if you are. The best we can do is try to make sure our presence is a positive impact and not a negative one." He sighed heavily, as if coming to terms with something in his own mind. "So what did you say that was?"

She raised her eyebrows at him. "A council of crows. I heard of them a long time ago, but I thought it was just an old wives' tale. They say the crows hold a court and pass judgment on one and then kill it."

"I'd say it looks to be true." He looked down at the raven in his arms. It stared back with a dazed gaze. "What were you guilty of, huh?"

ELEVEN

You can't keep it." Archer's voice sounded as though she was denying Jack permission.

"I don't intend to."

"Then what are you doing?"

"Just trying to help." The nutcracker breaking a walnut garbled Jack's words. "I'm just trying to give him a fighting chance."

Jack grunted as he struggled with another walnut. Archer could tell it was hard on him. She wondered how extensive his injuries had been. How far had he come to reach the point where he was walking around with a cane and struggling with walnuts? She could see a puckered scar on his neck, another on his left hand, one on his right forearm. Those were from bullet wounds.

The puckered effect happened as the wounds closed from the inside out. Doctors didn't stitch penetrating wounds shut, to avoid sealing in infection. There even looked to be one at his hairline, but it was hard to tell if that was from a bullet or not, being more of a linear scar. How many did he have?

"Let me do that, Jack." She offered to help. His hands shook as he cracked the walnut; he didn't answer.

He reached for another nut. "Jack, let me help you with that. Jack!" He ignored her. "Jack!"

"*JACK! JACK!*"

A coarse imitation of Archer's voice startled them both. They looked over at the raven. Nestled in a towel-lined cardboard box in the corner of the kitchen, its head was cocked sideways, looking at them with one eye. It blinked and called out again. "*JACK! JACK!*"

Jack looked from the raven to Archer. "He sounds remarkably like you."

Archer gave Jack a dirty look. "Thanks a lot."

65

"No, I mean, seriously. He's got a really good imitation of your voice."

"I do *not* sound like that."

Jack shrugged and scooped the crushed walnut meat into a small plastic bowl. He took the bowl over and placed it on the floor next to the bowl of water sitting in front of the raven. The raven blinked again, eyed the bowls, and then Jack.

"Well, if you aren't going to keep it, what are you going to do with it?"

"As soon as it gets up and flies around, I will open the door and let it go."

Archer shook her head exasperatedly and then waved one hand up towards the ceiling, punctuating a conversation she was having in her mind. After a moment, she sighed deeply and turned back to the man who was infuriating her in ways she didn't think had been possible. She composed herself and her face took on a business attitude.

"Okay. So back to why I originally came to see you. Toni was concerned that you hadn't come around the last couple of days, so she asked me to check on you. Seems you are doing okay—other than the fact you have decided that perhaps your uncle was murdered after all. Or did I misunderstand that before?"

Jack leaned back on the kitchen counter where he could look at both the woman and the bird. He was struck by how her black hair, pulled back tight and braided, shimmered iridescently in just the same way and with the same colors as the feathers on the raven. The similarities ended there, however. The bird's movements were quick and jerky, almost robot like, but Archer's were smooth and languid, nearly sensual, even in their casualness.

He realized she was staring at him, waiting for an answer. He was embarrassed to admit to himself he had no idea how long he had been staring at her. He cleared his throat, trying to feign a casual disinterest.

"No, that's right. I, uh, came across something that makes me think Toni was right about my uncle."

"Like what?"

"You don't mind me bouncing half-assed ideas off you?"

A hint of a smile crossed her lips. "That's what friends are for, right?"

He smiled back modestly, trying not to seem overly zealous. He felt weird about having noticed her like that. He had never thought he would favor any woman's attention other than Wendy's again.

The thought of Wendy clouded Jack's conscience. He cleared his throat in a bid for time to clear his mind.

"Okay. Toni had told me that her friend Judy died in a suspicious manner, shortly after looking into my uncle's death."

Archer nodded understanding, though admitted that she hadn't thought Toni was right.

"Well, I figured that was coincidental," he continued. "Accidents happen and people die all the time. Then I started poking around into other things."

Archer raised an eyebrow at him.

"I came across this purely accidentally," Jack said, "while I was doing other things.

"I want you to consider the odds on this. One," he held up a finger, "my uncle dies after telling Toni he thinks his brother-in-law was murdered, and that he thinks he is being watched. Two," another finger, "Judy claims my uncle was murdered and then she has a fatal accident. Three: the computer tech who installed my uncle's surveillance system drank himself to death, alone, after *leaving* a party, two days after Judy died. Four: the cable repairman, who installed the internet so that my uncle could have a surveillance system installed, drove his truck off a cliff and into the lake, killing himself and taking the last six months' worth of his office's records with him, at two o'clock in the morning on a *Wednesday*, the same night my uncle was found dead.

"What are the odds that *three* different people, who came into direct contact with my uncle, died in that short of a time span?" Jack wore a dour grimace now.

A single crinkle marked Archer's forehead between her pensive furrowed eyebrows. "Your uncle had a surveillance system?"

Jack nodded.

"Where is it?"

He rose. "I can show you where it used to be."

"See there? About halfway up, next to that black spot?" Jack pointed at the power-line pole and handed Archer the binoculars. She fiddled with the adjustments for a moment and then spotted the four holes forming a square pattern where screws had once held a camera in place. She gave him a bewildered look.

"How in the hell did you spot that?"

"I came out to look and thought about the best places to put cameras. This was really the only place to put one to watch the driveway and see who came and went."

"How many more did you find?"

"I only found two more. One over there, on that barn, pointed at the house, and one on the house, over here." He led her back to the house. "See that spot up there, where the paint doesn't match? You can see where the holes were puttied in and painted over." He sighed. "On the other side, back there, you can see another bad patch job where the internet cable was removed, and in the house there are two places where the coaxial cable plugs were removed and patched over."

Archer stopped with her hands on her hips and squinted up into the sky, tilting her head so that her hat's wide, flat brim kept the sun out of her eyes.

"That is some pretty interesting circumstantial evidence you have," she agreed. She shifted to look out over the lake and he followed her gaze. The water sparkled brightly. It was a calm day and what few ripples there were on the lake reflected the sun back at them like serpentine mirrors.

"You know, I peeked at the police report on your uncle's death," she glanced at him to gauge his reaction, "just to see if there was anything to Judy's claim, way back when. It didn't say anything about anything being stolen or disturbed. No sign of break-in. Nothing."

"Did you notice the report didn't say who found my uncle?" Archer frowned.

"I have a copy inside. I can show you. His body was found within hours of his death, but it doesn't say by whom."

Archer turned slowly and put the lake to her back, squinting up at the mountains where they had caught Big Mike and Little Mike poaching bear gallbladders three days ago.

"What makes you think your uncle didn't take the surveillance system down himself?"

Jack had pondered that question already. "It was installed three days before he died. The internet cable just a day before that."

She nodded distractedly. He could see her cop brain working behind her eyes by the way her gaze didn't appear to be on anything, but was focused on something inside rather than out. She was reaching the same conclusions he had.

His uncle's body had been discovered the same day he had died. Who could afford to take the time to cover up a crime scene so completely as to remove cameras and installed cable lines, let alone patch up and paint walls? Who could have been sure the police report would find no evidence of a break-in with that kind of work done after someone's death?

When her eyes went stone cold and her jaw set he knew she was there. Her body language dropped into the 'relaxed' position of a soldier 'at ease' as she centered her weight and met his eyes.

"Dirty cops," he murmured.

"Dirty cops," she confirmed.

TWELVE

When Jack and Archer walked back into the house, the raven was nowhere to be seen. The plastic bowls had been tipped, and water and walnuts were scattered on the floor. The towel that had lined the box had been pulled out and now lay soaked in the water puddle on the linoleum floor.

"I guess he's feeling better." Archer commented dryly.

With a disparaged nod, Jack propped the screen door open with an old kitchen chair.

"Hopefully he'll find his way out soon," Jack muttered as he bent to clean up the mess.

"Don't sit anywhere without checking for surprises."

He looked up at her quizzically with a handful of soaked towel and walnuts he was cleaning off the floor.

"Poop," Archer clarified, over-enunciating the word. "Birds poop. And they fly. And they poop when they fly. It could be anywhere."

Jack rolled his eyes and finished with the mess as Archer watched with a bemused 'I-told-you-so' smile.

"So, there is a little more I found out about my uncle, but I could really use some help with it," he commented absently as he finished with the mess.

"You know it is going to be really hard to find any evidence, let alone prove anything. If cops covered this up, they knew what to look for, what to hide, what doesn't matter …" Archer spread her hands helplessly.

"I know. But I think I found their mistake."

Archer raised an eyebrow at him.

"I went back through all of my uncle's mail, specifically the credit card bills. He made a few purchases right around the time of

71

his death, and I think they are related to the missing surveillance system."

He went to the refrigerator and pulled out a soda for himself and offered one to Archer. She shook her head.

"Can I get you a coffee instead?" he offered.

"Only if your cream and sugar jars are covered."

He gave her another quizzical look, then got it. "Where do you think he went?"

"It's a big house. It's probably taking a little time to come up with enough poop for all of the furniture."

"All right," Jack sighed. "Will you please help me look for him?"

"I thought you'd never ask!" She smiled and led the way out of the kitchen.

"So what did you find on the credit card bills?" she asked as she looked behind a couch.

Jack found himself staring at the way her pants pulled tight as she bent over. He blinked, twice, and then cleared his throat, trying to clear his mind. He hadn't really noticed a woman other than his wife in a long time, and he wasn't comfortable with the feeling.

He turned away to look behind a cabinet, but he wasn't really searching, just desperately trying to get his mind back on topic before he looked like an idiot.

"Uh, he bought more computer stuff than just the surveillance system from Rainbow Computers. He also went shopping in Sacramento, at that big computer store. I found a receipt tucked in with the bills that shows he bought a laptop and a wireless internet card." He grunted a little as he bent to look under the skirt of an end table.

"So? We already figured his computer was stolen or destroyed to get rid of whatever the surveillance cameras recorded." She said from under a dusty valence rife with cobwebs.

"Right. So I was thinking to myself, they took the cameras and the computer, so why take down the cable that brings the internet to the house? Why hide that it was ever here?" He moved into the room he thought of as the library and glanced around the top of all the shelves. The bird obviously wasn't down here. He headed up the stairs, speaking louder as he moved away from her. "That's when I realized why they killed the person from Rainbow Computers," he called as he moved into the room he had been sleeping in.

"Why?"

Her voice came from behind him, soft and electric, startling him. He jumped, not realizing she had followed him into the room. He swallowed hard and was grateful for the excuse of looking for the bird so he didn't have to look her in the eyes. He could almost feel her body heat even though she was three feet away. He struggled to keep his chain of thought.

She sensed his nervousness and smiled slyly. Looking around, she quipped, "So this is your room? Too bad there's probably poop on the bed, or we could try it out."

Jack glanced at the bed and swallowed, his ears burning as if they were on fire. He thought he saw her blush, too, as if she had surprised herself with such a crude and forward remark. Not sure how to respond, Jack tried to ignore it. "They killed him because he knew the system. He installed it and he knew where the data was being backed up."

"I don't follow you."

He stopped and met her gaze briefly.

"The kid at Rainbow Computers told me they had to have internet here to set up that kind of system. I didn't realize just what it was he had told me at first, but it sank in. Not all surveillance systems need internet access, but that one does, or it won't work right. And not only does it record the cameras to the hard drive on the computer, but it backs them up to the internet, for remote internet access."

"So they cut the internet to stop the backup from being saved to the internet." She nodded. "I'm with you so far."

"Well, my uncle went over the top. The people at Rainbow Computers warned him that the internet out here goes out two or three times a week for hours at a time, so he bought a backup plan for the internet, too."

"The laptop?" she asked. She kept more distance between them since her bedroom comment, but she still watched his reactions closely.

It gave him a thrill that was hard to ignore, but he tried. "The laptop had a wireless internet card, like its own cell phone, so that it could access the internet over cell phone towers when the ground line is out."

"So you think, even though they cut the internet line, the

camera footage was backed up to the internet over this wireless thing?"

He smiled at her. "That would account for the huge credit card bill charges, for going over the monthly data limit on the wireless internet card—on the day my uncle died."

"So you just download the data, you can see what happened, and you'll have your proof."

"That's where it gets a little sticky. Even though I was able to use his credit card statement to learn the name of the company he was using to back up his data, apparently there is a lot of controversy about the privacy of data, and even though I am next of kin, they won't release it. I have to have a warrant."

Archer frowned. "And if the cops here are dirty …" she started.

"Then going to a local judge will probably let them know I am on to something," he finished.

"I see your concern." Her mind was working and her gaze was distant. "So, what you want *me* to do is write up a warrant." She met his gaze flatly. Irritation glinted in her eyes.

"You can do that?"

She raised an eyebrow at him contemptuously.

"I didn't know you could do that. I was hoping you knew how I could get one …" He spread his hands wide and stepped back a little from the look in her eye.

"I'm feeling a little used here, Jack."

"I didn't know you could write a warrant. I was just going to ask if you knew how to get one so I didn't have to try to do it locally."

He suddenly felt very self-conscious, and didn't know what to say. He was saved by a raucous squawk. He turned just in time to see the raven fly past the doorway, back towards the kitchen.

Looking back to Archer, he tried to assure her one last time. "I'm not trying to use you. I didn't know you could write out a warrant. I thought judges had to do that."

She shook her head in irritation.

Jack sighed and went after the bird. By the time he made it to the bottom of the stairs, he had lost the raven.

He poked his head back into the library room, but didn't see it there.

"Jack!"

"Yeah! I'm over here, I lost it again."

"Jack!"

"Yeah?"

"Jack!"

He turned to see what Archer was calling about and spotted the raven on the railing at the bottom of the stairs. The feathers around its neck swelled and ruffled as it vocalized again.

"*Jack!*" The raven called his name in Archer's voice.

"Okay," Archer said from the top of the stairs, "maybe he sounds a *little* like me."

Archer and Jack stood on the cement steps shared by the kitchen's two back doors and watched the raven in the tree as it cocked its head and watched them.

"As long as you don't feed it, it won't stick around," Archer told him matter-of-factly.

"What if I want to feed it?"

"You shouldn't."

"What if I do?"

Archer gave him a sour look. "You *try* to get my goat, don't you?"

Jack didn't answer. He turned and went back into the kitchen. When she didn't follow, he brought out her cup of coffee. She made a point of ignoring him, watching the raven instead. He sat her coffee on the aged and cracked cement bench that was the only nearby furniture.

"I've been thinking about the warrant thing," he started.

"I'll bet you have." Her tone was flat.

He ignored it and continued. "It wouldn't be too much of a stretch to suspect my uncle was having problems with poachers. I mean Big Mike and Little Mike were poaching bear on his property, right?"

"Are you sure you didn't already have this in mind? I'm starting to get that 'being used' feeling again."

Jack met her gaze. "I'd be lying if I said I hadn't thought about this, but I had no idea you could get the warrant, I just had just wanted to get your opinion."

"But now?"

"But now, I realize you could say there is evidence of poaching and suspicion of more evidence on the video ..." His voice trailed off lamely.

After the silence between them had gone on for an uncomfortably long time, Archer picked up the coffee Jack had brought her. She took a drink, squinted up at the sun, and put her hat on.

"It's a good thing we decided we were friends, Jack. I don't like feeling used like this." She sat the coffee down and looked him over for a moment. "If you're going to use me, I can think of better ways ..."

As she walked coolly to her truck, Jack and the raven both watched her the whole way, heads cocked.

THIRTEEN

A light breeze blew in from the lake, ruffling Jack's hair. It smelled of fish. He paced back and forth on the old wooden porch, his cane all but forgotten where it leaned near the door. A group of migrant workers were fixing a tractor that had stopped two rows over in the walnut orchard. The smell of the lake was a welcome change to the smell of the pesticide the tractor had been spraying on the trees. He could hear the workers arguing in Spanish but he couldn't make out all of the conversation. It was mostly about the youngest man's inability to properly use his tools, pun intended.

Jack tried not to seem as though he was watching the workers, but he was. He was hyper-vigilant and he could hardly control himself. He wondered if the workers had been in on it? He had no way of knowing. He didn't know who he could trust and who was watching him. The mere thought of trying not to look as though he knew he was being watched had sent his anxiety to new levels.

As he paced, his steps and the creaks of the ancient boards made a steady rhythm that held the raven's attention. It sat perched on top of the custom-made birdhouse Jack had put on a pole just off the side of the porch.

The raven had shown no interest in leaving over the last three days. Jack felt obligated to set up a place for it to sleep after it had spent the first night on the porch next to the kitchen door. The woodworking had given him something to do to keep his mind busy, which he needed desperately. When he wasn't haunted by the faces of his dying family or worrying over the circumstances of his uncle's death, his mind inevitably would come back to Archer. He wasn't comfortable with that either.

He made the raven's house out of the trunk of a dead walnut

77

tree he found behind one of the barns. Miguel had shown him to the workshop where he found an amazing assortment of tools and equipment for tooling and machining. Jack was hard pressed to imagine what the old Gardner's Patch must have been like in its heyday, with workers making their own replacement parts for the tractors, the fruit driers, the grape presses, and who knew what other machinery.

Doing his best to stay out of the way of Miguel's son and the other workers who were beginning the process of setting up a winery, Jack had used the planer and the lathes to mock up a miniature version of the main house replete with the front porch he now paced. The raven had followed Jack like a puppy and watched it all with a keen eye, offering opinions from time to time in the form of strangled coughs, caws, and clicks interspersed with the occasional *"JACK!"* that made Jack turn to see if Archer was there. Talking nonsense with the bird reminded Jack of his favorite nonsensical commentator, Yogi Berra, and earned the bird the moniker of "Yogi."

He was actually proud of what he had made, though it didn't resemble the larger house as much as he had hoped. He had originally intended to paint the birdhouse to match its larger inspiration, but the walnut sanded up so beautifully that he left it bare. Besides, painting it would have left it unusable until it cured and the fumes were gone. Regrettably, the raven was currently working on painting it one splotch at a time in its own fashion. Jack found it ironic that the bird enjoyed the house as a perch as he had discovered, after finishing the birdhouse, that ravens don't use them.

Jack shook his head, ignoring the raven's indiscretions while he paced the porch and waited for Archer. Her warrant had worked. She had the information from the internet data storage company and she was on her way over with it. She had called and left a message on his cell phone while he had been in the shower.

Thank God for small favors, Jack thought to himself. *Who knows what would have happened if she would have called the house phone and left a message on the answering machine?* He tossed a quick and, he hoped, casual glance at the men working on the tractor. They seemed to be doing just what they were supposed to be doing.

He spotted her green truck on the highway approaching the driveway and his heart jumped. *How am I going to pull this off without giving away I know about it?* He needed to make sure he conveyed the information to her before she said anything, and the only idea he could come up with left him feeling scared, giddy, nervous, and worried.

As her truck pulled up to the house, he grabbed his cane from where it leaned against the house and hobbled out to meet her. Not too quickly, he hoped, this had to look natural, but he needed to meet her as far away from the house as possible. He did his best not to glance towards the workers in the orchard again.

"Hey there, Hop-A-Long." She grinned at him as she grabbed a small black bag from the front seat and sidled out of the truck. He was sure it was the data. He needed to interrupt her before she said anything about it.

"Hey yourself, Green Cheeks!" Jack tried to keep a very friendly smile on his face, knowing she had explicitly warned him against using Toni's nickname for her. He gambled she would take its use as some sort of indication that something was up and not just a dig at her. Nonetheless, he couldn't afford to take any chances and took advantage of the pause the name had caused by continuing to talk.

"I've been thinking about you! I really wanted to finish that conversation we started in my bedroom the other day!" He could tell by the narrowing of her eyes that she wasn't taking this the way he had hoped, but he was close enough now that, unless she was willing to make a big scene, it was going to work. He opened his arms wide, holding his cane so it wouldn't hit her, and stepped close to her body for a hug. She started to resist it, but he was already close enough he hoped her reaction wouldn't have shown to anyone watching. He buried his face into her neck and whispered. "We're being watched, my house was bugged."

He pulled back, grinning widely, the scent of her hair was strong in his nostrils, making him slightly heady and the memory of the feel of her body in his arms was disquieting. Her eyes were hard, displeased with his familiarity. *Please smile back*, he begged silently, his trepidation threatening to break through his plastered on smile. *Please. Please smile.*

It was taking too long. He must have whispered too quietly, too quickly for her to hear. Then her blue eyes flashed from cold steel to sharply intelligent, and then to soft and loving, all in less than a heartbeat.

"You mean the conversation about trying out your bed?" she purred.

Jack felt a little faint, not just with relief, but with the physical effect she had on his body.

Archer reached out to hook arms with him, starting him back towards the house at a slow gate. She put on a show and intentionally swung her hips wide, making sure she rubbed against his hip as they walked, forcing him to use his cane to steady each step.

"You know," she continued in a husky voice as they approached the steps, "I've had a lot of men hit on me in my day, but you ..." She stopped and turned to face him at the bottom stair. Her eyes went cold and flat, and so did her voice. "You are the absolute worst. No creativity, no flash, no flair. You weren't even the most blunt and direct. And I have to say the whole dead wife and kids thing was really so much more of a turn-off than a sympathy card. I highly recommend you don't try that one on anyone else."

Her hands were on her hips, her gun belt and uniform adding gravity to her indignation. "The next time you beg a ride home from some poor, unsuspecting girl, don't leave your crap in her car. You might not get it back!" She threw the small black bag at him and turned on one heel, nearly marching as she left. She stopped after a few feet and looked back. "Take a good look at my ass as I go. It's the last you're going to see of it, Mr. Uncouth."

Jack watched her all the way to the truck, speechless. He was sure it was just an act, but ... *holy shit!* He expected her to give him the bird as she pulled the truck through the driveway. No finger came, but she goosed the gas and threw gravel at him with spinning tires. Archer sped out of sight.

Yogi flapped his wings at Jack and made a noise that sounded like someone crumpling a plastic wrapper.

FOURTEEN

Jack the Observer wept silently. The end of the world was at hand, yet again.

Jack the Marionette was glad to be leaving work, glad to be with his family, and he was starting to feel the holiday spirit move him when the front doors burst open and an extremely short black man came running in with snow swirling all around him.

The man tripped on the doormat and fell sprawling onto the halfway house's stained carpet. He was tightly gripping a little pink backpack and he protected it as he scrambled to his feet.

"Bogie! Are you all right?" Wendy reached out to the man who was only slightly taller than Jamie, but he ignored her and pushed past to Jack.

"You gotta help me, Mr. Tabor! They gonna kill us!" His voice was high in feverish pitch as he pleaded and grabbed at the front of Jack's coat. "You gotta protect me!"

Jack grabbed Bogie's arm like a child and started pulling him down the hall towards Chuck. He looked over his shoulder at his wife and daughter, resplendent in their Christmas dresses with the red and green garland hanging on the walls behind them. "You guys go wait in my office, I'll be right there."

Wendy nodded at him and Jamie gave a resigned sigh and a half-hearted stomp of one foot. They were used to 'things that come up'. In a correctional facility full of inmates who could come and go pretty much at will, things always came up.

Little John took pity on Jamie's sad eyes and headed down the hall towards her and Wendy. "Come on, I'll keep you guys company, Little Jamie."

She perked up and caught his thick-fingered hand with her little one. "Can we play dominos?"

"Sure! Hold on. Lemme go back to my room and get 'em."

Wendy and Jamie stopped to wait while Little John headed down the side hall.

Jack and Chuck rolled their eyes at each other as Jack led Bogie past the front desk and towards the office where Alfonso was still on the phone.

"Need privacy, Alfonso, gotta go." Chuck grabbed the phone from Alfonso's hand and put it to his ear. "He'll call ya back," he said before hanging it up

"Hey!" Alfonso tried to object, but Chuck had him by the arm and out of his seat.

As Jack tried hurried Bogie into the room, Alfonso threw up a hand for a high-five with the newcomer. "Bogie!"

"Sancho!" Bogie looked desperate, but still took the time to slap the high-five. The two inmates stepped into each other for a hug, creating a traffic jam in the doorway.

While Jack the Marionette witnessed what appeared to be an emotional hug from a distraught man, Jack the Observer knew what was really happening. The little pink backpack passed from Bogie to Alfonso like a card vanishing up a magician's sleeve. Neither man acknowledged its existence or indicated it had exchanged hands. Nothing had happened between them, just a hug.

"Get out, Alfonso!" Chuck was a loud man when he wanted to be, but the inmate was used to being yelled at. A casual shrug and a sidestep and he was out of the office as if it had been his idea to leave. As he walked away, he carefully held the little pink backpack so that Chuck could not see it.

"Sit down!" Jack pointed at a chair and Bogie complied. "What the hell is going on? You know you are not supposed to be here if you're not a resident."

Bogie stammered. "I-I didn't know where else to go! Man, they gonna kill us!"

"Who's going to kill you?"

"The toppas!" Bogie saw the blank look on Jack's face and panicked. "The police, man! The po-po! The Five-O!" Jack's eyebrows knit grimly. "They ridin' dirty!" Bogie's voice squeaked with fear. "They bad cops! I swear!"

Bogie rose out of his seat, pleading. "Man, I know you clean! You they last problem! That's why I came here! I can't trust anyone else!"

Jack dropped into his chair and rubbed his tired eyes. He hadn't heard this particular one before, but he was used to any wild story that could be thought of to get out of trouble, and Bogie was definitely someone he had heard stories from before.

"I swear Mr. Tabor! I can prove it! That's why they want to kill me! I got proof!"

"Proof of what, exactly?"

"Proof that the cops are dirty!"

Jack rolled his eyes.

Voices in the hallway caught Bogie's attention and he paled and began to shake. "Fuck me, fuck me, fuck me ... "

Jack stood up and started to go see but Bogie grabbed at his shirt. "They gonna kill us!" He started to cry. "You gotta help me!"

Chuck stuck his head in the door. "There are a couple of officers out here who would like to speak with Bogie."

Jack nodded and stood up. "Come on in."

Bogie fell to his knees. "I swear to God, I am telling you the truth!"

"Get up, Bogie. Whatever you did, this act isn't going to help you any."

An officer poked his head in the door and saw Bogie on his knees. A smirk crossed his face as he entered the room with his hand on his holster. "Just the way we like 'em." He looked around quickly then he called back out the door. "He's in here, but I don't see it."

Jack the Marionette, stupidly unaware of the situation, asked, "See what?"

"Sit over there!" The officer pointed at a chair. Jack thought for sure the cop must be talking to Bogie, but the cop was looking at *him*.

Jack the Marionette became more confused and allowed his strings to walk him over to the chair and sit him down. "What's going on ...?" The police had never ordered him around before.

Jack the Observer tried to close his eyes, tried to look away, tried to not know what was going to happen next, but couldn't.

With his hand at the ready on his holster, the cop turned his attention back to Bogie. "Where is it?"

Bogie cried. On his knees, on the floor, he blubbered incoherently. The cop kicked him in the chest, hard, knocking him into the desks.

Jack jumped to his feet. "What the ..."

The cop pulled his gun and, with a smooth easy motion, shot Jack in the shoulder. "I said sit down!"

Jack fell back into the chair, unable to breathe. His heart pounded in his ears like ocean surf. His breath finally came, ragged and fast, uncontrollable like a dog panting in the summer. Bogie was screaming, but Jack couldn't hear him. He could hear shouting in the hall but he couldn't make any words out. His shoulder was on fire. The rest of his body was numb and wouldn't obey him.

The cop shot him again without even looking. His leg went out from under him and he fell on his face. He was sure his nose was broken, he could tell by the metallic smell, but he couldn't move. His strings had been cut and wouldn't lift him up again no matter how hard he tried.

He could only watch as the peace officer kicked Bogie towards the office door. Bogie's face was a bloody mess and he was losing teeth as the fourth or fifth kick finally pushed him through the doorway.

There was more shouting in the hallway, and he heard another gunshot, and a scream. Wendy. It was Wendy. Oh my God, Jamie. The Marionette's strings pulled at him and Jack somehow found the strength to stand.

Observer Jack was screaming at Marionette Jack. *Get up! This time will be different! You can save them!* But Observer Jack knew it wasn't true. He knew the Marionette couldn't hear him, couldn't change anything.

Marionette Jack somehow found the strength to crawl. His left arm wouldn't work. His right leg wouldn't work. But he grabbed at the desk legs and then the door frame with his right arm while his left leg twisted wildly trying to find any purchase to push against. After a lifetime of pain and numbness, screaming and silence, he finally got his head out of the door.

Bogie was dead. The hole in his head left no doubts. Wendy was screaming, hunched over trying to protect Jamie, holding Jamie's face pressed into her dress. Little John was standing against the wall, arms up in the air and eyes wide. Dominos lay scattered all around his feet. Chuck was hurriedly flipping pages in a notebook with a gun pressed to the back of his head, the officer holding the gun demanding to know where Sancho was, and what his real name was.

Four more police officers had their guns drawn, yelling at each other about the mess, and at Little John, Wendy, and Jamie, wanting to know where the pink backpack was. Wendy spotted Jack's bloody form crawling out of the doorway in his suit and Christmas tie. He saw the pain in her eyes as she saw what had happened to him.

"Jack!" She wailed, unable to contain her fear and pain.

Jamie squirmed her face out of the folds of her mother's green dress to see her father. "Daddy!"

The cop who had shot Jack looked away from his argument with the other officers and saw him. With a disgusted look on his face, he shot Jack twice, once in the chest, and once in the head.

Jack felt like a ragdoll on fire as his body spun out of control and landed on the floor, limp and useless.

"Daddy!" Jamie screamed and pulled away from Wendy, running towards her father as her mother fell to her knees in shock. Four shots rang out. Three of them entered Little John's chest as he dove to catch Jamie. The fourth hit Jamie and crimson blossomed across her green dress as she landed face to face with Jack, eyes wide with shock. She huffed once and closed her eyes.

Wendy tried to scream, but only a strangled noise came out as she furiously crawled to her husband and daughter. A single shot to the back of the head knocked her pillbox hat off and brought her crashing down on top of her daughter.

Time passed. Or didn't. It just was. Jack lay trapped in his body, unable to move. He was dead. He wasn't breathing. He couldn't breathe. He couldn't blink. He couldn't move his eyes. He couldn't hear his blood pounding in his ears anymore. All he could do was lie here in Hell and see his lovely wife and daughter dead.

Jamie looked peaceful with her eyes closed, happy, almost. Perhaps she had gone on to Heaven, he hoped, instead of Hell, as he knew he had. Wendy had gone to Hell, too. He could see it in her eyes. She was dead and gone, her eyes glazed, but the horror was forever etched into the lines on her face. She had watched her spouse and her baby die, just as he had, and she had gone to Hell, just as he had.

Was she trapped behind those eyes, watching, as he was? No. He was in Hell, and Hell was a solitary thing. If she was behind those eyes, they would have been in Hell together, and Hell would never allow a comfort like that, no matter how hollow. She was in her own Hell, somewhere else.

He tried to not feel too bad about Wendy going to Hell too and instead concentrated on Jamie's angelic face, trying to take comfort in knowing that she, at least, had gone to heaven.

Time continued to not pass.

After a while, Jack realized his ears worked in Hell too. He heard people walking around him, talking; the police officers. They were arguing again, discussing what to do. Part of him was listening. He heard their plans, the names they gave each other, and the insults they used. He heard the callous way they laughed at the people they had just killed. Part of him just cried.

Hell was a harsh mistress, Jack realized. As soon as he had started to accept forever looking into his daughter's innocent face, Hell had restarted time. Hell would never tolerate acceptance of one's fate. That was the nature of Hell; to punish through torture, not to allow acceptance or complacency. It was not enough to break your will, your spirit, you had to be continually broken, forever made to suffer.

The voices were discussing how Bogie and Sancho, now known to be Alfonso Robles, had planned this attack on the halfway house as a revenge thing. "Went postal," one of the voices called it. Another voice said something about fingerprints, gunpowder, guns …

Jack lost interest in the conversations as soon as he realized they were doing a frame up, and Hell was okay with that. Hell was happy knowing Jack knew the cops would get away with this and it allowed him to suffer with his grief in timelessness again.

Shots rang out. Hell came at Jack with a surprise attack. No complacency. He heard shots fired with loud *cracks* and bullets hitting with muffled *pht* sounds. A voice called out in a gleeful mock inner-city accent.

"Dat's fo you, fuckin' nigger!"

Wendy's body shook. He saw a hole appear in her dress. *Pht!* It had no effect on the Hell etched into her face, and he suspected it didn't affect her in her own private Hell, either.

"Dat's right! Dat's what you get, Bitch! You fuckin' ho!" The voice was on the verge of laughing, enjoying itself.

Two more shots sounded. Jack's body shook once, twice. He suspected he had been shot again, too.

"Ooops! Did I do dat? Fuckin' idiot!" A giggle escaped this time.

He realized they were going to shoot Jamie again too. It saddened him, but not too much. She was in Heaven, he was sure. They couldn't hurt her anymore. This was part of his private Hell, just for him, allowing him to know they would take away the solace he had taken in her angelic countenance.

Jamie's eyelids fluttered.

The Observer and the Marionette, now again one Jack, screamed in silence, in horror.

Oh my God. She's alive. She's still alive! And they're going to shoot her again.

FIFTEEN

Jack parked the little Toyota in the downtown Sacramento mall's parking garage. Sacramento had been more than a two-hour drive, but he needed to be sure of his privacy when he checked the discs Archer had given him. On the way, he had stopped for a drink at one fast food place, a burger at another, and a bathroom break at a third. He stopped at a rest area for good measure and made a show of walking around to stretch out his legs and back, which he had needed anyway. Modern GPS trackers could locate his car easily, which is why he had headed for the mall. He wished the mall would have been busier, but he was pretty sure he hadn't been followed.

The sound of the car door shutting echoed through the cement structure, as did the sound of the gravel under his shoes. He entered the mall through a department store and headed straight for the bathrooms. Once inside, he placed his satchel on the counter in front of the mirror and opened up the side flap. He pulled out a device about the size of a camera with a large view hole. He stepped back from the mirror so he could look at his own reflection through the optical and switched it on. He looked himself over carefully and then looked over his bag and cane.

Nothing reflected back at him. The laser finder would reflect back from the optics on any lenses, lighting up in the viewfinder and showing exactly where the camera was, had there been any. He sighed with relief. It would be hard to cover up his knowledge that he was being spied on if there was a camera recording him while he found it. Audio bugs were a bit easier to find without revealing you know about them.

He put away the camera finder and pulled out another device that detected transmitting frequencies of wireless audio and video bugs. He turned it on and let it do its job. Nothing happened. Jack sighed a little with relief. No one had managed to plant anything on his immediate person that broadcasted live. That didn't rule out something that recorded to a memory card that could be picked up later, but it meant that no one knew exactly what he was doing, exactly when he was doing it, and that would have to be good enough.

He put the bug detectors away and left the restroom, making his way through the department store and out into the long halls of the mall proper. Limping heavily on his cane, he made a beeline for the restrooms in the center of the mall, not slowing to look at anything, and then entered the long hallway that led to the back entrances of the stores and the mall restrooms. His thoughts were that anyone following him would have been hard pressed to keep up without giving themselves away, but he still didn't detect any kind of tail.

He let himself out the service door and into the delivery area behind the mall, squinting at the bright glare off the light tan bricks making the privacy wall that hid the dumpsters and doors from public view. He placed himself to the right of the double doors he had just exited, knowing that anyone following him out would open the door on the right with a push handle and not the one on the left that had sliding locks into the ceiling and floor. He fumbled in his satchel again and pulled out a stun gun. Then he latched the cover of the satchel and slid his left arm through the specially sewn-on elastic bands that allowed him to wear it like a shield. It was heavy on his arm, not only because it had his stuff in it, but because it was made to be protection from knives and bulletproof against most handguns.

Leaning against the warm bricks, he tried to breathe deep and calm down. A few minutes would be long enough to wait, he decided as he shifted his weight and leaned on the cane to try to make himself comfortable enough to stand still that long. He twisted the top of the cane and pressed a small button on the handle with his index finger. He felt the springs push against the handle and knew the shaft of the cane would now easily fall away revealing a wicked short blade, if needed.

Feeling scared and stupid at the same time, he both cursed and thanked his lawyer for making him take the self-defense classes and carry around all this spy junk. He felt stupid standing here at the ready for someone who probably didn't exist. He didn't really believe someone would come barging through that door when they realized he wasn't in the bathrooms, but he had to admit, Leif's precautions had already saved his life twice.

Jack took a deep breath and sighed, looking at the bulletproof satchel on his wrist. It was his second one. The first had been ruined by a couple of bullets that had been intended for him outside of the courthouse, after the preliminary hearings.

Jack still felt stupid, but he could live with that. He had promised Leif he would try to be careful and take precautions. Now it looked like Leif had been right to be so paranoid. Again.

After a few minutes, he pulled the satchel off his wrist and dropped the stun gun into an open pocket where he could reach it easily. He pushed the handle of the cane back onto its shaft until he felt it lock, then he headed out to find the bus.

SIXTEEN

The library was quiet, just as he had hoped. He had no problem finding a secluded spot to work. The cheap, secondhand laptop he had purchased on his way here was slow booting up, but at least he was sure it hadn't been tampered with. Archer had given him three discs that were labeled only with ID numbers that meant nothing to him, so he chose one at random and waited for the computer to do its thing.

The first disc had a lot of his uncle's paperwork on it. He had apparently been scanning in his bills and records and keeping digital copies as well as the original paper ones that had been forwarded to Jack.

That put a thought in Jack's mind. He hadn't even considered approaching the attorney who had settled his uncle's estate. That had mostly been done through Leif Postumaus' office. They generously took over most everything for Jack when his case had started to receive national attention. Leif had told him to consider it compensation for the publicity, no matter how the case settled.

Jack scrolled through the documents but didn't find anything unexpected: bills, will, deed to the property, service orders, and the like. A couple of them caught his eye. Apparently, his uncle had applied for permits to sell food at a farmer's market on Sundays, at a booth during the Rainbow Festival, and to host an event to raise money for the local volunteer Fire Department. How had he found time to do all of these things by himself? Jack shook his head in wonderment as he popped out the disc. Maybe he had the time because he had been alone. Jack certainly seemed to have more time on his hands now.

The next disc had footage taken from his uncle's security cameras. It was divided into hundreds of short clips that were dated and time stamped. After watching the first couple of short clips of his uncle walking past, Jack realized the system was motion activated to record and store footage. He glanced at the dates on the files. All of them were prior to his uncle's death. He didn't have the patience to sit through night vision shots of deer eating roses right now. He popped out the disc and hoped the last one had what he was looking for.

It was more time stamped clips, and he went straight to the last one, dated the day of his uncle's death. Taking several deep breaths, he steeled himself for the sight of his uncle's murder and clicked the file open.

It showed a face. Squinting and scowling, the face came up into the field of view and peered into and around the camera, looking first around one side and then the other. The face was revolting to Jack. *Is this the face of my uncle's killer?*

The face had thick black eyebrows, sweat dripping down its forehead, and a receding hairline. It was no one Jack had ever seen before. The man's upper lip curled in effort, and Jack imagined he could smell the stench of old alcohol on his breath as he revealed widely spaced, blocky teeth with enough gouges and grooves in them that each could have been carved of wood. Jack could tell the man was pulling on the camera, shaking it. He was trying to take it down, Jack realized.

The camera came loose and the field of view swung around wildly, showing Jack that the man was standing in the raised bucket of a truck just like the one the cable guy had used. Ugly Face dropped the camera into a bucket and the picture remained unchanging for a few seconds before the clip ended.

Jack sat and stared at the screen silently for a long moment. He hadn't seen what he was reading himself for, and yet, he had. He now had the face of a man with answers.

He took a couple of deep breaths and examined the time stamps on the files dated the day his uncle died. Most of them were stamped an hour prior to Ugly Face pulling down the camera. Jack selected the one that started the cluster and opened it.

The video was of the driveway and the cable truck with the lift bucket. The camera's field of view made details on the distant truck hard to make out but it did exactly what Jack had expected it to do. The truck pulled off the driveway into the weeds and then backed up to the pole. An undistinguishable figure exited the truck on the passenger side and managed to keep the truck between itself and the camera's view until the bucket started to lift up into the air. It was hard to tell who or what was in the bucket as the figure stayed hunched down inside, but Jack was pretty sure it would have been Ugly Face. It was easy to imagine his gnarly teeth in a crooked grin as he thought himself sly, avoiding the camera.

As the bucket reached the top of the pole, the figure reached out towards the wire with something and Jack thought he could make out the wire falling to the ground. The small smudge of a figure suddenly grew in size as it no longer felt the need to hide from a camera. It stayed, unmoving, in the bucket for a long moment and then the bucket began to descend.

A new vehicle entered the driveway. An old beat up Ford truck, just like Jack always imagined farmers using, came down the driveway, passing the cable truck without slowing, and pulled around the house out of the view of the camera. The angle of the camera prevented Jack from seeing into the cab of the truck, and it didn't have a license plate that could be seen, but the pattern of rust and unpainted primer would probably be as good as a finger print.

The video continued to run for several minutes, showing only the figure in the bucket truck as it re-entered the cab before ending.

Jack noticed the time stamp on the end of the video was later than the starting time stamp of the next file. He frowned and then recalled the system used multiple cameras. They must have been recording more than one thing at a time. He clicked on the next one. It was very short and only showed the farmer truck pull past a camera that had been aimed towards the other farm buildings. The next one was also very short, showing the farmer truck pull around past another camera's view. Jack clicked another and watched the truck pull back into the main driveway and park. They had circled the house to make sure no one else was there, Jack realized as he watched the grainy image of two men get out of the truck and walk to the bottom of the screen. Jack recognized they would have been walking up to the front porch.

As they approached the porch, they drew closer to the camera and consequently grew larger in the screen. One of them was an ox of a man; big and barrel chested. His massive arms swung wide out to his sides. The other was small next to the big man, but not next to the truck he was exiting, so Jack guessed the first man must be exceptionally large. Jack pressed the spacebar on the keyboard and paused the image to study the men's faces just before they were going to disappear off the bottom of the picture.

Ox's face and head were round with his hair and beard all cut to the same short length. His face was pretty generic and uninteresting, He wouldn't be easy to recognize if his head hadn't looked like a basketball sitting on a barrel.

The second man's face was just as nondescript, with the same short buzz cut hair and a goatee instead of a beard. Without the size difference the men could have been brothers, and the second man's lack of distinguishing features would have made it impossible for Jack to pick him out of a lineup of men with short hair and goatees.

Jack tapped the spacebar again. The men finished walking off the bottom of the screen and the security footage ended. The next few clips showed Ugly Face bringing his truck the rest of the way down the drive and circling the property. Each clip was from a different camera as Ugly Face pulled the truck up to each of the cameras, stuck his head out the window, and looked at each one before moving to the next. Jack shook his head in revulsion at Ugly Face each time a camera revealed a new angle of his toothy grimace.

Finally, Jack opened a file and Ox came back into view leaving the house with his back to the camera, carrying something under one arm. Jack's heart stopped and his breath caught as he realized it was his uncle. Ox had one arm around his uncle's neck and was dragging his limp form effortlessly along, like a kid dragging a backpack to school.

Anger and hate rose up in Jack as he watched the callous casualness of it.

The other man appeared at the bottom of the screen with his back to the camera. He gestured angrily at Ox, who stopped and casually flipped him the finger. Jack finally spotted the other man's distinguishing mark. A curving scar on the back of his skull that puckered the scalp and gave the impression of an evilly smirking smile, as if the man was laughing at you, daring you to test whether or not he could really see you with the back of his head. He pointed a finger at Ox and shook it violently, angrily.

Ox uncaringly dropped his burden by letting go. Jack felt his bile rise as his uncle's face landed in the gravel of the driveway. Ox made an exaggerated show of leaning against the truck and not doing anything else, while Scar became so enraged he practically began stomping his feet. Ox pretended to check his nails, then shifted his weight to his other foot, and finally crossed his arms and gazed off up into the sky.

Scar stomped off out of sight and then came back with a big rock in his hand. He yelled at Ox some more and was ignored. He finally lost all semblance of control and kicked the body at his feet twice before lifting the rock up and smashing it down on the back of Jack's uncle's head.

Jack vomited on his new laptop.

SEVENTEEN

It was a long drive home. Jack floated between the double orange reflectors down the center of the road and the white line as they shone back at him from the blackness of the night, the only things visible in his headlights. He numbly followed the serpentine path it illuminated for him, wandering this way, meandering that way. Occasionally a mile marker or an emergency call box went by his window, a streak of light in the dark, but he was alone.

Emptiness filled him. The darkness of the night blanketed his mind and his soul and swallowed him. He had briefly searched for the pain, for the anger, the rage, the hate, anything, but it wasn't there anymore. He was empty. Watching yet another member of his family murdered had broken something.

He had become the Marionette, but he had none of the emotions. There was no longer a part of him to be the Observer. Someone else was pulling the strings and his body was driving itself home. He was only dimly aware of the passage of time, of reflectors streaking by in the darkness.

* * *

The house was dark, and as the Prius' headlights moved across it, the house looked flat, like a paper cutout, propped up there by Satan himself to make Jack feel more at home in his private Hell.

Jack parked the car and killed the headlights. He stared at the glowing green clock on the dashboard for a long moment. It was nearly midnight. He wasn't sure where the day had gone, or even if he cared. He grabbed his cane without thinking and began limping towards the porch in the dark. He was a beaten man. The steps creaked under his weight. The door lock rattled loosely under his keys.

The smell of the house as the door opened made him sick. It was an old house, made mostly of redwood. It had a peculiar musty odor from being locked up in the sun; hot, dirty, and old. It was like the smell at the cancer ward in the hospital, if the patients had been houses; the smell of old, dying house.

He turned on a light and something moved behind him. A bright light of pain flashed in his eyes for the briefest moment before everything went black.

Oh my God. She's alive. She's still alive! And they are going to shoot her again. My Angel. My little baby.

Someone stepped into view. It was a cop. He was holding a gun and pointed it down at Little John. He turned the gun sideways in his hand and posed for a moment, getting a feel for how he wanted to look. "That's Right! That's what you get! Dumb ass! Stupid nigger. Died tryin' to save the little white girl." The gun bucked twice in his hand, the muzzle flash left a blue-green afterimage spot in Jack's peephole out of Hell.

Shouting came from somewhere far away. Someone had seen Alfonso and everyone was to join chase. Jacks hope flared! Jamie might live! *Please God! Let her live!*

Someone kicked at Wendy's body and rolled her off Jamie. Jack was sure that somewhere in her own Hell, she would be tortured with the knowledge that her final sacrifice was for nothing, that her body had proved an ineffectual shield for her daughter's life.

"Didn't think I would forget you, now didja, Princess?" The cop bent down to whisper wickedly. He glanced into Jack's face and in his black eyes Jack could see there truly was no bottom to the depths of Hell. The officer looked back to Jamie.

"Didja get to say good bye to Daddy?"

There was shouting from somewhere far away and the cop cursed under his breath. He stood up, fired twice into Jamie's back, turned on heel and hurried away.

He hadn't seen Jamie's eyes fly open with the impacts, bulging with pain and shock. He hadn't seen her mouth start to work like a fish out of water, trying to pull air into her damaged lungs. He hadn't stayed to shoot one more time, to finish the job.

Oh my God! Jamie! He watched in horror as she desperately gasped for air. She made eye contact with him and saw him for the first time.

"D-D-Daddy?" Her voice burbled and choked as she tried to breathe. Her lungs were working spasmodically, shaking her whole body. "Help me. Please, Daddy ... help me." She tried to reach a hand towards him, but she was too weak. Her hand shook spasmodically, out of her control. "Daddy?"

Jamie! Jamie! He screamed from his Hell in tortured silence. Finally, his chest heaved once, and air came in, tasting of dirt and blood. "Baby ..." He managed a hoarse whisper as tears started streaking his bloody face.

"Daddy?" Her wild eyes found his again. "Daddy, there's so much blood." She tried again to reach out to him, sliding her arm towards his face.

He tried to move but it was all he could do to look at her and breathe. He tried to tell her it was okay, but all he could do was make incoherent sobs.

"Why did they kill us, Daddy?" She choked on the words. "It hurts," she gasped.

They lay looking at each other, unable to move. He wanted so badly to reach over to her, to touch her, tell her everything would be all right. Every time he tried to say something, the spasms of his breathing ruined it. He stared at her, unable to do anything.

"Daddy?" she labored to get the words out. "How long does it take to die?"

The fear and pain in her eyes, looking to him for strength, pushed Jack off the precipice and into the deepest pits of Hell. Her body shook with pain as her eyes looked to him for help. Hell had found a way to make it worse. He sobbed as he began to pray she would die, that her pain would end, that she would escape this Hell and go to Heaven.

God ignored him. They lay eye to eye with their life forces draining away, unable to talk, unable to move, unable to die. Hell had claimed them all.

She finally whispered for help one last time with a quiet "Daddy?" and stopped breathing. Hell denied his last wish and forced him to live.

EIGHTEEN

Jack woke from the nightmare, on the floor, listening to distant voices in the darkness. The taste of blood was in his mouth. At first, he thought he was still lying next to Jamie, still in Hell, but then he realized he could breathe. Hell was continuing to reach out and touch him at will. He had little doubt that it would soon revoke his pass and drag him back. But for now, he found his body worked.

He focused on the arguing voices; men, angry, yet keeping their voices low. Their tones were dangerous and deadly.

The men who had killed his uncle must have come for him. He still didn't know why they had killed his uncle, why they had been watching him, or even who they were, but he knew that, given the slightest chance, Hell would take all options away from him again. He couldn't allow that. Not now, not ever. Never again.

For Jamie, he found the strength to start moving. For Wendy, he held his throat shut tight as a wave of nausea bobbed him in a swirling sea of floor, furniture, and walls. For pure spite of Hell, he stood up and looked around.

He could see fairly well in the dark room. Distant sodium lights on the outbuildings reached the windows of the house and cast an amber hue over everything. The clock on the mantle read ten after midnight. He hadn't been unconscious long. He steadied himself and spotted his cane and satchel still lying in the open doorway to the porch. The voices were out that door, on the front porch.

"The way I figure it, we're on the same team, and we want the same thing, so let's put the guns down and get it over with." The voice was cold and giving an order more than a suggestion.

"You ain't killin' him 'til I get what I want, first." The voice echoed in Jack's head. He had heard it before. "I get what I want,

103

then you kill him. I kill him. I don't care, but I ain't leaving without it, and he ain't dying 'til he gives it to me."

Jack fought nausea and rage as his head reeled. He knew that voice. He knew the face that went with it.

Didn't think I would forget you, now didja, Princess?

Jack wished he had a gun. For the first time in his life, he wanted a gun, he wanted to kill. He had refused to get a weapon permit when his lawyer was insisting on all of the protective measures. He had thought he would never be responsible for the death of another human being. But, now, here was the man who had made sure his wife was dead, had tried to kill him, and had killed his daughter. Now he was back to finally finish the job of killing Jack. Jack wished he had a gun. If there was anyone he felt he could pass judgment on, it was this man. And right now, he wanted to.

He did his best to pick up his satchel silently. He put his arm through the straps and turned it into a shield as he grabbed his cane and began backing away from the doorway, back into the house, away from the voices.

"You don't understand something here."

"I'm pretty sure it's you who ..." There was a strange noise and a heavy thump on the porch. Jack suspected one of the men had settled the argument. He didn't know which, but it didn't matter. They were both here to kill him, and in his mind, he had finally crossed a line. There was no going back. He promised himself he wouldn't kill unless he had to. *Promise*, he lied to himself.

Just as he slipped into the kitchen, the light behind him came on and he heard the man sigh in a heavy stage voice, intended for him to hear. "I know you're here, Jack."

Jack pressed himself into the wall next to the doorframe, trying to stay out of the light coming into the kitchen.

"To be honest, I can't believe you're alive." The voice was calm, almost reassuring. "That bump on your head must really hurt. If that idiot hadn't surprised me by sneaking up right behind you, my aim wouldn't have been off, and you'd be peacefully with your family right now. So I guess you can thank him for that."

Jack could hear the voice slowly moving around the room, clearing hiding places as it went.

"Of course, if I hadn't been here whacking you on the head, he would be torturing you for information right now, so I guess you can thank me for that. What a wondrous confluence of events for you. I suppose you must feel someone was watching out for you."

Jack heard the front door quietly click shut and the locks fall into place. He was being locked in. His would-be killer was making sure that Jack would have to make noise if he opened a door, as well as searching for him. Jack reasoned he would come here to the kitchen next, assuming that if Jack had gone upstairs, it would be impossible for him to get back by unnoticed.

Jack tried to come up with a plan, anything, but the only thing he could think of was misdirection. Silently, knowing it would have been done in the movies a million times and that this man probably wouldn't fall for it, he crept to one of the kitchen doors and carefully unlatched it, holding his breath, hoping his adversary hadn't heard. Apparently he had not, as he continued to talk in his soothing voice.

"I know all about your little bullet proof-satchel, Jack. Don't think it can help you. If you hold it up, I'll just shoot you in the gut. Hold it down and I'll shoot you in the face. Your choice, actually. I hear you've been shot enough you may actually have an opinion of which you'd prefer. How many times were you shot, Jack? Five? Six?"

The man's voice neared as Jack quietly moved away from the door he had opened and back into the darkest corner of the kitchen. Jack unsheathed the small sword from his cane.

"Sloppy work, if you ask me. Those boys really didn't know what they were doing. But, hey! More work for me. And in this time of economic crisis, that's a good thing." The man stepped through the doorway so quick that it startled Jack even though he had been expecting him.

Gun held at the ready, the tall, thin man moved off to the side of the doorway and blended into the shadows. If Jack hadn't seen the lean figure enter the room, he couldn't have spotted him in the darkness. The man scanned the room very quickly, obviously missing Jack in the darkness as he realized the door was open. The man cursed under his breath and started towards the door.

Then man stopped and cocked his head, listening. Jack could see him silhouetted in the doorway as he chuckled.

"Very good, Jack. Very good! You almost got me. But I know all about you, remember? I know about the leg they shot out from under you, and I can't imagine you would really take the chance that you could outrun me." He turned slowly and his eyes settled on Jack. "There you are." He smiled like a hungry shark, his white teeth bright in the gloom.

Jack stood ready with the blade in one hand and the stun gun in the other. The man had been right; the satchel really would have done little to no good against someone who knew what it was. He was glad he didn't have it strapped to his wrist, it would have been more hindrance than help.

"You really should have gone with a Taser rather than a stun gun. It's kind of hard to reach all the way over here with that thing." Jack could barely see the smile curl into a smirk in the darkness.

"What do you want with me?" Jack asked.

"You know why I'm here," he said soothingly. "Ah … But I see. You would like to know the details of how I came to be here." He flashed his lazy, wicked grin again. "I was hired, Jack; hired to kill you. You should be flattered. You are in rare company. I don't come cheap. You will be number forty-seven on my list of accomplishments. I hate to admit it, but this was my sloppiest. After so many government officials, visiting dignitaries, and well protected billionaires, I relaxed a little too much this time, got a little too careless."

His face grew serious. "I apologize to you for not making it a quick, clean, quiet death. After what you went through last time, you deserved at least that."

Jack thought the man actually believed the words, some sort of sick code of ethics. Jack knew there was no hope of escape, but he was not about to go down without trying. He tensed, ready to leap directly at the assassin, the only direction that would give him any hope of a chance.

"I also appreciate that you got rid of the bullet-proof satchel. It will allow me to make this painless for you." He raised the gun and pointed it at Jack's heart, his face no longer showing mirth or sympathy.

"*Jack!*" the voice came from the door, startling the assassin.

Jack leapt, swinging his sword down on the man's gun hand and stabbing the stun gun at the man's chest. Muzzle flash lit the room with a deafening roar and blue electric light crackled and snapped from the stun gun as the two men fell in a heap.

The noise startled the raven in the doorway and it took flight back into the night.

The gun fired again, wildly this time, as Jack stabbed the stun gun at the man again and again. Jack grunted with pain and effort as the man fought back. The man grunted hard each time the electric prongs made contact, but he held on tightly to the gun and continued to try to aim it at Jack. Jack was wishing he had bought a Taser. Each touch of the stun gun made the man flinch and jerk like he had been hit by a professional boxer, but the shocks were not incapacitating. In desperation, he brought the stun gun up to the man's temple and held the trigger down.

The man jerked spasmodically, his arms and legs flailed wildly and he finally dropped the gun. Jack held the stun gun on for a second longer than he thought was necessary, just to be sure. When he released the trigger, the room fell silent, broken only by the man's choked breathing.

Panting, Jack rolled off his would-be assassin. His leg hurt horribly from the fall and it had been a hell of a struggle, leaving him bruised all over. He just wanted to close his eyes and go to sleep, but he knew the man wouldn't stay incapacitated long. *Unless his brain is fried,* Jack halfheartedly hoped.

Jack carefully stood up and felt the soreness of his body. He reached up under his shirt and pulled out the satchel he had shoved there rather than dropping it. He glanced at it, shaking his head at the silvery smear of lead that stretched halfway across it. Twice now, a bulletproof satchel had saved his life.

He looked down at the unconscious man, too exhausted to feel hate or anger towards him. He tiredly kicked the gun away from the body, well out of reach.

He was trying to figure out what to do next when he remembered there had been two men. Not just any two men, but this man, and the son of a bitch who had killed his daughter. He nearly bent over and cried with exhaustion and stress. There was no way he would survive another fight tonight. He needed to do something fast.

Taking a cue from some movie he had seen years before, he tied the man up with an electrical cord. Unlike the hero in the movie, he had problems finding one. The toaster's was too short and so was the coffee pot's. He found a skinny vacuum cleaner in the closet. He tried to yank the cord from the end of the vacuum but only hurt his shoulder.

He took the whole thing over to the man's motionless form, rolled him on his side, and hog-tied him where he lay. It would have to do for now.

He got on his hands and knees and crawled under the kitchen table to find the gun he had kicked away. After a moment's fumbling in the dim light, he came out with the gun, grateful he hadn't shot himself accidentally. He checked the safety, and, not sure which way was on, decided to leave it alone.

His stomach knotted as he realized he now had a loaded weapon in his hands and he was going to look for the man who had killed his daughter.

He felt weak as a kitten and thought he might vomit from the stress. He took a deep breath and steadied himself before peeking back into the living room. The lights were impossibly bright as he squinted around the room. Not seeing anyone, he was reluctant to leave the cover of the dark and make a target of himself in that room, so he turned back to the kitchen and waited a moment for his eyes to re-adjust. Then he carefully stepped around the body and slipped out the open door that had almost fooled his attacker.

The night air was soothing, the darkness quietly welcoming without being overwhelming. Jack headed around the outside of the house, towards the front porch where he had heard the men arguing. He breathed and stepped as lightly as he could with the pains in his ribs and leg. He wished he had taken the time to find the shaft for his cane and reassembled it, but he also knew the longer he lingered the better chance his daughter's killer would come looking for him instead. *Unless he's already dead.*

As he came around the front of the house, he slowed; looking for signs there was anyone there. He was afraid his leg was going to give out on him and he would fall over out here in the bushes, but he pressed on. As the porch came into view, he could make out a lump lying on the steps. It was a man-sized lump and it wasn't moving.

Carefully watching for any other movements around him, he made his way over until he could see it was indeed another unconscious man he would have to deal with. He sighed with relief he wouldn't have to fight this one, too.

He looked down at the gun in his hand. Maybe it was disappointment he felt.

NINETEEN

The two killers sat facing each other on the old metal legged, vinyl seated kitchen chairs. Bound with extension cords, duct tape, and dish towels Jack had scrounged from the kitchen, they weren't going anywhere. The one who had killed Jack's daughter was named Brian Nazzaro. He had vomit on his chin, his lap, and his shoes. He was also cussing profusely.

The man who had tried to kill Jack carried no identification and refused to talk. He had blood on his forehead and chin, and Brian Nazzaro's spit and vomit everywhere Nazzaro had been able to spit it at him. The man took it stoically, but the hate in his eyes was palpable.

Jack leaned against the counter and watched them, trying to appear as stoic and cold as the assassin. He was waiting for Archer.

Nazzaro looked older, thinner, and craggier than Jack remembered. Although Jack hadn't known Nazzaro's name, life must have been hard on him after Jack had named other names in court. The other man looked healthy, well groomed, and would pass unnoticed in any suburban setting. *Except for the blood and Nazzaro's spit and vomit all over him.*

Jack considered killing them both, but the idea of being a murderer bothered him more than he had thought it would. As far as he was concerned, neither deserved to live, and, as neither would answer any of his questions, they were of no use to him. The problem with what to do afterwards vexed him even more. Disposing of the bodies just didn't seem like his thing.

He considered claiming self-defense, which would have been very close to the truth, but then calling the local police, whom he suspected had killed his uncle and may have sent this assassin here, didn't seem to be a good follow up to that plan.

109

He thought he would torture information out of them, but, once they began regaining consciousness, he found the reality of having two human beings tied up and completely at his mercy more than a little disquieting. He tried threatening Nazzaro, demanding to know why they continued to come after him, what the hell was in that pink backpack, and why he had killed his little girl. Nazzaro had refused to answer and Jack was the one who broke down at the memory of losing Wendy and Jamie. He just wasn't as cold and heartless as he had thought, or perhaps hoped, he had become.

He finally settled on asking Archer for help. He really needed help. He was out of his league here and overwhelmed. He had wanted so badly to kill Nazzaro, but he needed answers, from both men, and after he had shown his weakness by crying, he knew the assassin would never give in.

His eyes went to Nazzaro and his stomach churned. Reeking of vomit and cussing like a sailor's drunken uncle, he reminded Jack of the inmates at the halfway house whose lives his wife had tried so hard to help get straight again.

Of course, Wendy had never seen them like this. She had seen them when they were sober and remorseful, docile and subservient; willing to do whatever it took not to go back to jail or prison. Seeing them like this was his world, not hers. This is how he saw them when they violated their probation and parole, when they hated the world and themselves, when they were no longer the smooth criminal, but instead a trapped rat.

It wasn't hard to ignore Nazzaro's filthy obscenities and death threats. He had heard them all before, time and time again, from more inmates than he could remember. It didn't really matter that he knew Nazzaro was a dirty cop, and oddly, the pain of knowing he had shot Wendy and Jamie was growing more distant. Seeing him here, like the worthless bottom dregs of humanity he was, made him more familiar. He was no longer a bogeyman, a thing to be feared. He was pathetic and worthless.

The assassin, on the other hand, he was scary. Jack had come across a few inmates like him before. There was a quick and easy descriptor they used to warn each other about inmates like him: Psychopath. This man could be anything he wanted, whenever he wanted. He was only angry when he wanted to be. He was only friendly when it served his purposes. You were only alive until he decided you weren't.

Jack was very lucky to have survived his encounter with this monster. Both guns he had taken from his prisoners were in his possession. He dared not lay them down where they might again be used against him. He might also need them to defend himself again. These men would kill him in a heartbeat, given the slightest opportunity.

A quiet knock came on the back door. The knock was cursory as the door opened and Archer let herself in, gun drawn. Her bright eyes flashed, assessing the room and its occupants. Jack held still so as not to alarm her.

"What the shit is going on Jack?" Archer kept her gun pointed into the middle of the room where she could quickly cover both the men in the chairs and Jack.

Nazzaro instantly started screaming for help, begging for protection from Jack, calling him a madman, claiming he had been kidnapped. He kept insisting he was a peace officer and that Archer look at the badge in his wallet on the table.

Archer ignored him as she eyed the other man, as if she could sense his menace.

"Jack?" She repeated her inquiry, clearly not comfortable with the situation here. Jack had only told her it was an emergency and to come quickly before hanging up on her. She had had no idea what to expect.

"Archer, I'd like you to meet Brian Nazzaro." He waved a hand at the still pleading wretch and stated flatly, "He is the dirty cop who killed my daughter."

"And this one ...?" Archer gestured with her gun.

"I don't know his name. He said he was a professional assassin sent to kill me, but that's about all I know."

"Okay." She moved into the kitchen, carefully shutting the door behind her and making sure she never turned her back on any of the three men in the kitchen. "Take it from the top."

Jack nodded. "As near as I can tell, Mr. Assassin was waiting in the house for me to get home, so he could kill me. Mr. Nazzaro was waiting outside of the house for me to get home—so he could kill me. Neither seemed to know the other was there."

"I knew he was there! Professional assassin my ass! How the fuck do you think I found you?" Nazzaro apparently had decided to forgo the innocent routine with Archer. "I fucking followed his stupid ass all the way from Colorado. He never looked back once!"

Jack thought he saw the assassin's eyes widen slightly with surprise, but the man kept the rest of his face impassive.

"Dumbass!" Nazzaro spit at the other man again. "And you, you stupid sonofabitch!" He looked back at Jack. "Why couldn't you have just died like the rest of them, huh? Do you have any idea what a pain in the ass it was staking out your lawyer's office to find out where the fuck you were? If his stupid partner hadn't …"

The assassin's chair came apart with a squeal of twisted metal and popping screws as he stood up and pulled it apart with his bare hands. The back legs of the chair were still duct taped to his hands and he used one of them to bludgeon Nazzaro across the side of the head. Nazzaro and his chair went over sideways onto the floor. The assassin raised the chair leg to hit him again and Archer shot him.

The impact spun him sideways, but he couldn't drop the weapon taped to his hand. He teetered for a second and then regained his balance and turned to look at Archer. The bullet had shattered his upper left arm and it hung uselessly at his side. Blood began flowing down across his hand and dripping onto the floor. The chair legs were still taped onto his own legs and the seat of the chair dangled loosely from them.

"Are you going to kill me now, or what?" His voice quavered slightly with pain and effort, but it carried no emotion of any kind.

"That's all up to you." Archer held her gun on him. "You get to choose if you live or die by what you do next. I can call an ambulance just as easily as I can call a hearse."

The man considered the options for a moment before finally asking, "What do you want me to do?"

Jack wrapped the towels around the assassin's arm as carefully as he could while Archer kept her gun trained on him. His real name was William Roland Gray, he claimed. But, he also claimed that identity had been erased years ago and they would find nothing on him as he worked for a very secretive international organization that specialized in 'selective pruning of government branches'.

Archer called for the ambulance as soon as the man had started answering questions. Jack had argued against it, but as soon as he had started to remind her about the possibility of the local police being involved, she had shut him down with a warning look and then took charge of the situation, acting like a cop and treating him like a civilian. She had disarmed Jack and put him to work treating the prisoner's wounds. It was a good show for the benefit of the two prisoners. At least, he hoped it was just a show.

"If you are a political assassin, then what are you doing here? Why did you come for Jack?" Archer glanced at Nazzaro, who was still lying on the floor in his chair. He moaned a couple of times, but he had been effectively shut up.

"I was hired to, of course." He flinched a little and gave Jack a sour look as the makeshift tourniquet was pulled tight. "Look, I am feeling a little light headed from blood loss, so if you don't mind, I am going to hurry this along by telling you what I think you want to know.

"First, I would like to request protection. I am willing to testify against my employers and their clients, but you are going to need to get me in the witness protection program or I will be dead within days. Why, you ask? Obviously I am no longer fit for my job, as this situation so adroitly demonstrates. No offense, Mr. Tabor, you have proven an almost worthy adversary, but that … *Idiot*," he spat the word at the unconscious Nazzaro and shook his head in disgust. "Well, let's just say I never thought it would have been possible, and leave with the understanding that my employers would now be more than willing to have me terminated for incompetence." He swooned a little in his chair and took a deep breath, fighting the effects of the blood loss.

"You, Mr. Tabor, are obviously wanted dead by two separate parties. At least one is willing to pay very well, or my employer would not have bothered. The first is obvious. Your continued survival endangers several political careers, as I am sure you are aware. I cannot begin to guess which muckety-muck sent this *idiot*, but then, you know much more about why he is here than I do, so your guess will be better than mine. The second is not so obvious. Your lawyer did a good job of protecting you; your records are sealed, your properties are in the name of a trust that doesn't seem to tie back to you at all, and you two never seem to contact each other. It would have been quite hard to track you down if his partner hadn't handed me a copy of everything your lawyer was trying to keep secret."

Gray closed his eyes and leaned his head back with a sigh. "I am so tired. So, to sum up for those of us who are slow on the uptake. Your lawyer's partner wants you dead. I understand you need to take another look at the beneficiary of your trust, as it will fall to the law firm if you do not name someone. He wouldn't tell me how much he thought the civil suit settlement was going to be for, but I can tell you it gave him the giggles."

Sirens appeared in the distance and a small smile crossed his face. "I never thought I would be glad to hear that sound ..." The strength in his voice was fading and his words were starting to slur. "*Idiot* there probably knows more ... about who ... sent..." He was unconscious.

"Jesus, Jack." Archer shook her head in disbelief. "How many people want you dead?"

TWENTY

The Rainbow County Sheriff's Department was a new building, but it was still small enough you couldn't hold a meeting in it. It was mostly empty and mostly dark as the only office personnel working this time of night was the lone dispatcher. The chairs looked new and inviting, but Jack found them torturous.

The Sheriff was neither new nor inviting, and Jack found him torturous also. He had short bristly grey hair and a small potbelly that looked hard as a rock. His eyes were bloodshot from being woken up and called in at midnight. Jack suspected midnight was the only time you would ever see this man tired and the odds were in favor he was retired military serving out his second career behind a badge.

He didn't like Jack, and he took no pains to hide his disgust at being unable to access Jack's files. He also didn't like the fact Jack had called Warden Durante instead of calling 911 like most rational citizens. He seemed to not like a lot of things.

Jack suspected it was his name. He had chuckled at the joke made out of his lawyer's name, but he had to admit Beauregard Rambo was a bad name for anyone, let alone a country sheriff. Jack made damn sure he had kept a straight face when he had been introduced to Sheriff Rambo.

"So let me try to wrap my head around this one more time." The Sheriff hitched one leg up and sat on the corner of a desk while he spoke. He had a piece of paper in his hand he glanced at before turning a baleful eye on Jack. "This here says you are involved in litigious proceedings against the city of Arroyo and that, as a consequence of such, as possible law-enforcement corruption is involved, I am not allowed a copy of your record without a court order. Did I get that right?"

Jack nodded. "I believe so."

"And it is my understanding that you had not one, but two trespassing visitors tonight who were desirous of initiating your demise?"

Jack nodded again. The Sheriff sat silently for a moment, tapping the paper against his leg. "I'm having a hard time with this, son. You see, neither one of the men you, ah, apprehended? ... is cooperating right now. One has a severe concussion and some broken bones in his face and jaw and can't really talk right now, and the other is nearly dead from loss of blood after being shot in the arm. He has demanded witness protection before he'll talk, but ..." the Sheriff shrugged, "he hasn't been conscious enough to talk anyway.

"That leaves you and Warden Durante to fill in the blanks here, and this," he held up the piece of paper "prevents me from trusting anything you have to say. That leaves Warden Durante." His steely eyes drilled into Jack. "How well do you know Warden Durante? Obviously well enough you called her instead of 911, so don't hold back on me here, son."

Jack raised his eyebrows. He wasn't sure how to answer that question. He didn't really know her that well, but he couldn't really blurt out he had called her instead of the police because he suspected police involvement in his uncle's death. "She just happened to be one of the first people I met here and ..." he pointed to the piece of paper "I hope you don't take it personally, but I am having ... personal problems dealing with law enforcement officers right now."

"Let me tell you a little about Warden Durante. We here in Rainbow County, well, we're a little bit country, and she's a little bit rock and roll. We like to work together, and she likes to go it alone. I wouldn't go so far as to call her 'rogue', and don't misunderstand me, I understand a Warden's job is a solitary one, but let's just say she isn't known around here for team playing. You see where I'm coming from, son?"

Jack nodded again.

"Good. So here's how we like to do it out here in the country. You scratch my back, I'll scratch yours. I want you to start at the top of the story, starting with this." He held up the paper in his thick fingers.

Jack wondered where Archer was. A little moral support right now would have gone a long way. He decided that he didn't really have any choice but to tell the Sheriff about his family's murder, as both men in custody were related to the case. He found himself weary as he started to explain it all. The day had been long, too long for a normal human being to have to cope with, and he kept yawning in spite of the fact he was talking about the murder of his wife and daughter.

The Sheriff finally took mercy on him and left to go get a couple of cups of coffee. Jack was so tired he didn't bother to tell the Sheriff he didn't drink coffee. He was going to drink it in hopes the nasty flavor would keep him awake. He stood up and walked around the room, stretching his beat-up body and trying to wake up. That's when his eyes finally found the door to the Sheriff's office. It took him a long moment to realize what his brain was trying to tell him, but when his tired stream of conscious thought caught up with the sub-conscious recognition, his blood ran cold and he was no longer tired at all.

The door read: Beauregard Rambo Rainbow County Sheriff/Coroner.

Coroner. Is this the man who claimed Uncle Bobby's death was not a homicide? The man who had covered everything up?

The Sheriff walked back in with a steaming mug in each hand. Jack stretched casually again, faking a yawn as he took one of the mugs. Putting as much disinterest in his voice as possible, and faking a yawn in the middle of the question, he casually asked, "Where's Warden Durante?"

The Sheriff didn't even blink. "It's procedure to suspend an officer involved in a shooting," he said, "pending an investigation of the incident."

Jack turned on the computer as soon as he got home. He was plagued by the yawns now that it was nearly five in the morning, but he needed to know a little bit more about coroners. The internet was as full of useless vulgarities as ever, but he soon discovered that real life was still never like the movies.

In many places, the position of coroner was fulfilled by someone in law enforcement, with little or no medical training. The fancy forensic coroners were still mostly a thing of good detective novels and really big cities. In Rainbow County, it was part of the position of sheriff, who, while not directly responsible for performing an autopsy, was the initial person to decide cause of death and whether or not an autopsy should be done.

A quick search of his personal files brought up his uncle's death certificate, and there it was in black and white. Sheriff/Coroner Beauregard Rambo had signed and filled in the blanks stating Robert Ratchet had died of an apparent heart attack and resulting complications from striking his head upon falling.

He stared at that for a long time. *Is it possible that Sheriff Rambo had just been incompetent? He had included the head injury and called it a result of falling.*

Jack shook his head silently, fighting off the gorge rising in his throat. He had been a witness to his uncle's death, albeit a belated one, and there had been no exaggeration on the part of Toni's friend Judy when she had said the hole in his head was 'the size of your fist'. You would have to fall off a cliff headfirst to do that kind of damage to your skull.

Sheriff/Coroner Rambo had known. No one stupid enough to misinterpret the extent of the damage could have made it as a law enforcement officer, let alone as a sheriff.

Jack mentally added to the list of people responsible for his uncle's death: Ugly Face, Ox, Scar, and Sheriff/Coroner Beauregard Rambo.

He stared at his uncle's death certificate on the computer screen. It reminded him of something. Something important, but he just couldn't put his finger on it. The screen blurred as he yawned again. He was just too tired to figure it out now.

He turned off the computer and stood up stretching his arms wide, all the while discreetly looking for the two miniature cameras that had been placed in his kitchen. It took him a moment to spot them, but when he did, it was hard to keep from smiling. They had both been moved; subtly, to be sure, but definitely moved.

He tried hard to resist the urge, but gave in and glanced at the kitchen clock he had installed himself. It appeared untouched. That meant the camera in it would have captured video of whoever had checked the other two cameras while he was gone. He would have to find a surreptitious way to check his camera without being obvious to the other cameras. Tomorrow. He was too tired tonight.

He worried about Archer as he made his way up the stairs, but he knew no good could come from trying to contact her while she was under the watchful eye of Sheriff Rambo's County Inquisition into Officers who Shot Someone in the Line of Duty. She would contact him when she could, he was sure.

TWENTY-ONE

Jack! It's good to hear your voice. How are you?" Leif Postumaus sounded glad to take Jack's call.

"Been better, been worse."

"Oh, I hate it when you talk like that. What's going on?" Leif's voice became strictly professional.

"I had two different people try to kill me last night, and if they hadn't gotten in each other's way, they would have succeeded."

"I hate to ask you this over the phone, but, where are you?"

"I'm sitting in the CyberRainbow Café, talking to you from my laptop on their internet connection."

"That's not secure, Jack."

"It's more secure than my house, which has been bugged since the fifth or sixth day I got here."

"I can't believe they found you in less than a week. You must have done something wrong, slipped up somewhere."

"Yeah, I've been thinking about that. I didn't slip up." Jack let the statement hang in the air with silence.

"Don't make me guess, I charge by the hour, remember?"

"I can't talk about it until you move to a secure line and contact me."

"My line is secure."

"No, Leif, it isn't."

Jack logged in to a free games web site and waited for Leif's alias to show up in the chat room. It would probably be a while, but there were a couple of things he wanted to do on the computer

121

anyway.

He shrunk the chat window into the corner of his screen where he could keep an eye on it and pulled up his uncle's death certificate again. He felt like it was trying to tell him something. Just like last night when he had stared at the Sheriff's door for so long before realizing the Sheriff was also the coroner.

What is it? He eyed the document carefully. He didn't see anything obvious, no highlighted areas, no little 'sign here' arrows. It just felt familiar, like a déjà vu. Like something he had seen before. Like … a death certificate.

Like a different death certificate.

He started going through his uncle's files on each of the discs. He had been so concerned about the videos he had forgotten the document files. Quickly browsing thumbnail pictures and file names he found another death certificate. James Gardner's.

Jack opened it and his eyes immediately went to the coroner's signature. Beauregard Rambo. It listed the cause of death as crushing injuries from a tractor falling off its blocks as James Gardner had attempted to repair it.

His heart jumped at seeing Sheriff Rambo's signature, but then he realized the Sheriff's signature was going to be on all of the death certificates when any form of accident was involved. He stared at it for a while.

Any form of accident. That got him thinking. *How many 'accidents' had Sheriff Beauregard Rambo signed off on?* Jack could guess at least five: his uncle, Toni's friend Judy, the cable guy, the computer kid, and now Jim Gardner. That was a lot of looking the other way. Either the Sheriff was responsible for all of these deaths, or his pockets were being lined by someone else with very deep pockets.

How much would it cost to hire Ugly Face, Ox, Scar, and *Sheriff Rambo?* And not just for one murder, but five. Maybe more. Maybe a lot more. And for what? *What was valuable enough to spend so much money to kill so many people?* His mind was blank.

He tried to come at it from a different point of view. *What did all of these people have in common?* His uncle. *So why was my uncle killed?* His mind was blank on that too. He opened the notepad on the computer and listed the people who he suspected had died as a result of … whatever this was. Did they have anything else in common, other than his uncle? Cable guy, computer geek, mortician assistant. *Well, they were all from a small town. Small area, really not just the town, the county.*

"Rainbow fucking County!" He heard Toni's voice echo in his head. "Rainbow Valley, Rainbow City, Rainbow Lake and the goddamned Fucking Rainbow fuck Festival!"

That reminded him of the harvest festival Miguel wanted to have this fall. He had told Miguel he would get the permits for that. He should have done that when he went down to the courthouse to get permits for winemaking.

An idea tickled his mind. Permits. He had seen permits in his uncle's stuff. He went back to the thumbnail pictures and file names.

His uncle had applied for three permits. But the one to sell food at the farmer's market on Sundays and the one to sell at a booth at the Rainbow Festival had both been denied. Apparently, he had wanted to sell fresh fruits and nuts but had been rejected because his almonds were not pasteurized. Judging by the dates on the permits, they were from the previous fall and he had not had time to reapply for the permits before the season was over.

The third was more interesting. It was an application to host a fundraiser for the local fire department; a daylong event featuring a pasta feed, games, hayrides and ending with a bonfire. The application was dated four days before his uncle's death. It was a lot more thorough than the other applications had been, probably because it involved using his land for a public function. There was even a map with drawings of what parts of the land would be used for what.

He eyed the map for a minute. He vaguely remembered an approval letter that had been forwarded to him with his uncle's mail, but something felt wrong to him. It didn't look right. *Why doesn't it look right?*

The game chat website window popped up to the front of his computer screen with a cheerful 'bing!' announcing that LEAFKILLER101 had just signed on. Jack turned his attention to the chat box and made arrangements to contact his lawyer in a more secure manner.

TWENTY-TWO

"Okay, Jack. Why do you think my office line is not secure? You know how paranoid I am. I taught *you* how to be paranoid, remember? If there is a tap or a bug to be found, I have already found it. And I just went over everything again—it's clean." Leif's voice was tinny and a little distorted as a result of yet another trick Leif had taught Jack.

Not only had they both purchased disposable cell phones, Jack also called with a caller ID spoof card which allowed the user to send any name or number on the caller ID they wanted. This routed the call through the internet and made Jack's disposable cell phone virtually untraceable.

"It may be clean of bugs, but not of spies."

"You mean the morons staking out my office for the last month?"

"You knew about them?"

"Of course I did! I'm paranoid, remember?"

"Why didn't you do something about them?" Jack felt his ears start to burn. If Leif would have done something about them a month ago then Nazzaro wouldn't have had a chance at killing him last night.

"I was! I had my guys following them whenever they changed shifts. We have greatly increased our knowledge of who is involved in this! And I hate to say it, but it seems to get bigger every day!"

"You don't know the half of it." Jack walked along the bicycle path of Rainbow Valley State Park as he talked. He felt the need to make sure he wasn't somewhere anyone could be listening or had any surveillance set up. "They weren't the spies I was referring to. I was referring to your partner."

"Bullshit!" Leif spat into the phone so hard Jack flinched. "Are

125

you shittin' with me? This is not funny, Jack, I'm a busy man. I've got things to do. You can't be calling me up and …"

"Leif! I'm serious. There is bad juju on me. Two men tried to kill me last night!"

"All right! All right already! Why do you think my partner is spying on us?"

"Because the assassin told me so."

"I'm going to hang up the fucking phone right now, and you can go get a new lawyer, okay?"

"Just listen a minute, all right? I've stepped into a whole new hornet's nest out here and I'm still getting stung by the ones out there! My uncle was murdered and I think the people who did it have been thinking about killing me too, or they wouldn't have bugged my freaking house!"

"What the fuck, Jack!"

"Tell me about it!"

"Ahhh!" Leif growled in frustration, "Start at the beginning. I'm recording our conversation for my personal use, blah blah, client-attorney privileges, blah blah. Go."

"All right, here's the summary: Last night two men tried to kill me. One was Brian Nazzaro, who, by the way, is the man who killed my daughter." Jack took a deep breath. They had spent a long time trying to identify the officers involved in killing Jack's family, and they hadn't gotten very far. It was strange to finally have a name for the man he held most responsible in his mind.

"You sure about that, Jack?" Leif asked softly.

Jack nodded into the phone, afraid he wouldn't be able to keep talking if he dwelled on it. "The other was a professional assassin using the name William Roland Gray. He claimed he works for some big secret agency and we'll never get anything on him or them, but he's willing to turn state's evidence for witness protection. He also claimed that his agency was hired by your partner, and that your partner wants me dead because the settlement from the civil suit will revert to your offices and therefore to him. Both men claimed to have located me because of your partner. Both are currently in the custody of the Rainbow County Sheriff's Department. However, I'm not comfortable with that situation, as my uncle was murdered, I have the murder on video, I suspect—no, I *know* the Sheriff is in on it because he is also the coroner and there is no *fucking* way my uncle's smashed-in head was caused by a heart attack. I also suspect they killed at least three more people to cover up his murder, but I can't prove anything there. Does that sum it up?"

There was a long pause before Leif answered. "What do you think about calling in the FBI?"

"I'm not fucking joking!"

"I know you're not! But it sounds like you have the police in two different states trying to kill you! I'd call the US Marshall's office and try to get *you* into the witness protection program, but you don't fucking know anything to tell them so they would protect you! I don't know what the fuck to do!" Leif's frustration echoed through the tinny phone line as he yelled obscenities. "All right, Jack," he said after calming down, "did you put the clock up like I told you to?"

"Yeah, I hung it up first thing. Well, I peed first, but then I put it up."

"See? I told you it would come in handy. You need to get me that clock and the video of your uncle, then you need to get the hell out of there, go hide in Death Valley or something. Go hike the Appalachian Trail. Get somewhere where no one can find you until the next court date and let me sort out the rest of this shit."

Jack answered with determination in his voice. "I can't do that."

Frustration overtook Leif again and Jack listened to what could only have been the sound of Leif's phone flying through the air and hitting a wall. After a moment Leif's voice came back, sounding even tinnier than before. "Why the *fuck* not, Jack?"

"I can't walk away from my uncle's murder."

"No one is asking you to. Get me the videos. I'll get the one with your uncle's murder on CNN, your uncle's killer will fry, I'll get the other in evidence for us and bring charges against the guy who killed Jamie and Wendy, and he'll fry, and then we'll use it to put away the assassin guy too! See? No need for Jack to be out there getting killed!"

"I really don't think it's that simple. I think they have killed at least four people already to cover up whatever it is they are killing people for, and if we don't figure it out I think more people will get killed."

Leif sighed exasperatedly into the phone. "What makes you think they want to kill someone else?"

"They bugged my house!"

"People don't bug houses to kill someone, Jack. They do it to learn something. Or to see you naked. Is there someone there who wants to see you naked?"

Jack responded with a snort.

"All right then, what do they want to learn from you? Are you sure it wasn't the assassin or that dirty cop who bugged your place?"

"No, it couldn't have been them. The bugs showed up right after I got there. I think they were checking to see if I suspected foul play in my uncle's death."

"And did you?"

"Not until they bugged my house!"

"That should be on the video in the clock, right?"

"What, the one Joe Schmo they had put the bugs there? This is bigger than that and I need to get to the bottom of this. I'm not touching that clock until I have to. As soon as I do, whoever is spying on me will know I am on to them and I'll lose my only advantage."

Leif thought about it for a minute. "All right, if you're really going to do this, you need to figure out what changed to make them bug your house. How did they know you were there? Why would they care if you were there? Who knew you were there? You weren't there long, right? Two or three days? How many people did you interact with? Make a list of everyone. You can figure it out. It's not like you've lived there your whole life and it might have been the older brother of that girl you kissed in fourth grade."

Jack sat at his uncle's old wooden desk making a list of people he had met since his arrival. The scars and scratches on the desk made it easy for him to imagine it had been brought to California in the back of a covered wagon.

His list wasn't a long one, but it turned out to be useless. He started out with everyone he had met who could have known who he was or where he was staying. Toni, Archer, Miguel ...

That was where it had fallen apart. As soon as he listed Miguel, he realized that he had made the classic mistake of being aloof and overlooking the hired help.

He had no idea how many people were working this farm under Miguel's supervision, and although he liked Miguel, and in fact had been the one to contact Miguel and hire him to take care of the property, he had no way of knowing whether or not Miguel had been waiting to tell someone that Bobby Ratchet's nephew had shown up in person. The same went for Toni, and, as much as he didn't want to believe it, Archer. Maybe even the kid at the computer store was supposed to be watching for someone asking questions about the cameras that had been installed on the property.

Jack groaned in frustration. He was getting nowhere.

He began organizing the desk, cleaning up the things he had stacked there since his arrival. He came across the permit application for the winery he had promised Miguel and his son. He regarded the permit dismissively. *Why should I put out the effort to try to do this kind of crap when people are trying to kill me? When they killed my family? What's the point?*

Then he recalled his ride around the orchards and vineyards with Miguel in the ATV. Miguel had been straightforward, honest, earnest, and enthusiastic. How often had he had seen that dealing with convicted felons at the halfway house?

He grabbed his pen and started to scratch Miguel's name off his list. He would still have to take into account anyone working for Miguel, but his gut said Miguel was a good man. As good as they come.

He put down the pen without marking out Miguel, and picked up the application again. It was mostly filled out. He just hadn't finished the attachment for mapping out the location on the property. The man at the county office had assured him it would be all right to use a photocopy of the map he had purchased from their office, with the appropriate places marked on it.

He flipped through the pages and found the map and the aerial view he had bought at the Rainbow County Planning Department. He started to mark which buildings on the plat map would house the winery and the tasting room, but then thought better of writing on his one copy. He paused for a moment. He felt like he had a second one somewhere.

His uncle's application had one, an electronic copy. He could print that out. He stopped and looked at his copy again. Something was wrong.

He booted up his laptop and inserted one of his uncle's discs. He hoped it was the right one. After a moment, the disc pulled up its contents. It was.

He opened the file and stared at the map his uncle had used. Superficially, it was the same. It featured the same buildings on it, in the same places, but the outline was different. As was the name of the surveyor and the date listed in the corner. The one he had received from the county was dated about three years ago, the one his uncle had used was about twenty years older. He held them up to compare side by side. There was a chunk of land missing from the northeast quadrant of the newer one. He wasn't sure how big the affected area was, but it was noticeable. Several acres, at least.

He switched his computer over to internet access and pulled up a recent aerial view on Google maps. The part missing from the older map was a busy spot. There was a large building and several smaller ones, as well as a parking lot and a lot of motor homes, and a highway. The label on the map listed it as the Rainbow Casino and Bingo Parlor.

Again, something about this had bothered him before. He remembered. His uncle's mail had the approval for this application in it. He ran to the closet that had the duffle bag he had shoved all of his uncle's paperwork into. He pulled out a large stack of mail and started sorting. There it was. He pulled out the application and ran back to the desk.

He looked at the three different maps and then back to the computer screen. The casino was only out of place on his uncle's map. Why had his uncle used an old map? And why did his copy of the application have the old map while the approved copy from the county have the new one?

Jack looked at the dates on his uncle's application again. It had been turned in four days before his uncle's death. And it was returned with a different map than had been submitted. He thought for a moment. The bugs in his house showed up the day after he had visited the county courthouse. *Why? Is there a connection?*

After all, he had specifically asked for copies of their maps. If this was what had gotten his uncle murdered, he had shown up right in the middle of it and expressed interest.

What to do now? Find out when and how the map changed? How could he do that without going back to the county and raising more suspicions?

Frustration set in and he went out on the front porch and stared out into the orchard. A small flock of blackbirds was moving through the grass under the trees, hunting and pecking for food. He glanced at the birdhouse he had made for Yogi and hoped the bird was all right. He hadn't seen it since it had saved him from the assassin.

The only thing that stopped this place from being idyllic was the noise from the cars on the highway. And murder.

TWENTY-THREE

"Can we talk?" Jack's voice was hushed over the phone, although there was truly no need for it to be so. It just felt appropriate to whisper when he thought someone might be spying on him.

"This place is clean-clean. I went over every inch of it myself. And my partner is not here. He's out buying an engagement ring. Did I mention he's getting married? She's a nice girl. She keeps him busy. Too busy to hire an assassin." Leif said sardonically. "Anyway, I'm recording this, blah blah blah. How are you doing, Jack? Did you hole up in a safe place?"

"No. I'm still in Rainbow County."

Leif sighed heavily. "Okay. What do you need to talk about?"

"I am forwarding information to you. I have already mailed discs and now I am setting up a download site for you to get them, hopefully you'll get both."

"Okay. What kind of information?"

"Copies of the video of my uncle's murder, showing his killers, and copies of my uncle's records of this property compared with the county's records of it."

"Why the property records?"

"I am pretty sure that's what this is all about. Kind of. I don't know why, but this property is the only real connection between everyone who was killed, and the only thing weird I have found about the property is that a couple acres of it, no more than ten or twenty, changed hands about the time my uncle inherited it. The thing is—I don't think he knew about that, and I don't know how to look it up without going into the County Clerk and Recorder's Office and asking. I think going into those offices and asking about this property is what got him killed in the first place. Might not be so smart of me to just walk in there and ask. Any ideas?"

"No good ones. In a county that small there is probably only going to be one or two title companies and they are just as likely to be a cause of problems as the county." Jack could hear Leif's fingers drumming on the desk as he thought. "Okay, look. We are going to have to get a California lawyer involved sooner or later. Neither my partner nor I are set up to do anything there."

"About your partner …" Jack started.

"I know, I know what you said the bad guys said, but I trust my partner with my life. He didn't leak. Not on purpose, anyway. They are just trying to split our unified front. And it will work if you let it. Trust me to be right on this. He and I have been through a lot of shit together and having your settlement come to this law firm most definitely would not be enough to turn him to the dark side. Besides I asked him and he said he didn't."

It was Jack's turn to sigh heavily. "I would really like to leave my spy clock up a little longer, but I can take it down and see what it recorded those guys saying about your partner if you need me to …"

"Look, Jack. I know your job taught you not to trust anyone, so did mine. I know life has dealt you some shitty cards. But isn't there anyone out there you can still trust?" He was silent for a moment. "You trust me, right? Not everyone is a bad guy. Not everyone is out to get you."

Jack didn't answer.

"Well, maybe in your case everyone *is* out to get you."

Jack circled the casino for the third time before parking the rental car. It occurred to him that it was time to get rid of the rental. Most had GPS trackers in them now, and if law enforcement was trying to find him with it, they would. He resolved to go to a dealership and see about a short-term lease after he finished checking out the casino.

Rainbow Valley Casino and Bingo was surprisingly devoid of colors on the outside. In fact, it was surprisingly devoid of anything architecturally interesting. It appeared to be a hastily set up tent, although closer inspection showed it to be sturdier. It was a big white clamshell balloon, the type some sports teams use to practice in. The inside was no better.

Although the slot games flashed colored lights and made happy noises, the overall din was uninspired and irritating, while the ambiance and smell was that of a sweaty, smoky cave. Giant rainbow lights splayed across the ceiling, but did nothing to illuminate the gloom or disperse the desperation on the faces of the people slapping at buttons on the machines, drinking, and sucking on glowing sticks of stink.

One old lady reminded him of Toni with her drink and cigarette in one hand and another cigarette burning in the ashtray next to her. If she found any pleasure in the buttons and lights in front of her, it didn't show on her face.

He recoiled as a man in a one-piece jumpsuit walked by reeking so strongly the body odor was almost visible. The jumpsuit appeared to have once been a cream, or perhaps orange, color, but was now pushing past tan and looked as if it had never been washed.

He walked the perimeter of the casino and noted dealers standing idly at their tables with bored expressions. A Native American waitress walked by with a tray of drinks and flashed him a dazzling smile that was out of place with dull eyes.

He shook his head. There was nothing to see here. He'd had some vague idea of asking a manager to see their deed to the land or their lease, or whatever they did or didn't have, but the more he looked around, the more he was sure there was no one here who would have that information. He sighed and turned to leave.

Halfway to the door he spotted Big Mike and Little Mike wandering the rows of slot machines with beers in their hands. He was surprised to see them. They should have been in custody still. Jack didn't think there had even been enough time to post bail.

They spotted him and waved jovially.

"There's the Big Man!" called Little Mike, changing direction to talk to Jack.

"Can we buy you a beer?" Big Mike grinned.

"You know, to thank you." Little Mike grinned sheepishly and shifted his weight a little nervously when Jack didn't have an immediately forthcoming response.

"For what?" Jack asked.

"You know," Little Mike grinned sheepishly and whispered, "for not pressing charges against us."

"I don't know what you're talking about."

"Yeah! Right! Me neither!" Little Mike laughed nervously again and poked Big Mike in the ribs. "You neither, right?"

"Right!" grunted the large man. "But seriously, we more than keep our bargains. You scratched our back, and we'll scratch yours. Your secret is safe with us."

Jack frowned at them. *What secret?*

"Seriously," continued Big Mike in a reverberant voice. "We return favors in spades. We're good for more than keeping our mouths shut. We know those woods better'n our own backyards. If you ever run short of hired guns up there, we'll help fill in for you."

Jack stared at Big Mike. The man's lower lip protruded with the chewing tobacco that had stained his teeth yellow.

He took too long to answer and Little Mike stepped in. "Can't you see he don't want to talk about it here? Out in public is a bad place to talk business. Ain't that right?" He looked at Jack.

Jack returned what he hoped was a neutral smile.

"Well we oughtta get going." Little Mike shrugged nervously. He started to turn away, but stopped and looked back at Jack. "One more thing," he dropped his voice. "That Warden—I don't know how you leashed her. The Sheriff, I can see easy. But not her. You need to watch yourself. I don't trust her."

He grabbed Big Mike's arm and shuffled away, leaving Jack with a lot of unanswered questions.

Jack sat at the old wooden desk again and stared at his list. He hadn't managed to scratch out anyone's name. Was Leif right? Couldn't he find it in himself to trust anyone? He hadn't even scratched out Archer's name.

Why didn't he trust her? Was there something in the back of his mind? Did he subconsciously realize it? Could those two buffoons, Big Mike and Little Mike, actually be right? Was Archer playing switch-hitter for the other team? Why would she have given him the discs with the proof his uncle had been murdered? Why wouldn't she have just shot him when she had all the guns and two would-be assassins tied up in his kitchen to blame it on?

He wanted to believe she was on his side. He really, *really* wanted to. He liked her. Maybe Leif was right. Maybe there were some people you just needed to trust.

He reached down and scratched her name off the list. Hesitant at first, he vigorously blacked it out completely. He laid the pen down and picked up his cell phone.

If he was going to trust Archer, he was going to trust her all the way. He dialed her number to find out why Big Mike and Little Mike thought he hadn't pressed charges and to let her know what they had said about 'talking business' and not trusting her. Her phone gave him an 'unavailable' recording and didn't allow him to leave her a message.

He put the phone down and picked up the aerial view of the property he had bought from the county.

What is it up there the two Mikes had been talking about? It had to be close to where Archer had taken him. He squinted at the map trying to figure out where they had been. As his eyes traced the small line that was the dirt road, he remembered something Archer had said. The photo could have shown a pot farm.

Northern California was infamous for its hidden pot farms. The climate was perfect and there were vast wilderness areas to hide it in. He remembered hearing stories of people afraid to explore their own land out of fear of finding one and getting shot.

He looked at the photo again with renewed zeal, now that he knew what to look for and where to look. He moved the photo closer and further away from his face, wishing for a magnifying glass. He couldn't find anything; there wasn't enough detail. Not even whatever it was Archer had seen that told her the Mikes had a hunting camp set up there. He was surprised to see how close to the back of the casino that road had taken him and Archer. Frustrated, he tossed down the photo. There just wasn't enough detail to make anything out.

Archer had told him she had gotten her satellite photos off the internet. A quick search and an expensive credit card charge later, he was looking at very recent satellite photos at a much higher resolution.

Zooming in over the casino was the easiest way to find his property on the images. As he did so, he wondered again when the casino had acquired the land from this property. He quickly spotted what he suspected Archer had made out to be the Mikes' base of operations.

It wasn't as near the casino as he had suspected. It was up near the other edge of his uncle's land, butted up against not only the National Forest, but something called the Loquait Rancheria. He realized that made sense. More access to wilderness most people couldn't get near would make for better hunting. The Rainbow Casino and Bingo Parlor was also right on the edge of the Loquait Rancheria.

Out of curiosity, he typed in a search for the Loquait Rancheria and discovered it was, or had been, an Indian Reservation. The information was vague. He mentally shrugged and wondered if 'Rancheria' was some politically correct term for 'Reservation'.

He scanned the images for a while longer, but couldn't spot anything unusual. He felt a little better about Archer not having spotted anything. He knew something was there and couldn't find it, so why should she have? He was glad he had scratched her name off the list.

Still thinking about the land the casino was on, he saved the image to another file and pulled up his uncle's scanned documents. He used a photo program to merge the outline of the plat map over the satellite image to see just how much of the land had gone to the casino.

It was not a substantial area, only a few dozen acres to his untrained eye, less than a drop in the bucket for the amount of land that was left.

His disposable cell phone rang, startling him.

"Hey, Leif."

"So I was looking into the change on your uncle's property that you pointed out …"

"Yeah, I was looking at that just now, myself."

"I figured to come at it through the back door. Instead of looking when your uncle sold land, I was looking up when the casino acquired the land. That should be a little easier, right? It's federal when dealing with Indian lands and casino's and all that crap, right?"

"I guess …"

"Turns out it is a big fucking mess. California had to be different, just like always, and had these 'Rancheria' things that were like an Indian Reservation, but not. On top of that, I have learned some history. Back in the 1950's, the government decided to take all the land away from the Native American Indians again!

Did you know that? I don't remember that in school, do you? It really pisses me off, Jack. I heard a little about it in law school, with some of the lawsuits to reclaim land and status, but I didn't realize all the bullshit that was involved!"

Leif stopped ranting and took a deep breath. "Sorry. It just really gets to me. Anyway, all of the original stuff is messed up and confused, and nobody really knows shit. All they have are copies of the original treaties from way back when, that say things like 'to the tall oak and the Northern most edge of the Big Rock'. But there is tons of legal crap surrounding each one with what was changed and what wasn't, and I don't really think they apply anymore. So as near as I can tell, all of the maps and deeds and stuff are taken care of at the county level."

"Okay. So …?"

"So there was a fire in the Rainbow County Courthouse back in the 1950's and a lot of records were lost and had to be 're-established'. About three years ago they got around to 're-establishing' the borders of the Loquait Rancheria."

"Right about the same time Jim Gardner died?" Jack asked.

"Pretty much exactly the same time."

TWENTY-FOUR

The new car smell was both pleasant and oily. A Ford Hybrid Escape had been a good choice, Jack decided as he shifted his weight in the seat. He was on his way to go buy a GPS unit. It was considerably cheaper to buy one not pre-installed. Not to mention he wanted to make damn sure there was no GPS locater in his vehicle someone could use to find him, so he had gotten no extras.

He parked at the courthouse, marveling at a county small enough to always have parking available, and limped up the steps, leaning on his cane. The last couple of days had been hard on him.

The smell of the courthouse hit him again. It was hard to put a finger on what it was. Partly it smelled like creosote, as if they had used old railroad ties to build it.

He walked past the open doors of one of the two courtrooms on the main floor. A young man sat alone at one of the tables facing the judge's bench. He looked miserable, like he might throw up.

Fear, Jack thought to himself. *This place smells like motor oil and fear.*

Recalling Leif saying there had been a fire in the 1950's that had destroyed most of the records, he looked around at the wood for evidence of the fire. There wasn't any, but perhaps a lot of the undamaged wood had been recycled, reused to rebuild the new courthouse. That would account for the smell.

He limped past the rickety old elevator and made his way up the stairs, back to the planning department where the man with the bed-head hair had been. He still wasn't sure what he was going to say. He had no evidence, no proof that the man he had talked with before had anything to do with anything.

When he got to the counter, the man was nowhere in sight.

Instead, he was greeted by a girl young enough to be in high school. He turned over his application for the winery and asked for a second one for the harvest festival. The girl took the application, but couldn't find a blank one and had to go into the back offices for help. She returned following the man Jack had spoken with before.

This time he sported a two-inch rooster tail cowlick. The man started at the sight of Jack, but then smiled cordially. Saying nothing, he found the paperwork, handed it to the girl and promptly disappeared into the back again.

All for the best, Jack thought as he headed out with his new forms. He hadn't known what to say anyway.

⁂

Sheriff Beauregard Rambo happened to be walking past the courthouse as Jack hobbled out the main doors. Jack nodded to himself. Bed-head must have called him as soon as he had gone back into the offices. The sheriff spotted Jack and turned to greet him.

"Good afternoon, Mr. Tabor. Leg bothering you, today?" the sheriff's voice reminded Jack of a drill sergeant under orders to politely train enemy soldiers.

"I think it means it's going to rain." Jack smiled casually. He couldn't stop thinking that this man knew who had killed his uncle, had been in on it.

Instead of glancing up at the sky, as most people would have, the sheriff kept his eyes on Jack. "Not here. Not in the summertime. Stick around until the fall, then the clouds will roll in." He glanced meaningfully at the paperwork in Jack's hand. "What kind of mischief are you up to today?"

"Applying for a permit to have a festival. In the fall." Jack met the sheriff's gaze. He didn't think he could keep his hate out of his eyes so he did his best to fill them with contempt. Hopefully the sheriff would assume the look was all from the problems he was having with the police back home, but he wasn't going to bet on it.

The sheriff was used to staring people down. "I'm on my way to have lunch up here at the Grebe's Nest." He pointed over his shoulder with his thumb, at a café on the corner of the next block.

"You should join me."

Jack declined. "I still have errands to run."

"I have some more questions for you; It'll save you a trip to the station." The sheriff's tone left no room to decline his suggestion.

"Well, it is about lunchtime," Jack admitted. "Might as well kill two birds with one stone." He instantly regretted his choice of words.

The French onion soup at the Grebe's Nest would have been better had they actually put the bread and melted cheese on top. Instead, it was full of soggy croutons and cheese consisting of little floating unidentifiable white chunks. Jack wished he had ordered the patty melt the sheriff was having.

The sheriff ate methodically. When he was finished, he pushed his plate to the side, used a wet-wipe to clean his fingers and his chin, and eyeballed Jack.

"You're kinda quiet today, Mr. Tabor."

"I suppose I could say the same about you, Sheriff, but I suspected a busy man like you deserved a couple of quiet minutes to eat his lunch."

The sheriff nodded. "I appreciate that. Now, down to business." He leaned forward and rested his elbows on the table.

Jack leaned into the table also, resting his elbows the way Rambo did, and bringing his nose within eight inches of the sheriff's.

"So you are planning on staying around?"

"For now, at least."

The sheriff nodded. "Good. Then I won't have to track you down and get a court order to bring you back to deal with the two yahoos you put in the hospital."

"I didn't put them in the hospital."

The sheriff waved his hand. "Technicalities. You are up to your eyeballs with those two. The one with the busted jaw keeps scribbling on his writing pad that he is going to sue you. Apparently he thinks you have a lot of money."

"Not yet."

"Why not yet?"

"If the City of Arroyo follows through with their proposed settlement, then I will have a lot of money. As of now, I do not."

"The other guy, the assassin you called him, he still won't talk unless it is to Witness Protection. What's your take on him?"

Jack could tell the sheriff was not looking for any real answers; he was sizing Jack up, trying to decide what to do with him.

"Only what I already told you. He claimed to be a hired killer."

"Sent by your lawyer's partner." The sheriff stared at him for a while before asking, "Where is Warden Durante?"

Jack furrowed his eyebrows, genuinely surprised for the first time in the conversation. "I don't know. You said she was on suspension."

"She hasn't contacted you for follow up paperwork?"

Jack shook his head. "No."

The sheriff must have seen the truth in Jack's eyes. He leaned back and spoke again.

"I told you she wasn't a team player. How the hell am I supposed to conduct an investigation when she goes sulking off somewhere? She'll be lucky if she doesn't have charges brought against her, the way she refuses to do what she should." The sheriff sighed, and for the briefest moment, Jack saw the tired and worried man behind the mask.

But the mask returned as the sheriff stood up. "If you see her, tell her I'm looking for her. Then do yourself a favor and distance yourself from her, she is nothing but trouble." The sheriff put on his hat and left Jack with the bill.

TWENTY-FIVE

The sun hung low in the sky, turning the clouds orange. A distinctive birdcall floated in from the lake, and Jack recognized it instantly. A grebe. Miguel had told him about them when they had been standing out on the dock watching the bass swim by in the water. Grebes were famous for carrying their young on their backs while swimming and for running on the water during courtship. The sound came again, more distant this time. It reminded Jack of a loud monotone cricket with a short fast chirp.

He was walking, trying to clear his head. The lake view was pleasant, and he hadn't walked this road since he had arrived.

Yogi, the raven, followed him for a while, calling out his name in Archer's voice, but it stayed behind once he moved past the orchard and out near open shoreline. The bird had finally returned, and he was glad to see it again. At the same time, he had slowly come to resent the bird's company, because every squawk it made reminded him of Archer.

He had no idea what had happened to her. She hadn't returned his calls. Toni hadn't seen her, either. The thought that she might be dead, murdered like his uncle and the others, flitted through his mind occasionally, but he kept pushing it aside. He was worried about her.

He had forgotten about the dead deer until he was upon it.

It had only been a week, but the sun and the heat had bloated the carcass. He could smell the rotting stench, but only within a step or two. The eyes, long gone, no longer beckoned to him, for which he was grateful, but as he noticed how the neck and the head had twisted up and pulled back into the classic death pose, unbidden thoughts of his daughter in her grave came to his mind. *Has the same thing happened to her body? Is her skin dried out and pulled*

145

tight?

He shook his head to clear the image. He hated when his mind ran amok through horrors he had not previously imagined.

He picked up his pace and walked past the dead animal. He glanced quickly up at Toni's house as he walked by. He really didn't want to talk to her right now. He didn't want to talk to anyone. A funk had set in and he wasn't sure what to do anymore.

He was considering Leif's advice. Not that he wanted to hike the Appalachian Trail or go to Death Valley, but he was coming to the conclusion he should leave. He hadn't enjoyed the conversation with Sheriff Rambo, and he wasn't sure he could do anything more here than he had already done. He had given Leif copies of all of the evidence of his uncle's murder and told him all of his suspicions of the other murders and who might be involved. Leif now knew more about the history of his uncle's property than he did and was in the process of working with a California-based attorney. What was left to do? He had no idea where to start looking for any more evidence, or even what he was looking for evidence of.

He knew people had been killed. He knew it had to do with the land. He had the proof of his uncle's murder, as well as good evidence to back the theory it was over the land. *Now what? Could I possibly get any evidence about the other murders?* He wasn't the police, and he didn't know the people, so he doubted he would get very far asking questions. Not to mention he was certain the police were involved and would notice as soon as he started poking around.

The only thing holding him back was Archer. Where was she? Was she all right? The fact that Rambo didn't know where she was gave Jack hope that she was alive, but left him confused. If she wasn't hurt, where was she?

The sun faded behind the top of the mountains, and the clouds above turned a vivid pink, lighting the lake with a pastel hue. A large carp jumped nearby, slapping the water hard as it landed.

He leaned on his cane and sighed.

As he approached the house, Jack slowed his stride, taking care to watch his step. He had lingered too long on the sunset and was forced to come back in the dark. Lights from the other buildings cast long shadows through the orchard, and the passing headlights from the highway moved the shadows of the trees across the ground in eerie unison.

He paused at the bottom step remembering what had happened the last time he had come home in the dark. He nervously glanced over his shoulder. There was nothing there, and it was actually a relief not to have the raven announcing his arrival.

He cursed himself for being jumpy, but he couldn't bring himself to climb the steps to the front door. He shuffled around the side of the house and let himself in through the kitchen door instead.

The ATV, had tight controls. It responded to Jack's movements a little too well. Every bump jerked his arms and every jerk of his arms changed Max's course, which, of course, bumped Jack and made him jerk his arms.

Miguel rode in the passenger seat this time, showing Jack how to use the two sticks for steering. Jack maneuvered through the orchard as the raven followed them around calling his name.

Miguel laughed at the bird as Jack came to a stop in the shade of a tree. "It's like a puppy!"

"Better. It's not chewing the furniture."

"Noisy though. Reminds me of my wife." Miguel grinned.

Jack smiled to show he appreciated the humor, but the mention of a wife made him think of Wendy. A wave of guilt washed quickly through him as he realized he had not thought of his wife for the last day. He had been focused on finding Archer.

Hence the ATV lesson. He had told Miguel he wanted to explore the property, but in reality, he was heading for the spot Archer had come out of the woods with Big Mike, Little Mike, and another guy whose name he never heard. The two Mikes had offered to help him with something up there, so he figured that something had to be close to where they had been captured. Whatever it was.

It was the only idea Jack had left to search for Archer. He didn't think Archer was the kind of person to just vanish, and if Rambo didn't know where she was, he hadn't hurt her. So who else might have? Someone hiding whatever it was up there was the only thing he could come up with. Big Mike and Little Mike may have had a similar conversation with someone who agreed with them that Archer was trouble.

"Thanks again for applying for the permits." Miguel brought Jack out of his thoughts. "My son is walking on clouds at the chance to do this. It really is a once in a lifetime opportunity for him. You won't regret it."

"I know I won't, but we still have to wait and see if the permits are approved."

Miguel waved the doubt away. "It's all good. You'll see." He pointed to the gate. "Drive me over, and I'll get out and open it for you. We can leave it open so you don't have to get in and out when you come back. I'll have one of the guys close it later."

Jack sped up the dirt road, kicking up dust behind him. The ATV went faster than he anticipated; faster than he felt safe, but the wind was at his back and he was trying to stay ahead of the dust. Besides, it felt good to go fast. It made Jack feel alive and a part of the world with the wind blowing in his face. It felt good to have an objective, a goal. Nothing might come of it, but at least it was an arrow pointing out a direction.

When the road curved up around the mountain and the wind blew the dust away from him, he slowed and began looking through the trees for signs of anything that looked different. The vegetation was thick in some places, thin in others, and mostly made up of tall weeds, grasses, and bushes, with trees scattered farther apart than he would have thought. There was nothing to differentiate any part of it until he came around to the northern side of the mountain.

Here the forest began to take over. The vegetation thickened and changed, becoming greener and containing a wider variety of trees. It was harder to see up into the thickets here, but Jack could still see well enough that he didn't think there was anything unusual to be found.

The motor droned as loud as a motorcycle and Jack was glad

for the silence when he finally shut it off. Parking in the same sheltered area where he and Archer had parked, he glanced up the road where he had taken his walk and then up the side of the hill where Archer had gone. Neither seemed the way to go. He decided his best bet was to go between the two, the direction Archer had marched the three men back from.

He looked around for the raven, but it hadn't followed him up the mountain. If there was something up here, it wouldn't be a good thing to have the bird following him around calling his name.

He pulled out his satellite photos. They were similar to the one Archer had used, though his were better. Not just because they had cost him so much to get access to, but because he had needed to print so many pages to fit just this area of the property in. He flipped through the pages until he found the ones that clearly showed the road he had just come up.

He examined the pages and then the hill he had watched Archer walk up. He recalled the sight of her in the pale morning light, as she had started up that hill, so self-confident and self-reliant that he had been intimidated by her. Not that he would admit that to her, but her sheer, raw personal presence was amazing. He hoped she was all right.

Turning the photographs over in his hands until they lined up with where he was looking, he was pretty sure he could identify where he was sitting and his immediate surroundings. He began scanning the photographs for anything that might have caught Archer's attention in the direction she had come back from.

Never been good at hidden picture games, he was feeling frustrated when he finally spotted it: A shadow, with straight edges that came from nowhere … some kind of camouflaged building. It blended into the forest well, but the shadow's sharp lines stood out once you noticed them.

Pulling out the old compass he had found in his uncle's stuff, he marked the direction he thought he needed to go to find the building. He hoped it would be no more than a couple of miles; the terrain looked rough.

Jack started the ATV up again and slowly steered it into the forest ahead. He picked his way carefully around the trees and the bushes, checking the compass often, fearful of getting too far off course. The ATV had no problems climbing through the grassy thickets.

Going uphill was much easier on his body than going downhill. When going down, the seatbelt held uncomfortably tight across his waist, and he had to brace his weight with his sore leg. He ducked an occasional tree branch and scraped his arm on a bush that reached too far into the ATV as he drove past. Once, a hill with loose gravel gave him some problems, and he thought he would be going down it backwards, but somehow the six wheels found traction in the sparse clumps of grass and pulled him up. His hips and back were sore from all of the jostling when he finally spotted the little shack.

He had been searching for an hour and had almost given up when the sun glinting off something caught his attention. It looked like a beer can. It was lying in front of a rickety lean-to type building built between two trees, made out of weathered two-by-sixes and covered in camouflage netting.

He killed the motor and stiffly climbed out of the vehicle. He stumbled, caught himself, then took a deep breath and stretched slowly, trying not to irritate anything that didn't already hurt.

It was peaceful here. Quiet. The wind gently ruffled the dried leaves that collected under the scrub oak bushes. The sound of a raven echoed in the distance. Jack idly wondered if it was Yogi.

He circled the small shelter, amazed Archer had managed to spot it in her satellite photos. It was hardly big enough to fit three people, especially considering how big Big Mike was. The three men must have been miserably cramped in there.

Jack continued to walk around the camping spot in wider and wider circles focusing his attention outwards for whatever *it* was that the two Mikes had been talking about. Out here in the middle of nowhere, it would be hard to judge how close or far they thought something was. A person might be on top of something without even noticing it.

He spotted the bear trap Archer had mentioned. It was the kind used by the authorities to trap bear alive. Looking like a giant barrel on a small trailer, it had a front gate that would slam down when the pressure pad inside the barrel was stepped on. Archer said they had been baiting it with doughnuts. It was shut now, and there were no doughnuts in sight.

He looked at the tires on the trap. They were old and bald, but not rotting from disuse. The trap couldn't have been here longer than a couple of years at the most, not without the tires starting to crack and sink into the dirt.

No campfire, Jack realized. That was the odd thing about this campsite. Other than the beer can, it hadn't really been used. He didn't see a campfire or places where shovels had been used to cover refuse. Not that he really thought the two Mikes would fastidiously bury any evidence of their passing, but there was so little sign that they had ever been here.

He went back to the tires on the trailer and looked closer. There was no grass growing under the trailer. It had been here long enough to kill the grass underneath and leave bare dirt. *Two summers at least then*, he thought.

But the camp looks hardly used. Why? *Because they never stay here.* Why? He leaned his head back and grimaced.

Why didn't they stay here? They couldn't. Or they didn't need to. Or they didn't want to. Too much human scent would keep bears away. But they baited it with doughnuts. They would have to check the trap regularly. Replace the doughnuts after the squirrels ran off with them.

This isn't a main camp. It would be ideal to go out from a central camp in several directions to check multiple traps. Jack scratched his head. *Where is the main camp, then?*

TWENTY-SIX

Archer came out of her daydream at the sound of the motor. Her legs were asleep, and it hurt to straighten up out of the prone position she had been lying in. She had held the position for the most of two days, leaving her self-appointed post only rarely to relieve herself in the woods behind her.

She had built herself a small lean-to on a rocky ledge overlooking Jack's property, working at night to avoid being seen. The little shelter not only gave her protection from the sun and kept the chill out at night, but made her nearly impossible to spot and reduced the chances of any reflections off the lenses of her equipment giving her away.

Her night vision scope, which she had taped lens to lens to a video camera so she could record what she saw, had helped her see someone going around the side of Jack's house last night, but the resolution on the night scope wasn't good enough to make out who it had been. She was sure it had been Jack, though, as the figure had limped and hadn't tried to move stealthily. And she had seen Jack go off on a walk he likely was returning from.

She raised her spotting scope now, making sure the lens never stuck out of the shadow of her shelter, to look at the green six-wheeled ATV buzzing quickly across the highway to the gated dirt road on her side. She had also attached a camera to the spotting scope, so she could photograph what she saw. It was much more powerful than the night vision scope and she easily recognized Jack as the driver of the vehicle, which she thought was odd. One of the other people working the farm wouldn't really have caught her attention, but Jack?

What's he up to? She wondered.

During the last two days, the only suspicious activity she had noted was two Rainbow County Sheriff Patrol cars that took turns going by the Gardner's Patch every half hour or so during the day. That seemed excessive to her. She identified the driver of one of those patrol cars as the man with a crescent shaped scar across the back of his head; the man from the surveillance video who brutally murdered Jack's uncle.

A Deputy Sheriff. A murderer. It explained better what had transpired between her and Sheriff Rambo. Rambo had been furious, with no evident reason for his fury. Was she in his jurisdiction? Sure. But it was hers, too, and she was a peace officer just as much as he was. They were in different departments, on different watches, but she was just as obligated to deal with any crimes she encountered as he was. Some might argue he had authority over her, being Sheriff. Others might argue that she superseded him, being a state-level employee, not county.

They were supposed to work together, but there had been problems butting heads with his office since she arrived in this county. Until now, she had assumed it was because she was a woman and they resented her, but she couldn't ignore the fact that he had released, and dropped all charges against, the three men she had brought in on Federal charges for poaching bear gallbladders.

He didn't have the authority to do that. That was the District Attorney's job, and, as the DA had not officially looked at the case yet, which she knew he hadn't, as it was her case, the DA couldn't have dismissed them, either.

Strange things are afoot, she thought as she watched Jack drive out of sight up the dirt road, a cloud of dust in the air marking his passage.

Within five minutes, a Rainbow County Sheriff's Patrol car pulled into Jack's driveway. Archer followed the car with the spotting scope and snapped a couple of photos of the deputy with the scar as he got out. He had something in his hands, but she couldn't tell what it was. Her digital camera made electronic clicking sounds as she snapped a couple more photographs.

The deputy looked around impatiently before spotting a tall, lanky worker with shaggy hair. Archer couldn't tell if he was Hispanic or Native American from this distance, but her camera clicked away as he gave the deputy a thumbs up signal and the deputy entered Jack's house. The lanky worker leaned against the corner of the house and kept watch back towards the other buildings as Archer's camera clicked again. The deputy came back out and Archer took as many photos as she could, hoping to get a clear image of the small black plastic things in his hands.

She continued to lie hidden and watch as she contemplated that for the next hour or so. It was the sound of automatic weapon fire that startled her into action.

Jack had all of his satellite photos spread on the ground, laid together to form one giant photo. The breeze was gentle, but nonetheless he had to keep scrounging up more rocks to hold the corners down, and the more rocks he used the more of his photo he hid from his own scrutiny.

He had pinpointed his own location and was now scouring the images in an ever-widening circle for anything out of the ordinary. At first, he had not bothered searching back towards the road he had come from, but then he decided it was best not to leave anything out. Other than the road, and of course the little building he had just found, the only thing that stood out at all was a dry creek bed not too far away from his present position.

Wishing he had the foresight to have taped all of the photos together, he carefully picked them up in order so he would be able to lay them out more quickly next time. He shook the dirt, pine needles, and an acorn husk off the pile of photos and tossed them into the ATV.

He was lifting his sore leg over the sidewall and into the machine when something hit the dirt to his left. Several somethings. They all hit with soft *pft* sounds. Then a distant quick *brrrat!* sound kicked his brain into gear.

"Shit!" He fell where he was. He was being shot at! He tried to curl into a ball, pulling himself mostly under the ATV.

He lay in the dirt, holding his breath, waiting for more *pft* sounds, waiting for one to hit him and hurt like hell, maybe end it all.

The dust in the air swirled slowly as he opened his eyes. No more bullets had thumped into the ground around him. He waited with his forehead against a tire and the oily smell of the machine thick in his nostrils.

He stayed sitting in what he hoped was a protected area behind Max. He presumed whoever had fired had ceased due to lack of a clear sightline. That led to the thought that they must be moving to get a better shot, which meant Jack needed to move before they got a clear shot at him. He knew the approximate direction the bullets had come from, based on where he had heard the noise of the automatic weapon. If nothing else, he knew he couldn't stay where he was.

He put an arm up and over the side of the ATV and grabbed his bullet-proof satchel. He expected bullets to chase his movement as he pulled it to his chest. None came. He breathed harshly as he snaked his hand out to grab his fallen cane.

There had been a significant time lag between the hail of bullets hitting the ground around him and the sound of the rifle reports, which made him hope he had a few minutes until someone caught up with him, but sooner or later, someone would show up and see if they got him, and finish the job if they hadn't. It was time to go. He wished he could take the ATV, but he would be a sitting duck trying to get in and start it.

He slid the satchel all the way up one arm, wishing he could wear it like a backpack. With a deep breath, he crawled hastily into the nearest bunch of scrub oak. The branches scraped at his face and he winced to protect his eyes, but he pushed through. He skittered behind a tree too small to hide behind, laying prone in hopes of making himself a smaller target.

He glanced ahead and realized he was near the crest of a small hill topped by a large pile of boulders. There was no way he could outrun anyone, especially in the forest, but he hoped he could out-think them. They would expect him to top the hill and keep going as fast as he could—unless they knew he couldn't run. If he could find a suitable place in the pile of boulders, perhaps he could pull off an ambush. A loud branch cracked loudly somewhere down below, spurring him to move again.

He scrambled up the hill, not aiming for the rocks, hoping to top the hill and then come back to them once he was out of sight. He fell, picked himself up and fell again. He wiped at something on his face and his hand came away bloody, but he managed to stumble over the top of the hill and fall down again.

He rolled sideways, away from the boulders, so that he could head back towards the rocks, hopefully unseen. Clumsily, and making way too much noise in the dried leaves, he crawled, trying to position himself where he thought the rocks would be between him and his pursuer. Scrambling up some loose scree, he slipped and hit his knee painfully on a fist-sized rock. Grimacing, he continued on all fours back up towards the top of the rock pile. He slipped again as he finally reached the larger boulders.

There was no good place to hide. Panting, he threw his back against the boulders and looked up. The rocks went up for another six feet, but he didn't see a way to climb up. Not that he could have, anyway. His leg muscles shook violently and he dropped to the ground.

He pulled the satchel around to the front of his body and covered his chest with it. He opened the side pocket and pulled out the Taser the assassin had recommended he purchase. He was pleased with himself for taking some good advice, even if it came from a bad source. *Next time, though, I'm getting a gun.*

He started covering himself with leaves and debris. The Taser had an effective range of only fifteen feet; he hoped he could hide himself well enough to prevent getting shot from a farther distance.

None too soon, he thought as he heard heavy puffing and heavy footfalls coming towards him. Whoever was chasing him was pushing hard and fast.

Jack readied the Taser and pressed himself against the rocks and the dirt, willing himself invisible, hoping they would run right on by and never see him. Maybe he could make it back to the ATV and get enough of a head start to get off the mountain before getting shot.

The footfalls slowed as they neared the rocks, but the huffing grew louder and was interspersed with coughs and chuffs. Jack frowned once he realized his pursuer was going to stop to rest at the rocks. The sounds of movement came closer. The coughing and chuffing increased and Jack feebly prayed it was the onset of a heart attack. Then something made Jack's blood run cold; a vocalization not producible by a human throat. A bear rounded the rocks sniffing out Jack's scent.

TWENTY-SEVEN

Archer ran as hard and fast as she ever remembered, trying to get up over the saddle top of the mountain that was between her and where she thought the gunfire had come from. It had to be Jack. She had camped up here for two days and hadn't heard a sound from the forest behind her. But then Jack drives up the road and an hour later she hears automatic weapon fire. *Not a coincidence.* She cursed herself for not following him when she had seen him drive by. The whole reason she was up here was to watch him and see if she could figure out what the hell was going on.

Her heart pounded as she pulled herself up the steep slope, using rocks and branches as steps and handholds. Branches grabbed at the M1A rifle slung over her back, but she ignored them. Once, the .40 caliber Glock holstered on her hip caught on an unforgiving branch and spun her around, landing her hard on her butt. She brushed the pine needles off while she ran, cursing the one that stuck in her palm.

She was grateful for the pine needles, in an odd way. This part of the forest, with the coniferous trees, was easier to run through than the forest on the mountains less than a mile away. There, the mountains were covered with tall grasses, thistles, and weeds interspersed with the scrub oak brush, oak, and madrone trees, creating a thick, dry, slippery ground cover, which was great at hiding rocks and squirrel holes that could easily snap her ankle. Here the pine needles kept the ground clear of most of the brush and weeds, allowing much better visibility of the next place to put her rapidly pumping feet.

She slipped and fell again. She got up, pushing herself as hard as she dared, pushing herself hard enough she couldn't pay attention to anything but where she was going; hard enough she couldn't think about what had happened to Jack when someone had unloaded an automatic rifle into his body.

*   *   *   *   *
*   *   *   *   *

Jack stopped breathing when he saw the bear. It was a big one; at least eight feet tall. He pointed his Taser at it even though he didn't think the Taser's prongs would be able to penetrate the bear's thick hide.

The bear put its nose to the ground and snuffled. What was it doing? Sniffing for …

Oh, yeah, thought Jack, as the blood from the scratch on his forehead trickled into his left eye. He tried to blink it away, but it was mixed with sweat and the dirt he had used to cover himself, and it burned. He held as still as he could, trying even not to breathe, but something gave him away.

The bear turned and looked right at him. Jack saw the hate in the bear's eyes. He also felt the bear's roar vibrate in his chest as it charged.

Jack's hand trembled as he tried to aim the Taser. *Oh God. How close is fifteen feet?* Too close when you are watching a bear charge at you.

The bear leapt. Jack pulled the trigger.

*   *   *   *   *
*   *   *   *   *

Archer crested the mountain not ten minutes after having heard the gunfire and pulled her mini binoculars from her thigh pocket. Wheezing, she scanned the hills ahead, looking for any clue as to which way to go now. A bear's roar echoed below her, and she tracked the noise back to its origin. The movement caught her eye, just in time to see a brown blur … the bear pouncing.

She then saw a tangle of arms and legs. Whatever the bear had pounced on had human limbs that flailed out wildly.

"Oh, Jesus …" she whispered aloud.

*   *   *   *   *
*   *   *   *   *

The bear stiffened, mid-leap, under the shock from the Taser. Its whole body went rigid and unyielding as all of the muscles contracted at once. It uttered weird moan-like growl, as if the wind had been knocked out of it.

To Jack, it felt like a rock covered in fur landed on him. He kicked and pushed to get the bear off him. His efforts were no good; he had no hope of moving the animal. It easily weighed three times what Jack did.

Then the Taser finished discharging and the bear went limp before rolling off Jack. Jack gasped in pain as the massive weight rolled across his body. The bear was dazed for a heartbeat, and then it snarled as it twisted to right itself, raised a massive paw, and swiped at Jack.

As Jack tried to roll out of the way, the claws shredded the first couple of inches of the back of his shirt before snagging on his jeans. The bear lifted Jack up into the air, flinging him onto the rocks. Pain lanced through Jack as he struggled to get up. The bear staggered to one side, still slightly dazed. Jack spotted the Taser in the leaves, its cables still trailing to where the barbs had imbedded in the bear's muzzle. He made a desperate leap for the weapon and landed with his hand on it as the bear pulled a paw back for another swipe.

Jack squeezed the trigger and the bear went rigid again. Overbalanced on three legs, it toppled and rolled over once, twisting and snapping the wire leads that connected it to the gun. Jack fell to the ground, clutching the weapon tight, as the bear tried to right itself again. The gun's drive stun was sparking, now that it wasn't feeding the current down the lines. Jack knew the weapon was all but useless now, and desperately hoped the bear would run away.

A shot rang out and the bear jumped away from Jack. Jack forgot all about the Taser. He scrambled back around the rocks, back towards the direction he had come from, desperately wanting to avoid both the bear and the shooter. He dove into the scant cover provided by the scrub oak brush. He forced his aching body to army crawl across the top of the hill, at a right angle to the direction he had been fleeing before.

A large rock gave way underneath him, sending him tumbling down the hill into thorny wild blackberry bushes. Blood was sticky on his fingers and face as he winced and tried to get out of the thicket. The wicked thorns were worse than any rosebush he had ever seen, and they tore at his face mercilessly. His satchel snagged and caught until he was finally forced to let go of it and leave it behind.

Tiny knives stabbed all over his body as he stumbled through the brambles. A few of the thorns sliced across his forearms and one tore at his ear, but he hit the bottom of the hill running for his life.

He panted as he considered his options; up the next hill, or up or down the ravine between the two hills. He didn't know the area at all so he wasn't even sure which way the lake was anymore. His best guess was that downhill would eventually take him there. His leg gave out and he stumbled, sprawling out in the sandy bed of a dry creek.

He drew a ragged breath, wincing at the pain from a broken rib. He looked down at himself as he climbed to his feet. He was covered in blood. *How badly had the bear hurt him? Where was the bear?* He looked back up the hill, but couldn't see anything from here. If it was still after him, it should have caught him by now. Hopefully it was eating the guy with the gun.

His back stung where the claws had struck, his ribs hurt when he tried to breathe, and his legs refused to do his bidding. There was so much blood, he was sure he would start to fade soon. There was no way he could outrun someone, he had to out-think them.

His only chance would be to get back to the ATV and get to help soon.

He hoped he could fool anyone trying to track him. He stumbled down the hill and into the dry, sandy rock bed, intentionally disturbing the rocks as much as possible, picking up golf-ball-sized rocks as he went. He found a larger pile of rocks that stuck up out of the sand, walked past them making obvious tracks, and then backtracked to them as best as he could without making a new trail. He stood on them and threw rocks at the ground as far ahead as he could, hoping it would make it look like he had gone on down the gully.

Carefully, he moved up onto the far side of the hill and backtracked, hoping to circle up and around, back to the ATV.

TWENTY-EIGHT

Archer kept her scope trained on the bear, but it did not rise. She did not like having to kill it, but it had attacked a human, and once they did that, they tended not to stop. Besides, it had been attacking Jack. When she was sure the bear wasn't going to get back up, she swung the scope around trying to find Jack, but there wasn't any sign of him. The blood in the leaves and on the dirt and rocks was apparent in her scope, even from this distance. Silently, she prayed Jack was alive and started out to find him.

Wishing he had thought to pull his cell phone out of the satchel before he had dropped it, Jack finally gave in and tried to hide himself in some scrub oak overlooking the way he thought a pursuer might come. Exhaustion was setting in and the thorns that had broken off into his skin were becoming unbearable. He sat and began to pull out the stickers in his pants that were making it almost impossible to continue. When he leaned against a tree, sharp pains shot up his back from the thorns, the injury from the bear's claws, and his ribs. He reached behind his back and probed at his wounds with searching fingers.

The claw marks on his back didn't feel like anything too serious, just deep scrapes. He sighed with relief. He had been imagining his ribs and spine were exposed. He looked at his blood-covered arms. There was too much blood. Even inspecting his still bleeding cuts, he couldn't account for it. He sighed with relief as he realized he wasn't feeling woozy from loss of blood, only from exhaustion.

But if all the blood isn't mine, it has to be the bear's. He was amazed at what the Taser had done to it, but there was no way it had caused the bear to bleed like that. It must have already been injured. Or shot.

Someone had shot it. Maybe they hadn't been shooting at Jack after all, maybe they were shooting at the bear, and Jack had just been in the distant line of fire.

Gall bladders. It was probably those idiots Big Mike and Little Mike, or that other guy that had been with them. They got out of trouble and instantly went right back to poaching bear.

He looked again at his bloodied arms and hands and then reached up to tenderly feel the ear the brambles had caught at. *Damn them!*

Archer slowed as she finally reached the bear carcass. She was sure it was dead, but it was always better to be safe than sorry.

She circled the carcass and spotted the exit wound from her shot. It was easy to spot—a large part of its skull was missing. She winced. She had been aiming for a kill shot at the shoulder. It had worked, but she had hoped she would have been a better shot under pressure. Then she noticed the pooling blood under the bear's chest.

She leaned in for a closer look. The bear had been gut-shot. She no longer felt so bad for having killed it. It had been the walking dead, mortally wounded.

Someone up here was using an automatic weapon. If they were using it to hunt bear, then they were likely to be close and would be coming for the gall bladder. Unless they had heard her shot and turned tail.

She looked at the bear's wound again. *How far could it have run, gut-shot, before it encountered Jack? Was that even Jack I saw?* She had thought it was, but realized it might have been the poacher.

She noticed the silver barbs sticking out of the bear's nose and muzzle. She traced the thin broken wires with her eyes and then spotted the Taser half-buried in the leaves. No self-respecting poacher would be caught dead with a Taser, it had to be Jack.

Her suspicion was confirmed when she spotted his cane. She picked it up and poked the bear in the nose with it.

Hopefully I have enough time to find Jack before someone else shows up.

She started around the boulders, stopped, and looked back at the bear. "Hmp!" She grunted to herself. "I'll be damned—he shot it with a Taser."

Jack had almost convinced himself that there really wasn't anything to be afraid of, that it had been an unfortunate hunting accident, when he heard the sounds of rocks tumbling down the slope he had so desperately escaped down. He flattened himself and hid as best as he could, hoping that his diversion tactics would hold up.

Someone was carefully picking their way around the brambles, but the brush Jack was hiding in blocked his view. The figure stopped and bent over to retrieve his satchel and his heart leapt. *It's Archer!*

Relief flowed over him. He started to jump up and shout her name, but it caught in his throat. She had been missing for nearly three days, now, for no reason he could think of, here she was, out in the middle of the forest, following his bloody tracks, carrying what looked like an automatic weapon—after someone had shot at him.

He decided to stay right where he was, hold his breath, and pray.

Archer carefully followed the blood trail through the flattened blackberry bushes while doing her best to stay out of them. When she spotted the satchel and pulled it out of the brambles, her heart went out to Jack. Those thorns were razor sharp and wickedly large. He must be torn to shreds.

She stopped, pulled his cane out from where she had stuck it through her backpack straps, took off her backpack and put his satchel in it. She took a long drink from her canteen, and then put everything away and started following his tracks again. She followed them all the way to where Jack had stood on the rocks and thrown stones. There she stopped and puzzled over how his trail had changed.

She was so intent on the unusual disturbances in the sand that the rifle slug slamming into her back caught her completely off guard.

Jack had been watching Archer follow his trail when the loud shot rang out not fifty yards from where he was hiding. The impact hurled her forward to land, unmoving, on her face.

"Yee-Haw!" A shout came from where Jack had heard the shot. "Nailed her!"

"Nice shootin', Tex!" A second voice followed the first. "You sure she's dead?"

"If she ain't she will be."

"What if she was wearing a bullet proof vest?"

"Those are good for pistols, not high powered rifles. My bullet went clean through. Probably left a big hole on the other side."

"Wanna go make sure that was her?"

"Hell no! I ain't goin' near the body! I don't give a shit what Rambo says, I don't trust him, and I ain't leavin' no evidence I was ever near that body! Not one damned hair, skin cell, or footprint! He wanted her dead if she ever came back up here, he can come get the fucking body himself. I'll tell him where it is, but I ain't gettin' close enough for him to get any evidence he can pin on me unless he has to admit I was over here doing his dirty work! Besides, how many women you know gonna be up here pokin' around dressed like that? Besides your mamma, I mean."

"Fuck you!"

A scuffling sound was followed by some muffled laughter. Jack imagined the two men were punching each other in the arms. He felt numb inside. He couldn't take his eyes off Archer's unmoving form lying face down in the dirt. Tears began welling in his eyes as he realized she most definitely had not been involved in whatever was going on up here. *She must have seen me drive up and followed. Probably to protect me.*

Tears burned his cheeks. *It's my fault she's dead. If I hadn't hidden from her …*

He tried to control himself, tried to stay calm, a sob or a choke would give him away and then he would be dead too.

He couldn't take his eyes off her.

"You think she was alone?" one of the voices asked.

"Yeah, the Wardens almost always work alone, unless they are in the middle of a bust. Then this place would have been crawling with them."

The second voice grunted agreement, then asked, "Should we go back and get that six-wheeled thing?"

"Man, you don't understand shit do you? I ain't touching nothin'. I ain't even *lookin'* at nothin'. I was never here. And neither were you, you understand? If we get busted for anything, we ain't never been over here. We always just stayed over there and took care of the shit, and that's all we ever did. We don't know nothin' about this, ever. Don't never tell no one. Ever!"

"But you said we was going to tell Rambo we did what he told us to." Confusion on the part of the second man and his tone of voice led Jack to believe he wasn't the brightest of the two.

"I am! But you ain't! You just forget ..."

The voices started moving away and Jack snuck out to follow. His grief was morphing as fast as he could wipe away his tears. He was filling with something darker than anger and colder than rage.

Hate.

As he looked out at Archer's body, his vision swam with memories of his wife and daughter, shot down in cold-blooded murder. Just like Archer.

Archer had a rifle. He had seen it. He would get it. He would get it, and he would kill those murdering sons of bitches.

TWENTY-NINE

Waiting until the men were far enough away they wouldn't hear him, but still close enough to follow, Jack did his best to sneak back towards Archer's body and retrieve her weapon. The scrapes, scratches, cuts and bruises he could ignore, but his bad leg, which had been through so much already today, he could not. It continually buckled under his weight, and he had to plan his movements so that he did not land face first when it happened.

When he finally had gone as far as he could without exposing himself openly, he dropped into a crawl and carefully snuck out towards Archer's body with his eyes back up the gully, searching for any sign they might still be looking this way. When he was sure no one was watching, he turned his attention towards the body lying at his knees.

Her rifle had been slung across her back with her backpack and his cane; he would have to lift her head to get the strap off. He didn't want to touch her. Touching her would make it more real, if that was possible. If it was any more real, he was afraid his sanity, what was left of it, would snap, leaving him nothing more than the feral animal he could feel trapped inside his cage of hate and desire for revenge.

He slid his cane out from the straps, able to grab it without touching her. He momentarily thought about using the sword blade to cut the strap on the rifle to free it, but realized he needed it. He was going to need the cane to walk and his other hand would be needed for more than just holding a rifle all the time. He steeled himself and reached out.

He gently worked his hand under her throat and shoulders to lift her, grimacing all the while. Tears began to well in his eyes and blur his vision as he tried to ignore how warm she was. He was grateful her face was away from him, he didn't want it burned into his memory as his wife's and daughter's had been.

When she moaned, he nearly dropped her face first back into the sand.

Jack held her tight; all reservations about touching her were gone. "I gotcha," he whispered as he lay face to face with her, cradling her head and stroking her hair. "I gotcha. Everything's going to be okay." He rocked her gently and spoke soothingly to her. Tears rolled down his cheeks leaving clean streaks in the blood and dirt. She was dazed and still coming back into consciousness. He didn't try to hurry her. He held her and continued murmuring softly.

Her eyes came into focus and she recognized him. "Jack?" With recognition came awareness, which brought pain. She groaned. "My back hurts, Jack," she told him matter-of-factly. "And my head."

"Shhhh …" he shushed her as he continued stroking her face. "It's going to be all right."

"What happened?" She met his eyes and saw his tears and bloodied face. "Are you hurt?"

He shook his head as he shushed her again. A quick sob caught in his throat.

"Am I hurt bad?" She was starting to remember. "The bear!" She tried to sit up but he gently held her and shushed her again. "What the hell happened? Let me up, Jack!"

She pushed against him, and the tone of her voice brought Jack back to his senses. He had been somewhere, somewhere else, he realized. Somewhere not good. He had been here, but not here. He had been right. Touching her had cost him his sanity, but not in the way he had expected.

"Shit!" Archer grunted through clenched teeth as she rolled over. "I think I broke some ribs." Jack did his best to help her sit up, his leg hardly responding anymore. She wheezed a couple of times before getting on her knees and then forcing herself to stand. "What happened, Jack?"

"They shot you. In the back." His voice was dry.

Archer immediately came alert and dropped her hand to her holster, scanning the hills with her piercing blue eyes. Turning around obviously hurt her, but she held steady in her search for her assailants.

"Where are they?"

"They went that way, about ten minutes ago."

She relaxed but didn't take her hand off her holstered Glock. "I don't remember."

"You never saw it. You never had a chance."

"The last thing I remember was the bear. And you. I was trying to find you. I found your bag." She dropped her backpack off with a grimace of pain and flipped it around to her front so she could open it.

The hole in the backpack wasn't readily apparent, but when she pulled out his satchel, the deformation caused by the high powered round was obvious. The satchel was ruined.

"I'm gonna take that damned thing home and build a shrine around it." Jack whispered hoarsely.

"How bad is it?" Archer turned her back to him and tried to raise the back of her jacket but couldn't, the pain was too much. "Did it go in? Am I shot?"

Jack used his cane to push himself closer to her. He could see the rip in her shirt and the long smear of lead across the bullet resistant vest underneath it. A second rent of fabric showed below her arm.

"I think it ricocheted." He tried to lift the vest, but it was too snug and elicited a grunt of pain from Archer.

"Don't bother. I just realized there would be blood everywhere. Although," she grunted in pain again, "I can't really rule out internal bleeding." She turned around to face him. "So this is what it feels like to get shot," she grimaced. "It hurts."

She noticed him leaning on his cane. "I suppose it hurt a bit more when you got shot."

He shook his head. "I mostly remember being numb, couldn't feel anything. The pain came later."

She eyed him for a moment. "How bad are you hurt? You're covered in blood."

"It's not all mine."

"Yeah, I know. The bear was already shot when it got to you, but you're cut up pretty bad. You need to get to a doctor, get checked out." She grunted in pain as she tried to move. "So do I."

"I don't think it's safe for you to go to the local hospital."

She looked at him and he explained. "I heard those guys talking. They knew it was you. They shot you *because* they knew it was you. Rambo told them to."

"What?!"

"I heard them say that Rambo had told them to kill you if you ever came up here again."

"That son of a bitch!" She winced, regretting the force she had put into words. "Well," she whispered angrily, "that explains a lot." She pulled out her cell phone.

Jack leaned on his cane and studied her strong features. He saw so much personal strength and determination that he admired them. He was developing a deep respect for this woman.

When he had first seen her, he never would have imagined she would actually have been able to re-awaken the part of him that would be attracted to a woman. He had thought that part of him had died with his family, along with any desire to be close to anyone. But here she was, standing strong and proud against man and nature, filthy with the grime of days in the forest, bloody, with injuries to her face from falling into the dirt after being shot in the back, and she was striking. He felt a growing admiration for her, and more.

"No service." She said flatly as she turned the phone back off and put it away. "Help me put this back on, would you?" She held out the backpack and he took it, helping her put her arms through the straps. After he cinched it, she turned to look at him.

"Are you going to be able to get back to your ATV?"

He furrowed his brows at her. "Where are you going?"

"I'm going to go get the son of a bitch who shot me."

THIRTY

I'm coming with you."

Archer turned to face Jack, her piercing. blue eyes commanding. "You need to get to the ATV and go see a doctor. I'm a big girl. I can handle myself. Besides, this is my job. It's what I do."

Jack met her gaze flatly, as only someone who had seen as much pain as he had could muster. "I'm coming with you. If Sheriff Rambo decided it is not too much of a risk to have a Warden murdered, then it can't be long until he has me swatted like a fly. Not to mention I am unarmed and injured. If we split up and I run into those guys first, I won't survive it. I have just as much, if not more, at stake here. I'm coming with you."

She held his gaze stone-faced for a long instant. "You're right. My first priority should be to get you to safety."

"Bullshit. We're not letting those bastards get away. We don't follow them now, we'll never know for sure who shot you in the back, and I've enough of that bullshit in my life already." Jack shifted his weight. "You know I'm right."

He could see her debating. She wanted to catch up with the shooter as much, if not more, than he did.

He forced the issue. "Screw it. I'll follow them myself." He turned and started walking.

"And just what the hell are you going to do?"

"Free country. Free citizen. My land."

"Did you get shot in the head, or what?"

Jack whirled, anger twisting his face ugly. "They fucking shot you! In the back! I thought you were dead, Archer! Do you have any idea what that felt like? I was living through my worst hell all over again. All over again. Fuck them. I'm going to go kill those sonsofbitches." New tears, angry ones this time, rolled down his

173

cheeks.

Archer glowered at him and came to a decision. "All right. Christ. Don't make me sorry." She grunted and bent over, lifting a pant leg to pull out a small Glock 30 from an ankle holster. She handed it to him, butt first.

Jack took it from her. "I gotta get me one of these. That Taser didn't work out so well …"

"Remind me when your birthday comes around. Do you know how to use it?"

"Yeah. Is there one in the chamber?"

"Not supposed to be, but there is. No good having a hidden last resort if you have to muck around with it before you can use it."

"Living dangerously." He *tsked* at her as he struggled to find a comfortable place to carry the gun.

"No other way to live. Don't stick it down the front of your pants and shoot yourself in the dick, Don Adams."

"First I was Gimpy, then Wrong-Way, now I'm Don Adams. I'd rather you called me Whiskey Jack … Green Cheeks."

Archer glowered. "You cry like a little girl because you think I'm dead, then you demand revenge on my attacker, and now you start sexually harassing me, calling me the one name I asked you not to. What kind of friend are you?"

Jack gave her a wry smile. "The kind that you can be sure will watch your back."

Jack struggled to keep up, but Archer said nothing. She stopped from time to time to examine a footprint or broken twig, mostly to let him catch up, but also to catch her own breath. She was sure she had cracked at least one rib, probably more, but she wasn't about to play with them and find out. If they were broken and going to puncture something, they would have done so already.

No point in dwelling on it. She had to do what she had to do, and if Jack was right, she had to know who shot her. Capturing them might well be the only tenuous evidence she would ever lay her hands on to prove Rambo was playing for the wrong team. If she didn't prove it fast enough, he would kill her himself. Especially if his boys came back saying she was dead and then she came limping back into town. He would know she knew something was up.

She tried not to keep glancing at Jack. Not only because she didn't want him to feel like he was dragging her down any more than he already knew he was, but also because she was fascinated by his tenacity. No, fascination wasn't the right word, and she knew it. She was attracted to it. She was attracted to a strength and determination she had seen in very few people.

She stopped when she spotted blood on the trail of tracks and waited for Jack to catch up. She ignored his panting, hoping he would ignore hers, and pointed out the tracks to him.

"There are their original tracks, see where they followed the blood and bear tracks? They looped back to the path they came in on and followed it back. I suspect that means they have a specific destination in mind, like they are going right back to where they came from." She pointed in the direction they likely had gone.

"That's where the gunfire came from," Jack pointed. "The bullets hit around me up there at the ATV." He pointed out the machine parked up the hill from them a couple hundred feet.

Archer silently chided herself for not having seen the green ATV sooner. She wasn't paying close enough attention to her surroundings, and it was going to get them killed.

"You sure you don't want to take the ATV and go to the hospital?" She asked him.

"As soon as I fire that motor up, they will know someone is here and come running."

She nodded at him. "That might be a good back up plan. Let's keep it in mind. Meanwhile, we need a real plan."

They followed the footprints and blood trail more slowly now, fearing detection as they grew closer to what Archer suspected would be the base camp. They had gone back to the ATV and retrieved Jack's satellite photos before proceeding, and Archer had spotted something in them Jack had missed.

"See here, where it looks like just more grass and bushes?" She pointed to a spot on the photo they had determined was the area they were headed to. "Notice the regular spacing of these bushes, here, here, and here."

"It just looks like bushes to me."

"It's supposed to, but it's camouflage. They have it spread over such a huge area that you can see the pattern repeated here, here and here. See this one is right angle to that one, and this one is opposite, but these bushes are spaced in the same pattern, same distance as these others."

"I see it. What do you think it means?"

"Pot farm. There is no other reason I know of to hide a couple of acres of land. Pretty nervy to do it this way, too. Most of them are much smaller and they grow the marijuana plants in with the trees and bushes so they don't stand out." She sighed as she gazed down the trail they were going to follow. "We're going to have to watch out closely for those guys. They're probably guards living up here in a camouflaged shelter, and the whole place is probably booby trapped."

"Great," Jack mumbled as they put away the photos and resumed their search.

Archer had been right. He stopped when she threw up a hand in a closed fist. He had seen enough movies to know that meant he was supposed to stop. She pointed at the ground in front of her feet and then at the leaves on the brush next to them.

Waving him closer, she whispered. "See the blood on the leaves and the ground? This is where the bear was shot. We must be pretty close now."

He nodded at her; then something caught his eye. "Look," he pointed to a thin line running about two inches above the ground. "Booby trap."

Archer followed the line. One end was tied to a tree, the other was connected to an automatic rifle pointed right at them. Archer shook her head as she motioned Jack to stand aside while she disarmed the trap. The bear had been randomly shot by hitting a tripwire. The two guards had come to investigate and found her by dumb luck.

If Archer hadn't followed him, and if he had survived the bear, likely they would have shot him instead of her. Archer glanced at Jack as she pocketed the ammunition she had taken out of the assault weapon mounted on the tree. He could tell by the look on her face she was thinking the same thing.

He started to say something to her but she threw her hand up again, silently ordering him to be quiet. She pointed to her ear. Voices.

Jack nodded understanding.

Archer came in behind them from the right, and Jack came in from the left. Archer held her M1A leveled. Jack had the small Glock in his hand, but resolutely refused to put his finger inside the trigger guard out of fear he might nervously twitch and shoot accidentally. Not that he had any qualms about shooting either of the two men, who were hunched over working on some sort of tank with water pipes coming out of it, but he didn't want to give himself away too soon.

When Jack thought she couldn't possibly get any closer without being noticed, Archer stopped.

"Don't move! Hands in the air! You're under arrest!"

Both men jumped with surprise. One reached for the assault rifle leaning against the nearby tree.

"Don't try it!" Jack's voice from another direction was enough to stop the man.

The two men slumped in defeat as Archer quickly zip-tied their hands. They both wore scraggly beards and were dressed in overalls and muddy work boots. They could nearly have been twins, and Jack found it easiest to tell them apart by the color of their coveralls. One wore brown and the other wore blue. Neither man spoke as she took them separately to trees a few feet apart and tied them with their arms behind their backs around tree trunks, facing the men so they couldn't see one another. She backed up and started walking a circle around them to look them over. The one in the blue eyed her defiantly, the other looked abashed, but neither spoke.

Jack stood where he could see both men and keep them covered with his gun. He had been full of anger and hate, but now, just as when he had his own would-be assassins tied up in his kitchen, he found he did not have it in him to kill.

He watched Archer as she circled them, trying to read her face. They had planned how to make these guys talk, how to get information about Rambo, but he no longer felt he had the nerve for it. Did Archer?

He could tell when she reached a decision, and he could tell she didn't like it, but he had no idea what it was until she walked to him and asked for the gun back.

"We caught them. They're not going anywhere. Are you sure you want to cross this line?" he asked as he handed her the gun.

"I already have," she answered flatly, as she took the weapon and checked to see it was ready to fire. He nodded and stepped a little closer to show he was willing to support her.

She turned back to the two men, who both now refused to make eye contact with her. She sighed wearily before confronting them.

"This is how this is going to work," she started. "I am going to kill one of you and the other is going to sing like a bird if he wants to live."

That got her a glance from the one in brown. He then quickly glanced at Jack, as if looking for confirmation that it was true. Jack kept his jaw set and hoped he could do what Archer was expecting him to.

"Now, I know one of you two shot me in the back, unprovoked and without warning. I'm not too happy about that. I'm going to give the other one of you the chance to be the one who lives by telling me who shot me."

"We ain't tellin' you nothing, bitch!" The man in the brown overalls shouted so hard spittle flew from his lips.

"Shut up, idiot! She ain't gonna kill us!" the other scolded.

The voices and the attitudes gave it away to Jack. He recognized the shooter's voice and the condescending way he had spoken to the other. "That one," he said quietly and walked around the trees and pointed to the one who had rebuked the other. "He's the one who shot you in the back."

Archer followed and raised her gun, pointing it at the face of her assailant. His confidence faded and fear took its place. "Are you the one who shot me in the back?"

"Fuck you!"

The man in brown started squirming to see what was going on, but he couldn't get his head far enough around the tree.

"No. Fuck you." Archer fired the gun into the tree above the man's head and Jack used his cane like a golf club, teeing off to the man's groin. The man cried out in a strangled agony.

At the sound of the man's cry, the other man cried out in fear and desperation. "Billy! Billy! You okay?"

Jack prevented Billy from answering by shoving a wad of bloody cloth he had torn from his undershirt into the man's mouth and using a couple of Archer's zip-tie handcuffs together to hold the gag in his mouth. The man tried to head-butt Jack, but only managed a glancing blow. Jack gave him a quick knee to the groin and took the rest of the fight out of him.

The indistinct muffled groans and curses only served to agitate his partner more. "Billy!" He twisted and squirmed but still couldn't see what was going on.

Archer, with the gun still prominently held in her hand, left the gagged man and walked back to the squirming man. He genuinely looked scared now. She eyed him dispassionately before glancing at her gun. "You already used up your first stay-alive free card by not telling me he was the one who shot me. You have one left. I hope you use it wisely. Tell me all about this place and what Sheriff Rambo has to do with it."

The man shook his head violently. "I ain't talking! I won't never talk!"

Jack put his head in his hands and rubbed his face wearily. He had been afraid of this. This was the hole in the plan to make them talk. They had tried to come up with a better idea to get information from the men, but other than hoping they would try to bargain for lesser sentences, they had no way of getting information from them. Jack had been worried they would be too afraid of Sheriff Rambo and his dirty police force to testify against them. He had convinced Archer this would be the best way to get information from them, but their ace in the hole was a bluff.

Now he regretted putting the idea in her head.

He swiped his hands through his dirty matted hair in frustration and nearly yelped as he went over both the cut on his head and his torn ear. He pulled his hands away with more blood on them. They must have both re-opened when he had scuffled putting the gag on 'Billy'. He looked at the blood on his hands and had an idea.

He reached up to his ear and scalp again and tried to get as much blood as he could on his hands without wiping it back off into his hair, and then he walked back to Archer and to where the other man could see him.

With an eerie stillness in her voice that was even convincing to

Jack, Archer quietly and calmly asked about Sheriff Rambo for what she claimed was the last time. When no response came, Jack walked over to them with his bloody hands held out in front of himself, as if he was looking for some place to wipe them off.

"I tried to staunch the blood flow. I was hoping he might live long enough to tell us something useful, but I don't think he's going to make it. Next time you decide to kill someone, just shoot them in the head, not in the dick, I felt like some kind of pervert trying to put his junk back together. I gave up and threw it up there on the hill." He walked closer to the man as he spoke and, when he gestured up the hill, he made sure he waved his bloody hand just under the man's nose before casually using the man's shirt as a towel.

"I like shooting men in the dick." Archer's mouth was a hard line as she spoke matter-of-factly.

The man quivered and it appeared he might retch, cry, or both. Jack stopped and looked him in the face, not looking at him, but through him, as if he weren't there.

"You know what?" He asked to the man's face, but then turned around to show the man meant nothing to him, he was talking to Archer. "Fuck this. We already killed that guy. Kill this guy, and we'll go get that asshole Rambo, bring him up here, make it look like he did this shit, then fucking kill him too."

Archer lowered her gun, considering. "That could work. We'd just have to get it done by tonight so all the bodies looked like they died at the same time." She pointed her gun towards the gagged man. "He won't die for a while yet, and it could have been possible he shot Rambo before he died …" She nodded her head with a growing enthusiasm. "Yeah," she said with a smile. "We can do that."

"I'll talk! I'll talk! Don't shoot me in the dick!"

THIRTY-ONE

Archer left Jack watching over the two men while she climbed to the top of the ridge to find a place where her cell phone would work. Eschewing protocol and explaining the involvement of the local authorities, she placed her call directly to the FBI, which also added several hours to the time it would take for backup to arrive. Once she was back from making the call, she used that time to survey and photograph the marijuana farm. She couldn't tell how big it was, but it certainly was the biggest she had seen. The camouflage nets only covered a small part of it. The rest was mixed into the surrounding trees and brush as she had seen others do before.

The man who had talked, Marshall, wasn't too pleased when he found out Billy was still alive, but that hadn't shut him up. Once he had broken, he was a flood of information. Unfortunately, it wasn't much more information than could be expected of a lackey in his position. He was intimately familiar with the pot farm and its workings, but he tended to get fuzzy when it came to much more, other than Sheriff Rambo was the boss and some of his deputies were in on it. He didn't even know what happened to the marijuana after it was harvested.

Marshall seemed eager to please, and Jack wondered if the man had mental problems. He acted as though he was smitten with Archer. Jack rolled his eyes at Archer when she decided to take Marshall along to guide her around the pot farm.

As Archer walked carefully around the hidden fields, Marshall,

181

hands still zip-tied, led the way to show her where the booby traps were. Archer cautiously disarmed and photographed each one as they circled back and forth under the camouflage nets and around the marijuana plants. The technical prowess that had gone into designing the whole thing amazed her.

"Where does the water come from?" she asked Marshall as she took pictures of the complicated timer and valve systems.

Marshall walked her up the hill to a small water tank buried in the ground so it would be hard to notice. "See this?" he pointed. "This is one of our storage tanks for the water. We gravity flow from here down to drip irrigate everything. They're not very big tanks," he smiled apologetically, "but we have a lot of them."

Archer nodded and smiled at him. "But how do you fill the tanks?" she asked as she snapped more photos.

"From the casino," he pointed off to the east. "It's only about a mile that way."

"From the casino?" She was taken aback.

"Yeah," he chuckled. "Where else?"

"Why would you run water all the way out here from the casino?"

"Well, I guess they tried pumping it up from the lake, but ol' man Gardner found out about it." He leaned towards Archer conspiratorially and whispered, "I heard that's why they bumped him off."

"That's why *who* bumped him off, Marshall?"

"I dunno," he shrugged. "Whoever the sheriff works for."

"I thought you said he was the boss."

"No. He's *my* boss. And that's all I know."

"What about the other people they killed?"

"I only heard rumors." He was clamming up and Archer realized she was pushing him too hard.

"I don't mind hearing rumors." She reached out and touched his arm, hating herself for doing it, but it worked.

"I heard they killed that other guy who inherited the farm and a couple of other people, to shut them up, but that's all. I didn't hear no details."

Archer glanced away, disappointed. He had confirmed all of Jack's suspicions, but couldn't give her anything to work with that might prove them.

Sorry he had disappointed her, Marshall offered more

information to cheer her up. "I know that's why they wanted you dead. They said you been hanging around with the new guy that owns the land, and that you would be suspicious when they killed him."

Archer grunted in pain as she sat down next to Jack. He was eating a cold can of Spaghetti-O's he had scrounged from Billy and Marshall's supplies. He had given Billy water earlier, but the profanities and insults had prompted him to but the gag back on and he hadn't offered to share the food. He spotted the hungry way Marshall watched him eat and took pity on him. After all, he had been cooperating.

"I'll get you some when I finish." Jack told him.

Marshall nodded and looked grateful. "Mostly, I really gotta pee."

Jack looked at Archer who shook her head. "I'm out of zip ties. That's why I didn't tie him back up to the tree."

"Sorry, man, you're going to have to hold it."

"I can't hold it. I gotta go." Marshall wiggled desperately.

Jack shook his head. "I've seen too many movies. Your hands are staying cuffed."

"Can't you just …"

Jack stared at him. "Just what? Hold it for you? That ain't gonna happen."

Marshall looked at Archer desperately.

"Don't look at me." Her hand went to the gun in her holster.

Billy snorted a laugh through his gag.

"I'm sorry, Marshall. A couple of hours ago you guys tried to kill her, and I'm sure you would have killed me if you'd have known I was there. I'm not going to give you that chance again. If you have to go that bad, go in your pants."

Marshall hung his head. Billy tried to muffle something through his gag.

"You've got nothing to say I want to hear," Jack told him and went back to eating cold Spaghetti-O's.

He offered Archer a bite. She grimaced at it and then resignedly took a mouthful off his fork.

"I'm sorry I talked you into pushing these guys for information." He stared into the can of pasta so that he wouldn't have to meet her eyes. "I know it wasn't the right way to handle things."

She was quiet for a minute. "Well," she sighed after she swallowed, "I'm glad you had a plan. When I saw that son of a bitch smirk at me, I thought I was going to kill him. If I hadn't had your plan to fall back on, I might have."

They shared the rest of the can in silence. When they finished eating, Archer told Jack what she had learned. "Marshall pretty much confirmed all of your suspicions. They killed your uncle and old Jim Gardner, and others, to hide this place."

"How big is it?"

"I don't know. It's huge. Biggest I've ever seen or even heard of. Those nets only cover places where they were worried about people or equipment being spotted by airplane. They hid the water tanks, the fertilizer tanks, and the flophouse; pretty much only the areas where a person could regularly be spotted while they took care of this place. The drip lines go off in all directions. There must be miles of them. They pipe the water all the way from the casino, because the springs here have too much boron in them, it kills the plants.

"Marshall said they used to pump it up from the lake, but that Jim Gardner discovered it, and that's why they killed him. He also said he had heard they killed your uncle and some other people, but he didn't know anything about it."

They sat in silence for a few minutes, ignoring Billy's muffled curses. Marshall sat dejectedly and ignored them.

"I think they killed my uncle because of the casino." Jack finally broke the silence with his speculation. "He had put in for a permit using an old map that showed the land the casino is on belonged to the Gardners. When the application was returned to him in the mail, post mortem, it had an updated map on it, not the one he had submitted."

"But what does the casino have to do with all of this." Archer waved her hand at the pot farm around them. "Why risk a lucrative business like a casino on something like growing pot? Heads are going to roll as soon as we point out the casino is supplying the water for this."

Jack shook his head. *Water. Why would someone risk all of that for water?* Then something Miguel had told him came to memory. This property had riparian rights and water rights to the lake were rare and hard to come by. "Water!" he blurted. "That's what this is all about!"

Archer wrinkled her forehead at him.

"Hey, Marshall? Where does the casino get its water from?" Jack asked.

Marshall refused to look at him.

"I will find a solution to your pee problem if you tell me," he bargained.

Marshall sighed. "It comes from the spring up on the hill here. It fills a big tank that flows down to the casino, where they filter the boron out, and then it gets piped back up here. They put the little pipe that comes back here with the filtered water inside the big pipe that takes the dirty water to the casino so that no one would notice it. Now can I pee?"

Jack ignored him and turned to Archer. "It's all about the water. The casino was built to get water to this place, to have a water source that wouldn't attract attention."

Archer shook her head. "It takes a lot to build a casino. There's no way ..." her voice trailed off as she considered the possibilities.

"I gotta pee!"

Jack sighed and fought with his leg to stand up. He handed the small pistol to Archer. "Cover me," he said as he limped over to Marshall and helped him up. He walked Marshall over a couple of feet to a tree and then yanked down Marshall's pants.

"Hey!" Marshall practically screamed, "What are you doing?"

"I told you I wasn't going to hold it for you. Lean forward against the tree so you don't pee on your feet." Jack reached out and put his hand on Marshall's shoulder to help him lean forward and then stepped away, leaving Marshall leaning shoulder first into the tree.

Billy's muffled noises through his gag could have been laughter or complaints. "Shut up." Jack told him. "You can just sit there and piss yourself. You shot her in the fucking back, asshole."

He limped back over to Archer to explain his revelation. "The pot farm was here first. They put it here because they could access the lake water without anyone really noticing. The Gardner's Patch was one of the only places that had riparian rights, so no one would think twice if there was a pipe in the water there, but a pipe anywhere else would be noticed. The only one who would really notice was Jim Gardner, and unfortunately for him, he noticed. So they killed him. They probably kept using the lake water, but realized that anyone who owned the property would eventually notice a pipeline running across it that didn't belong, so they annexed a part of his land that had spring water on it, built something on it that had a legitimate reason to have a lot of filtered water, and then started piping the water back to the pot farm."

Archer thought about that for a minute. "I still can't believe they built a whole casino to get water to a pot farm."

"I'm done!" called Marshall from the tree.

"And when my uncle submitted a permit using an old map that showed the casino was on land that should have belonged to him, they killed him, assuming he would figure it out sooner or later."

"I'm done!" Marshall called again.

"And now they're going to kill you because you noticed."

Jack nodded. "The only thing that doesn't make sense is why didn't they kill me right off the bat? Why bug my house and spy on me."

"I'M DONE!"

THIRTY-TWO

The FBI arrived en masse and descended upon the pot farm with a vengeance. It had taken them a couple of hours to arrive, for which an agent named Pitrone apologized profusely and explained they had come all the way from Sacramento. Agent Pitrone and Agent Kelly then proceeded to grill Archer and Jack, both together and separately, for a couple of hours while twenty or so other agents took possession of Billy and Marshall and began destroying the marijuana farm.

It was dusk by the time Archer and Jack had answered questions to Pitrone and Kelly's satisfaction. They were standing behind the casino, looking at the water pipe leading to the pot farm. The casino parking lot was full of black sedans and black vans. The FBI had set up base in the casino parking lot, as it was the closest place to park to walk into the pot farm, and after Archer had explained the water situation, it seemed the FBI might be there awhile.

Agent Kelly finished calling in for a warrant for the casino and hung up his cellphone. "They're faxing it now," Kelly reported.

"Okay," said Agent Pitrone as he hung up his own cell phone and turned to Archer. "A warrant has been issued for Sheriff Rambo's arrest, and agents are on the way to take him into custody. You'd better be right." Pitrone's dark eyes reflected the flashing lights from the small army of cars the agents had arrived in. "If Billy and Marshall decide not to give testimony, Rambo will be free in hours and he will be pissed."

Archer nodded. "Thank you."

Jack nodded his thanks, too. He was leaning heavily on his cane, looking so tired no one would have been surprised to see him fall over.

"Are you sure you won't let the paramedics check you out?" Agent Pitrone asked.

"They won't diagnose me or stitch up Jack," she explained. "They'll just transport us to the hospital where we would be the doctor's problem, not theirs. Besides there are still unknown officers under Rambo's thumb who can't be trusted, and we don't want to get cornered at the hospital."

"I still don't understand why you didn't turn in the video of his uncle's murder as soon as you realized the killer was a cop." Kelly gestured towards Jack while asking Archer.

"We didn't have enough information about what was going on. There was motive behind the murder, we were sure, but we just didn't understand," Archer explained. "Now that we do, I'll get you copies of the video and everything else we have, first thing in the morning."

"You need a ride out of here?" Pitrone asked.

Archer shook her head and pointed to her truck. She had parked in the casino parking lot three days ago, before hiking down to her secluded lookout spot above Jack's farm. "I've got my truck. Thank you, though. It's a nice gesture."

Pitrone nodded, then he and Kelly headed back towards the casino. Jack limped along after Archer, following her to the truck.

"My place or yours?" Archer asked Jack as she gingerly slid behind the wheel and shut the door. It was well after dark now, and the silence in the cab was deafening after the din of the evening.

"Whose place is closer?" Jack asked tiredly.

"Yours. It's just down the hill and around the bend from here."

"Mine then. You'll have to excuse the mess, this morning was so long ago, I don't really remember if I cleaned anything up or if I was painting the living room."

Archer started the truck and drove out of the parking lot. "Are you okay?" she asked.

"Long day at the office," he mumbled. "You?"

"Naw. I love my job. But what I really meant was; do I need to take you to the hospital? The nearest one I think we would be safe to go to is in Ukiah. I hear they're really good there."

"No. Other than my usual problems, I've just got cuts and bruises. Probably could stand a couple of stitches, but by the time we get there ... Hell, I'm halfway healed already. Mostly need to worry about infection from those damned thorns. And I think I got poison oak."

"What about your leg?"

"Pffht! It's the same old thing it always was, they can't do anything for it. I just need to wait for it to get better again." He paused for a moment as he realized she might be looking for an excuse to get herself to the hospital. "What about your ribs? Do we need to get you checked out?"

"Pffht!" she imitated him. "I broke a rib in college. They don't even wrap them anymore. If it punctured anything I'm pretty sure I would know by now."

They rode in silence for the remaining few minutes it took to get back to the farm Jack had inherited. Archer pulled into the circle drive and put the truck in park. "You need me to help you in?" she asked.

"It's been a long day, Archer, don't play games. Turn off the truck and come in. You're staying here tonight, end of story, no arguments or false modesty." He opened the door and started getting out without waiting for her reply.

She hesitated for a couple of seconds, then turned off the motor and followed him. Catching his elbow and helping balance him as he maneuvered up the wooden steps, she grunted with pain as taking his weight put stress on her ribs.

"Dumbass," Jack muttered as he fished out keys and unlocked the door.

"I'd laugh, but it hurts."

"Yeah, my wife used to say my sense of humor was painful too."

Archer fell silent and Jack looked anywhere but at her. He had no idea why he had brought up his wife like that, but he had, and it was done.

He shut the door and looked up at the stairs. "I'm tempted to forego the stairs and just sleep in the chair and let you have the couch, but the shower is up there and I have a lot of blood and dirt I really want to wash off. It itches." He stopped and looked at her. "And you smell like you haven't had a shower in three days. Stay off my couch until you're clean." He pointed a finger at her and started up the stairs.

Archer followed him up the stairs. From her lower vantage, she could see where the bear had raked its claws across his lower back. It looked red and inflamed; worse than she remembered.

"Do you have any antiseptics or antibiotic ointments?" she asked.

"I think there is a first aid kit on the wall in the kitchen, by the door. By the door by the oven," he answered, chuckling half-heartedly. "Why? Are you okay?"

"Just a little worried about infection," she answered as she turned back down the stairs.

When she came back up the stairs, Jack was already in the shower. She chose a different bathroom and luxuriated in the warm shower. The bruise on her back was a thing of beauty she wished she could admire more clearly, but it hurt too much to twist around enough to see it in the mirror.

Her clothes were filthy, so she wrapped herself in a towel and wrapped another one around her wet hair. Scooping up the supplies she had scavenged from the first aid kit, she went to find Jack and dress his wounds.

He was still in the shower. The door was open, but she knocked anyway. "Are you okay in there?"

Jack grunted an unintelligible reply.

"What's going on, Jack? Are you all right?"

"I can't get these damn thorns out. I was hoping they would soften in the water."

"What? Let me see." She stepped in and opened the shower curtain without waiting for permission.

The sight of his scarred body surprised her. She had expected scrapes and even gashes from the thorns and the bear, but the old bullet scars were more than she had anticipated. She winced inadvertently, and hoping he hadn't noticed. She didn't want him to think she didn't find him attractive.

Many of the bramble thorns had broken off and embedded into his skin. She couldn't help but notice even his scrotum hadn't been spared the abuse.

"Jesus, Jack, how did you manage all day like this?"

"What? This?" He didn't bother to look at her as he worried at a thorn on his shoulder. "This ain't nothin'. You should try getting shot and left for dead sometime."

She chuckled. "I did. It wasn't so bad, I guess …" She painfully turned and lowered the back of her towel so he could see the bruise.

"Yeah, well, they shot me six times. It hurt a little more."

"I thought you said you just went numb."

"After the first three or so, yeah. Just couldn't really hurt any more than that, I guess."

"Do you have any tweezers? I'll help you with those."

"I'd appreciate that. They're over there in my shaving kit." He shut off the water and grabbed a towel as she started rummaging through the kit.

"This is like a woman's purse. What don't you have in here? What's this? Monistat? Jack is there something you want to tell me?" She giggled.

"It was my daughter's," he answered somberly. "She always seemed to have problems whenever we went out of town, so I started carrying that to make sure we had it when we needed it."

"I'm sorry," she said sincerely as she put it back and found the tweezers.

"Don't be. I've got a lot of baggage and a lot of issues. You've been a good friend so far, better than anyone could have hoped for."

"So far." She mocked him. "Go sit on the bed so I can reach with these tweezers, and we'll see how you feel about me in a couple of minutes."

She followed him to the bed where they sat awkwardly side by side while she tried to get the thorn tips from his back. "I can't twist like this, it hurts my ribs. I need you to lie down."

Jack lay on his stomach and she climbed up onto the bed on her knees to get a better reach. He jerked a couple of times as she pulled out particularly nasty thorns but he didn't say anything.

"You know what, Jack?" She asked as she delicately tried to remove a thorn tip from inside one of the gashes the bear had left on his back. "I kind of like being your friend. Thanks for asking me to accept the position. No one ever offered me the position like that before." He jerked a little as she poured some peroxide on the claw marks. "Sorry," she whispered gently.

"Anyway. I was thinking about what you said about having a lot of baggage. I think I would like to try to help you carry it for a while." She smiled as she grabbed the antibiotic ointment. "I mean,

I know we haven't known each other that long, but I enjoy your company. You know what I mean?"

Jack snored.

THIRTY-THREE

Jack woke up naked and alone. He wondered for a moment if something had happened between Archer and himself, but dismissed the thought. His body was stiff and sore and it was hard to get out of bed. It was even harder to put on clothes.

He limped down the stairs to the kitchen and took some ibuprofen, hoping he would find Archer down there. He didn't. He peeked out the window and saw that her truck was gone. He suspected last night had been a missed opportunity, but he wasn't sure he was ready for it, anyway. He really liked Archer, more than liked actually, but life was complicated.

Something caught his eye on the table by the front door. He walked over and found Archer's ankle holster with the small Glock 30 in it and a note saying 'Happy Birthday, Gimpy'. It was signed 'a friend'.

Smiling to himself, he sat down and put the ankle holster on. He was stiff and it was hard to stay bent over long enough to strap in on. It felt like he re-opened the gash on his back trying. When it was on, he stood and took a few steps to see what it felt like. It would take some getting used to.

He sighed, thinking about Archer and missed opportunities, then tried to distract himself with some breakfast. He was putting away the dishes when the doorbell chimed. Peeking through the window, he was surprised to see it was Toni. Her grandmotherly face looked grim. He answered the door with a smile, but she didn't return it.

"Jack! Jack!" the raven cried as it flew down and landed on the porch railing next to Toni, startling her so much she almost fell. Jack grabbed her.

"That's Yogi. We saved each other's lives, and we're best

193

buddies now," he told her, as if that explained everything.

Recomposing herself, Toni said in a pinched voice, "Archer's been arrested. She used her one phone call to tell me you need to watch your ass."

His mouth gaped open. "What? What happened?"

"She said they were waiting for her when she got home. She wanted you to know Sheriff Rambo wasn't arrested, and they dropped the warrant for him."

Jack was at a loss. "Why? Did she say?"

Toni shrugged. Her voice was shaky. "Something about excessive force, coercion, and falsifying evidence. She didn't really get a chance to explain before they made her hang up. She did say this was her one phone call and asked if you would see about getting her a lawyer from out of the county. The last thing she said was she didn't think they were playing by the rules with her and she wasn't going to be able to post bail."

Toni looked him in the eye. "She's scared. I ain't never seen anything rattle her cage before, Jack, and it worries me. Do you have any idea what's going on?"

Jack felt like a great weight was crushing down on him. His mind had been only on Archer since he woke up and he hadn't thought about the previous day's events at all. He rubbed his eyes wearily. He realized he was still standing in the doorway and stepped back to let Toni in. Yogi accepted the invitation and hopped through the door.

Jack started to talk, but then remembered his house was bugged and shut his mouth again. He looked at Toni, put a lip to his fingers to warn her to silence and then gestured for her to move back outside. He already knew from experience not to bother trying to chase Yogi out so he left the door ajar as they moved out of the house.

He looked around trying to think of a safe place to talk. He didn't want Toni to end up on the list of people who knew too much and had to be eliminated.

He spotted her car and pointed at it, asking without words if it was all right to talk in there. Toni looked at him as though she thought he had lost his mind, but she went back around to the driver's seat and got in. He got in the passenger seat and waved her off again when she started to talk. With an exasperated look, she started the car and drove out onto the highway.

"Sorry," he apologized. "My house was bugged right after I moved in. You were right, my uncle was murdered, and I can prove it. Sheriff Rambo is in on it. He was also in on the murder of Jim Gardner and some other people, but I can't prove that. Yesterday Archer was shot in the back by a man Rambo told to kill her. She's okay, she wore a vest," he assured Toni when he saw the look on her face. He decided not to tell her how close of a call it had actually been.

"So we tracked down the guy who shot her and scared him, actually his friend, into telling us everything they knew about Sheriff Rambo. It wasn't much, not enough to prove anything. Then we called in the FBI to deal with the pot farm the guys who shot Archer were protecting. We also told them about Sheriff Rambo and they said they were going to arrest him. I don't know what happened after that, other than what you just told me.

"I mean, yeah, we 'coerced' him into talking to us, and I hit the bastard in the nuts. A couple of times, maybe. But I don't know why they arrested her." He thought about it for a moment.

"If this was all about that pot farm. I can't imagine they would still feel the need to kill me, I mean, I think that was the whole reason they had come after Jim Gardner, my uncle, and now me. To keep it secret, I mean." He chewed his lip while he thought.

"So you guys busted a pot farm yesterday," Toni finally spoke up, "that Sheriff Rambo had his fingers in. You fingered him for it. He somehow slipped the hook, and you don't think he's going to be pissed?"

"Can I use your cell phone?" Jack asked.

Toni rummaged in her purse with one hand and then tossed it to him.

"Is it all right if I call long distance?"

"What is this? A wasted minutes commercial? Use the fucking phone!"

He dialed the phone.

"Hey Leif, it's Jack. I need the best damn legal team you can get."

THIRTY-FOUR

"Jack Tabor?" The man walked over to the hard wooden bench Jack was sitting on. He was average height, wearing immaculate brown hair and an expensive business suit. He didn't fit in with the courthouse surrounding him; he was overdressed and overly professional for the run down Rainbow County Courthouse.

"Yeah?" Jack looked up wearily. His eyes were dark and sunken, his face leaner and gaunter than it had been.

"I'm Bill Addison." He held his hand out to Jack, who stood up and shook it.

"Nice to finally meet you. Are you going to be able to help?" Jack looked into the man's eyes and was glad to see self-confidence and presence of being in them.

"I'll be honest with you, it's a mess. When Leif contacted me, he didn't know half the story. Assuming what you two have claimed is true; they have a damn good frame up job going on here. It's going to be hard to prove Archer didn't do the things they accused her of. She's not getting out anytime soon. The judge refused bail."

Jack turned and looked back at the closed double doors of the courtroom he had not been allowed to enter. Archer was in there, or had been until a few moments ago. The officer at the door had refused Jack entry, saying it was a closed hearing. The officer still guarded the door with a bored look on his face. Jack hung his head. "This is so wrong …"

The lawyer reached out and put a hand on Jack's shoulder, unable to withhold a comforting gesture from someone so obviously in need of one.

Jack took a deep breath and looked up again, "So why haven't they arrested me yet?"

Bill shook his head. "They refuse to discuss it. They said you are only peripherally relevant to their case at this time and any charges they may or may not have pending against you will most likely be a separate case."

"That doesn't make any sense! I'm the one …! They …!" Jack shook his cane in frustration. "Why are we in this courthouse and not a Federal Courthouse?"

"The Feds aren't the ones pressing charges—yet."

"FUCK! I'm telling you, these people are all in on it! She is going to get screwed here! Can't you tell they are all full of shit?" Jack yelled. Bill Addison winced hard enough Jack was embarrassed. He shut up and sat down back down on the wooden bench. The full attention of the police officer at the double doors was on him now.

"I admit it feels unusual, but I don't see anything I can definitely say is improper or unwarranted." Bill waved his hands helplessly. "They have a lot of evidence to back up their allegations."

"This is all my fault. If I would have just minded my own business, she would never have been in this mess! She had nothing to do with any of it!" He clenched his teeth and raged silently for a moment. "What about the fucking video of those assholes killing my uncle, huh?" he hissed. He could feel the police officer's eyes on him. It felt like he was listening in, spying on the conversation.

"I told you, if it's a frame up, it's a good one. Those three guys in the videos? Two of them are on record saying they were forced to do it by Warden Durante, and the third, the one who actually used the rock, was found dead last week—by suicide."

"*Forced* to do it? How the fuck do they explain that?"

"The same way those other four guys are: She found their pot farm and threatened to arrest them if they didn't cut her in and do what she said."

"What other four guys?" Jack was incredulous. His stomach knotted and he started to feel lightheaded.

"The two you helped capture and a couple of guys both named Mike."

"Big Mike and Little Mike?"

Bill nodded his head.

"They're all copping to being in on the pot farm? They're taking the fall for it?"

Bill nodded again. "And Billy Johnson even admitted to shooting Archer in the back and leaving her for dead. He claims he was trying to get rid of her because of all the things she made them do, because she was taking too big of a cut of the profits and not doing anything but threatening them. He says she called the FBI and exposed the farm because she was pissed he shot her."

Jack stared at the lawyer in disbelief. *Why would all of those guys come together against her like this?*

"Is it possible she was playing you, too?" Bill asked softly.

It was the same thought Jack just had.

Was it possible? Could Archer have been playing for the other team? This wasn't the first time this possibility had come up. Big Mike and Little Mike had seemed to think she was in on it, and they obviously weren't. They had thought he was in on it. They had even offered to work for him.

"When they searched her place they found a couple hundred thousand in cash and some unregistered weapons. They also confiscated some spy cameras and microphones with recordings still on them. The recordings were all of you and your house. She was spying on you."

"She was spying on me? Ha!" He tossed an involuntary glance at the officer he was sure was spying on them right now. "What about the people following me now? Everywhere I go, someone is tailing me. Didn't Leif mention that to you?"

"Yeah, he did. I don't know whether or not you noticed, hopefully he's good enough you didn't, but we put our best man on it and he followed you around for a while too. He reported everyone he spotted watching you was a police officer. They have you under surveillance. Not surprising really, since they seem to think you were targeted by Warden Durante for some reason. They're probably hoping to find out why she was spying on you."

"No." Jack shook his head firmly and smiled grimly. "No. It wasn't her. I know they are full of shit." Jack grabbed Bill by the arm and led him away from the officer guarding the courtroom door. When they were out of earshot, he whispered, "I can't prove anything when it's our word against theirs, but I might be able to prove this one."

"How's that?"

"I forgot about it with all the shit that's been going on, but I knew I was bugged, and Archer knew I knew, because I told her. What I didn't tell anyone was that I had my own camera set up from the moment I got in the house."

"You already had a spy camera set up in your own house? Why on earth would you do that?"

"It was Leif's idea. There had already been at least one attempt on my life," he shrugged, "make that one more, after my family was killed, and he suspected there would be another. It's kind of morbid, but I agreed that if they did kill me, I wanted some kind of hard proof that could be used against them, because, whoever 'they' are, 'they' are connected to the murder of my family.

"I've been so caught up with Archer's arrest and the videos of my uncle's murder that I forgot about it, but I bet it recorded something that will put a hole in the idea that Archer was the one who put the other cameras there."

THIRTY-FIVE

Jack carefully climbed down from the counter with the spy clock in his hands. His legs weren't working as well as they had when he had put it up there, so it took some effort to get it down.

The camera was another expensive doohickey he had gotten from Leif when the lawyer had pressed him to carry the bulletproof satchel and stun gun. Jack promised himself he was going to give Leif a big hug next time he saw him. Leif's foresight and insistence had saved Jack's life multiple times, it had saved Archer's life, and now it might prove her innocence.

The clock was a self-contained unit with a hard drive for storing hundreds of hours of footage. The camera hidden in the clock was not only on a motion detector, but filmed in night vision and recorded sound as well. It should have caught everything that happened in the kitchen since the moment he had installed it when he arrived that first night. It should show the bug being placed in his kitchen, Brian Nazzaro and the assassin, Archer helping him search for the raven ...

He felt a fearful sadness crash over him. Archer had been in custody for four days and he couldn't get in to see her, couldn't help her, couldn't do anything. They hadn't even allowed him in the courtroom. He clenched his jaw and hoped the clock would have answers he could use.

He started for the door to take the clock to Billy Addison, but thought of the 'police officers' he kept spotting wherever he went. He wasn't sure who he could trust and was sure he shouldn't trust anyone. He needed to back up all of the information from the hard drive before he handed it over. In fact, he should make multiple copies; send one off to Leif, maybe one to Toni or anyone else he could think of to trust with it. He felt paranoid, but had good reason to, after all that had happened.

He turned on the computer and wondered if he had enough discs to copy whatever was on the clock's hard drive when he heard the distinctive sound of a cocking pistol.

"Turn around, son, and keep your hands where I can see them." Sheriff Beauregard Rambo aimed the six-shooter from his hip. He was in full uniform and wore a bored yet smug look on his face. A deputy stood behind him, his weapon also drawn. "Where is it?" the sheriff asked the deputy over his shoulder without taking his eyes off Jack.

"It's in that clock he's got on the desk there." The deputy pointed with the semi-automatic pistol he held in his hand.

"Cuff him and get it." The Sheriff's hard, steely grey eyes never left Jack's face as the deputy handcuffed and picked up the clock.

The deputy turned the clock over and looked at the back of it then showed it to Sheriff Rambo.

"Pretty nifty hiding spot," the Sheriff commented dryly. He waved his gun towards the door. "Let's go. Grab those spycams and bring them, too. Hurry up! It's going to get dark soon."

Jack seethed as he watched the deputy grab hidden cameras from the house. He had forgotten to check for new spy cameras and had revealed his only ace in the hole. The deputy must have been waiting somewhere close by, watching his every move on a remote video screen.

Jack took a deep breath and steeled himself. He knew Rambo hadn't come to arrest him, he could see it in the Sheriff's eyes. They had come to wrap up the last of the loose ends. The deputy headed for the door and Jack stumbled as the sheriff shoved him to follow.

As they cleared the threshold, the raven flew down calling his name in Archer's voice. "Jack! Jack!"

The deputy's head whipped around to see the bird. Jack stepped backwards to use a reverse head-butt on the sheriff. The sheriff dodged easily and kicked Jack in his bad knee. Jack dropped to the porch face first, unable to break his fall.

"What kind of idiot do you think I am?" The sheriff kicked him in the gut and sent him rolling down the porch steps, his head hitting the steps as he went. Blood filled Jack's sinuses. He knew his nose was broken.

"The dead kind of idiot," said a calm voice as the sheriff landed next to Jack at the bottom of the steps.

The deputy made a startled cry and there was a thump on the wooden porch.

Jack twisted, trying to see what was happening. He rolled over just in time to see William Roland Gray, the assassin, pick up the deputy's gun and aim it out towards the orchard.

"Fucking bird," Gray said coldly and fired the gun once.

The sun was going down and Miguel and all of his workers were gone for the day. The highway was silent, empty of cars. Golden sunlight streamed through the trees as the sunset turned the orchard into a wonderland of green and gold, light and shadow. Jack looked out into the trees just in time to see a puff of black feathers frozen in time in the golden light of the sunset.

A satisfied grin crawled across the face of the assassin and he bent over, cocking his head to look at Jack's sprawled form. "Well, now. We meet again." The man's left arm was in a cast and sling, held tightly to his body with Velcro. "Things are a bit different this time, though, hey?"

Jack struggled, trying to get his feet under him, trying to get up, but his head swam, and he was nauseous from his fall down the stairs.

"There, there. Don't panic, you'll just hurt yourself more. I'm not here to kill you—this time." He patted Jack on the stomach with his good hand before helping Jack up, maneuvering him over to the steps and sitting him down. "I've even brought you a present."

He walked over to the two Rainbow County Sheriff's Department patrol cars parked in the driveway and opened the back door on the rearmost car. A limp form tumbled out and he caught it deftly by the shirt collar. He dragged the body over to Jack's feet and dropped it there. It was Brian Nazzaro, the man who had put the final bullets into his wife and daughter.

"See? I knew you would appreciate that." Gray smiled unemotionally.

Blood dripped from Jack's swelling nose as he stared at the lifeless eyes of the man who had killed his family. He obviously had died recently, but his eyes weren't pleading, they were just empty, cold, and dead.

Listening to the patter of the blood droplets falling from his nose and hitting the porch between his feet, Jack waited to hear his daughter's voice pleading *How long does it take to die, Daddy?* but it didn't come.

He looked into the dead eyes of the man he held responsible for destroying his life and asked himself the question his daughter could no longer ask. *How long does it take to die?*

"Not long enough," he heard himself mumble through the blood on his lips. The son of a bitch had not taken long enough to die.

Apparently not only hearing but also understanding the sentiment, the assassin apologized. "I understand, and I am sorry, but I was working under a time constraint, and at a disadvantage." He pointed to his injured arm. "But we do what we can, now don't we?"

Gray walked over to the spy clock the deputy had dropped on the porch. "Is this it?" he looked at Jack. "Is this what all of the commotion was about?"

Jack tore his eyes away from the dead man to see what was being referred to and then nodded numbly.

"Hm." Gray picked it up and turned it over. "Ah! I see. You hid the hard drive in the back. Perfect!

"You know," he raised an eyebrow and nodded at Jack, "you were very convincing when you questioned Idiot about this thing. You convinced me you didn't have it, didn't even know what it was, and I … Well, I can't remember the last time someone fooled me." He grinned wide. "You could have been an Oscar winner!"

Jack frowned, confused by the assassin's words, but Gray didn't notice as he tucked the clock under his sling.

"We're almost done here now." He told Jack as he collected the Sheriff's gun from where it had fallen and laid it next to where he had placed the deputy's gun on the railing. Next, he dug handcuff keys out of the Sheriff's pocket and walked over to Jack. He sat on the step next to him.

He seemed to want to say something to Jack, but didn't know what it was. Finally, he fished in his pocket for something while nodding towards the dead body of Brian Nazzaro at their feet.

"I can't honestly say I did that all for you. Truth be told, I despised that idiot. He botched up my contract with you, he couldn't keep his mouth shut about things he wasn't supposed to know, and to top it all off, he was a little prick."

Jack jumped in surprise as the assassin plunged a syringe into his arm and injected him with something. He jumped up to get away. Gray didn't pursue.

"Don't worry!" he called after Jack. "If I had wanted you dead, I would have already killed you! It's just a sedative! You'll like it!"

Jack felt the stuff taking hold already and stopped running lest he fall face first into the ground again. He turned slowly back around to face the house and the sunset. The golden light was warm on his bloodied face.

Gray stood up and jingled the handcuff keys out in front of himself for Jack to see. "Come on back, I'll un-cuff you."

Jack looked at him and then back off into the sunset. The drugs were taking hold and he stumbled slightly before deciding to walk back to the assassin and the three bodies. It was true; Gray could have killed him already, if he had wanted to. He felt dizzy and queasy and it was getting worse as the sedative did its job. He had spent weeks in the hospital in the cotton fog of drugs. He didn't like it then, and he didn't like it now.

The pain was better. Pain was real.

But the sunset was spectacular. The sky was turning purple, the clouds burned with heavenly luminescence and the sun was so warm, so inviting.

It would have been easy to give in to the sedative, but he took a couple of deep breaths to keep his head clear and walked back to the man with the keys. Gray took him by a shoulder and gently turned him so that he could unlock the handcuffs, which he then tossed on top of the Sheriff's still form. "I just needed to make sure you were calm enough you wouldn't panic and think I was going to hurt you," the assassin assured him in that calm, hypnotic voice. "I needed to make sure you knew we're friends now."

Jack wiped the blood off his face with his sleeve and winced at the pain in his nose that momentarily lifted the drug fog. Gray returned to the railing and picked up the Sheriff's pistol and tucked it in his pants, then picked up the deputy's semi-automatic and walked back over to Jack.

Jack's cheeks were numb. He rubbed his wrists absently, trying to restore feeling to them while he took deep breaths trying to keep his head clear. The only thing he could really feel was the distant throbbing of his broken nose and his aching knee, but even those were growing more distant.

Gray held out the deputy's gun. "Would you help me with this?

Sam Knight

I don't have enough hands," he smiled apologetically and nodded at his arm in the sling.

Jack took the gun, thinking it was getting too hot out.

"Are you feeling all right?" Gray asked in that calm, friendly, reassuring voice. "Here, let me help."

He stepped in behind Jack, reaching his hand out to cover Jack's own as it held the gun. Quickly, he pulled Jack's arm around, pointed it at the sheriff's head and pulled the trigger with Jack's finger on it.

Jack was still looking dumbly at the hole that had appeared in the sheriff's forehead when his hand holding the gun was aimed at the deputy and fired twice. Before he could look at the deputy, the gun was aimed at Brian Nazzaro and the trigger was pulled repeatedly until the chamber clicked empty.

"There! Don't you feel better." The assassin chuckled and let go of him.

Jack stumbled and plopped down on the steps, still holding the deputy's gun, and again found himself staring at the body of the man who had killed his daughter. His body was numb and his mind was full of cotton, but he realized what had just happened to him and he didn't like it.

This man had just done to Nazzaro's body, to the sheriff and deputy, what Nazzaro had done to Jack's family. It was all so cold and calculated. How many people had this hit man killed this way? He was just as bad, or worse, than Nazzaro had been. Where was the justice in that? How could he find peace and justice in another murder?

Jack found no satisfaction in seeing the body of the man responsible for his family's death, let alone in that of the sheriff or his deputy. There was going to be no sense of justice or of peace. It wasn't just the drugs addling his thoughts, it was more than that. It was a disbelief in the callousness of it all.

The assassin pulled the sheriff's pistol out of his pocket and put it in the sheriff's hand, knowing Jack wouldn't be able to go get it. He went back and picked up the clock, tucking it back into his sling.

"By the way, I lied," he clucked his tongue. "That was a lethal dose I gave you. I'm actually a little surprised you're still conscious." His little smirk was maddening, even in Jack's drug addled haze.

Cold rage burned deep inside of Jack, fighting to make it up past the drug fog. Jack raised the empty gun and pointed it at the man who had stolen any true justice he might have ever gotten for the murder of his family.

The man laughed at the attempt. "Is that the thanks I get for saving your life? They were going to kill us, you know. You, me, and Idiot there," he nodded at Nazzaro's body. "They were going to take us out to put bullets in the back of our heads and bury the bodies. We were loose ends. You were too, but they were waiting on you. Watching you, waiting for you to slip up and show them where this was." He hefted the clock up in front of him.

"You just happened to finally reveal where you had hidden this right when Rambo was on the way to finish off Idiot and myself, so he stopped to get you too. Not that I am complaining, mind you." He leaned over and, reaching past the impotent gun pointed at him, ruffled Jack's hair impudently. "You gave me the opportunity to escape."

The gun was growing heavier in Jack's hand and he finally let it drop to his lap.

Gray stood admiring the pastel colored clouds for a moment. "I had hoped to escape, to make a plan, but that syringe I took from the hospital was the only weapon I managed to conceal from them, and I knew it would be way too slow acting for just any opportunity. But, hey! This way worked out great, don't you think?"

He looked back at Jack with a mock look of sadness. "Sure you're going to die now, but look!" His countenance brightened as he waved his hand at the bodies, "You got your revenge on the people responsible for the death of your family! Isn't that worth it?"

He stopped and frowned, then pursed his lips. "Maybe you hadn't figured that part out." He squatted on his heels to look Jack in the eyes and explained as though talking to a child. "They killed your family. They wanted your family dead so that when they killed your uncle this land would go into probate without any heirs and they could acquire it easily." He stood up and clucked his tongue again. "But you just wouldn't die. How many times did they try to kill you? Four? Five? Counting me?

"You almost blew my perfect record, but we've fixed that now, haven't we. We had to, since I'm retiring. Did I mention I was retiring? It's all thanks to you. My employer has decided I am a liability and I need to be terminated." He chuckled and smiled down at Jack. "I hear that in the movies all the time. Never got to say it before."

He turned, stepped off the porch, and held up the clock. "So thank you for this. It will be my insurance policy against termination. And don't worry, unlike you, I do have the encryption key for it, so if anything happens to me, your revenge will be complete." He smiled pleasantly again, "See? Such a fortunate happenstance this was, us running into each other again like this. We all get what we wanted. Mostly." He stepped back closer to the porch and reached down to check Jack's wrist pulse. "Won't be long now," he assured Jack and patted him lightly on the cheek. "Enjoy the sunset."

Through the haze of the drugs in his system, Jack hated him. It wasn't just the injustice of it all; it was the lack of justice. In spite of the hit man's words, there was no justice to be found here, only murder. Justice needed to be something more than murder. It needed purpose and meaning. But most of all, Jack now understood, it needed regret and remorse. It needed the people who carried out justice to have regret and remorse that the act was one of necessity, not a cold callous, heartless, uncaring act. It was something that had to be done no matter how much you didn't want to do it, something you would regret no matter how badly you wanted to do it. Justice was tempered, murder was raw.

He stared into the eyes of the cold-hearted hit man who would never understand justice as anything more than an eye for an eye. Justice would be stopping this man from killing again, bringing all of this insanity to an end. No matter how much he didn't want to be a killer, justice would be best served by ridding the world of this man in the only manner left to him. No matter how badly he wanted to kill this man, he knew he would regret it forever. There would be justice here.

Jack feebly raised the gun with unresponsive hands, and pulled the trigger. Nothing happened. The gun was still empty.

The man smiled a wicked smile at him and shook his finger as though Jack had been a naughty boy. He turned then, and walked out of the shadow of the house, into the last vestiges of the golden rays of the sunset.

Jack watched him go with the smile burnt into his numb mind, the only thing he could see. He was back in Hell. He tried to pull the trigger again, but still nothing happened. His legs were numb, his lips thick, the drugs had taken his body. This man had done the worst thing he ever could have to Jack; he had put him back into Hell.

A tear trickled down his cheek as he thought of the last time he had been in Hell. His wife and daughter had been there with him, together, but not; each in their own private, yet shared Hell. Now he was back and truly alone this time.

A grebe called out on the lake and the sound of the lapping waves gave him hope he was perhaps on his way to a better place this time. Maybe he would see his wife and daughter there.

He thought he could see his wife smiling at him, enjoying the thought of a family reunion. He wondered what she would have to say about Archer. He frowned at the thought, but felt he could almost hear his wife saying Archer was a good woman, that she had protected him. She had protected him and now he needed to protect her.

Protect Archer. Poor Archer was going to prison. How can I protect her? Archer needed protection.

Protection.

The gun. Archer's gun. He remembered she had given him a gun for protection.

He blinked. The light of the sun was almost gone; the assassin was halfway down the long driveway as Jack began to fumble at the ankle holster with thick fingers. Numbly he pulled it out and was grateful Archer had taught by example that it was all right to keep one in the chamber, even though you weren't supposed to. He raised his wobbly arm and took aim at the receding figure. Knowing his aim would be poor, he used the porch railing to steady the gun. Squinting one eye, he aimed for the middle of the man's back and pulled the trigger.

When his ears stopped ringing and the smoke cleared from his eye, he tried to look for the man, to see what had happened. It took a moment to spot the form lying in the long shadows of the trees in the driveway.

He twisted his body, tricking it into rolling him onto his hands and knees so he could stand up. Drunkenly, he stumbled out towards the body, still clutching the gun. He took deep breaths, trying to keep his mind clear, trying to fight off the drugs just long enough to see this through.

When he arrived at the body, it took him a long time to remember what he was doing before he realized the man was dead. A perfect shot in the back of the head.

Jack's body swayed as he looked down at his first murder victim. Maybe he had been wrong about justice, about needing to feel remorse. He didn't feel any at all. Maybe it was the drugs. Good thing he had aimed for the back and not the head.

"I took your advice on the Taser," Jack mumbled at the body, his words nearly unintelligible through his thick numb lips, "and I think this worked out so much better, don't you?" He dropped the gun next to the body and turned away.

The sun was gone and it was growing colder. A lone cloud still blazing orange in the purple sky hung over the lake like a castle in heaven. It made him smile.

I'm coming, he thought to his wife and daughter. *I'm on my way*.

He stumbled off the driveway and over to a tree and collapsed. Watching the cloud castle, he leaned back against the tree and waited to die.

How long does it take to die, Daddy?

Too long, Honey. It takes too long.

THIRTY-SIX

Smothering hot air was slowly suffocating Jack. It was old and stale and stank like burning things, bad things. The darkness was oppressive, overwhelming, and there was a great sense of Nothingness.

He was back in Hell, and he wept. His wife and daughter were not here. Hell had denied him yet again. It would always deny him; that is the nature of Hell. Even in death his torment continued. He couldn't move, he felt sick, he ached, his head hurt—everything Hell should be.

Somewhere off in the Nothing he could hear the bellowing roar of a great fire and clanking metal sounds, like medieval torture devices. Sounds of distant screaming came from far away. A booming voice rumbled over the screaming. The voice may have been laughing or crying, or yelling; he couldn't tell but it was definitely a voice over all the other horrible sounds.

This was his punishment for murder. He had murdered the assassin, shot him in the back when he wasn't looking. It didn't matter why he had done it, he had and that was all that mattered, and now he was in Hell.

Hot tears trickled down the side of his cheeks and across his ear, tickling like a bug. He flinched, just a little but it was enough. He wasn't dead. He found a perverse comfort in the flinch, a comfort Hell would never allow; a comfort that showed he was still in a body that could feel. Even when he had been lying, watching his daughter die, he had not been able to feel anything other than distant pain, but now he could. He had felt a tickle. He was not in Hell after all. He couldn't be; Hell offered no gleams of hope.

But then he remembered he had seen his daughter was not dead after all—right before she was shot again. He was wrong. Hell would gladly offer Hope so it could dash it away again.

His body shook with great choking sobs as tears and snot congested his airway and he convulsed into a coughing fit that proved he did have a body.

The sound of the distant voice changed and he knew he had attracted its attention. He clenched his teeth and swallowed hard and repeatedly, fending off more coughing, trying to remain silent. The voice came closer, no longer booming now but muffled. He could start to make out words.

"… just a camera set up of some kind! I'm telling you it's not the hard drive we were looking for! Yes! Goddammit! I'll bring it over as soon as I am done here!" The voice was very close now. Jack held his breath.

White light seared across Jack's eyes, blinding him with pain and intensity. He tried to throw a hand up to protect his face but only managed a small flop of his arm.

"Fuck me," the voice bellowed over Jack's face. "Tabor is still alive."

Jack rolled his eyes wildly trying to figure out where he was and what was happening. His mind was fuzzy and it was hard to think.

"What am I supposed to do? Huh? Cremate him alive? I don't do that shit! You want him dealt with you come over here and do it yourself, Dickhead!" The man on the phone turned his back to Jack and began pacing the room angrily.

As Jack's eyes adjusted, he could tell he was lying inside some sort of heavy cardboard box. He tried to sit up, but his body was weak and shaky and wouldn't obey him. He was groggy and tired. His mind felt slow and drunken, but his heart began racing and panic set in as he realized the man on the phone was talking about killing him.

"No! Wait! I got it!" The man on the phone raised his voice in excitement. "Send over Chuck and Louie. Let them talk to him. I bet they can find out where the hard drive is. They're already getting paid a shitload, you might as well get a little more work out of them."

The conversation paused for a moment, and Jack could make out the roaring of a furnace and a radio playing abstract music. No wonder he had thought he was in Hell.

The man continued his conversation on the phone, his voice calmer now. "You think? I don't know. Everyone already thinks he's dead … Yeah, maybe. I don't know. There's really not that big of a hurry. No, just Deputy Stith. I still got the other three. Well, think on it, but send over Chuck and Louie. If they can find out where it is, it won't matter. All right. Yeah, I can deal with him."

The man hung up the phone and leaned over to look Jack in the face. "You don't look so much like your Uncle. At least not right now. When we get done with you, I expect you will look exactly the same!" His chuckle was slow and menacing. Jack didn't recognize him but this had to be the crematorium at the funeral home, the one Toni's friend Judy had worked in, so this man must be the one who had cremated his uncle's body.

The man patted Jack on the chest, smiling grimly "I'll be right back, sweetheart, don't go anywhere." Jack tried to answer, but only managed to grimace. The other man grinned.

He fought to move, to regain control of his body, and even managed to sit up before overbalancing his cardboard casket and tumbling to the floor, sending the gurney flying across the room on its wheels.

"Son of a bitch!"

He heard the man curse and come running back towards him. He tried to get up but was distracted by the man's boot kicking him in the head.

The throbbing in Jack's head woke him up slowly. Gently at first, but then becoming an insistent pain, it made him wince and want use his hands to squeeze his head back together. But he couldn't. His hands were bound at the wrists, tied to the arms of a wooden chair, and numb from lack of blood flow.

"He's awake."

Jack squinted up at the man who had spoken. A sick feeling came to his stomach. He knew this man, this face. The revelation made his body shake with emotions. This was the man who had killed his uncle.

"Well now," Scar said with a husky voice full of menace as he squatted in front of Jack to look him in the eyes, "you look like you've got something you want to say."

Jack tried to talk but his voice cracked and his parched throat constricted in an unintelligible hoarse rasping noise. "I thought you were dead," Jack finally croaked.

"Yeah, been getting that a lot lately," he grinned wryly. "I'm thinking of changing my name to Plissken." He waited a moment then frowned in disgust. "How come nobody gets my joke?"

"Because you're too old. Nobody remembers that stupid movie." The mortician who had kicked Jack peered over Scar's shoulder. Scar scowled and gave him a hateful look.

"Chuck!" Scar called over his shoulder without taking his eyes off the mortician. "Bring the dead man a glass of water, would you? His mouth seems a bit dry."

Shuffling feet and the sound of a faucet happened out of Jack's view, then another figure came up behind Scar with a cup of water in his hand. Jack recognized him, too. Ox—the man who had dragged his uncle out of his house by the neck. Ox handed Scar the water. "Here you go, Louie."

"Thanks, Chuck." Scar's voice was condescending, as though he thought Ox had somehow gotten the water the wrong way. Ox didn't seem to notice the slight.

"Hey, the gangs nearly all here. Where's Ugly?" Jack impertinently asked the three men. "Getting his teeth fixed? I hope."

Scar looked at the water thoughtfully for a moment and then reached up and pulled Jack's head back by a handful of hair. He poured the water into Jack's mouth, gagging him.

"You know," Scar said with mock patience, "I thought you were dead, too. Quite a coincidence, huh? What do you think happens when two dead men meet? Think they cancel each other out, maybe?" He smirked a little.

"Come on, Louie. Let's get this shit over with." Ox sounded bored and impatient, like a child on a long road trip.

"Uh-uh, Chuck. I've been dreaming of this moment every day I had to stay hidden and pretend I was dead, I thought of what I would do if I ever got my hands on him. I never thought it could possibly happen, but now that it's here, I want to savor it." He reached to his side and pulled a hunting knife from a sheath attached to his belt. He twirled it slowly, reflecting light from the blade so that it moved across Jack's eyes. He chewed lightly at his bottom lip thoughtfully then slowly used the knife to cut a deep gash along the outside of Jack's little finger.

Jack sat still and stared Scar in the eyes. His hands were completely numb from the bindings so he hadn't felt anything. Even so, he had been to Hell enough times that he wasn't afraid of this man, or any other for that matter. He was ready to die, ready to go to his family. Jack just waited and stared back.

Jack's lack of reaction seemed to surprise Scar a little, but the mortician was visibly unnerved and turned away.

"Tough guy, huh?" Scar ran the blade lightly across the back of Jack's hand, just deep enough to make the blood well out freely, never taking his eyes off Jack's.

Jack met his gaze flatly. He had already been through so much worse.

Scar's lips twitched revealing his frustration and he angrily stabbed the blade down through the top of Jack's hand, pinning it to the wooden armrest. Jack jumped as the sharp pain shot through him, but the ties prevented him from pulling his hand away. Scar's eyes were wild and his body twitched here and there with uncontrolled agitation. He looked ready to kill Jack.

"What the hell are you doing, Louie?" The mortician demanded. Ox stepped in and put a rough hand on Scar's shoulder. Scar whipped around and snarled in Ox's face, almost out of control.

Ox held his hands up calmly and smiled softly at Scar. "You haven't even asked him about the hard drive yet. You can't kill him without at least asking."

"If you mess this up, you're done!" The mortician chastised Scar with a pointed finger. "How much more do you think we are going to put up with from you? Huh?"

Ox looked at the mortician with pleading eyes and then back at Scar with a set chin. "You need to keep in control of yourself, Louie. Just like we talked about."

Resentment and hate flashed across Scar's face. He ground his teeth as he brought himself under control and slowly turned back to Jack. He stood up straight and sniffed loudly before reaching down and pulling the knife out of Jack's hand.

Jack flinched at the pain.

Scar wiped the bloody knife off across the bridge of Jack's nose, making sure the tip came close to each eye as he wiped first one side and then the other. Then, slowly, he brought his snarling face close to Jack's and put the tip of the blade to Jack's throat.

"Where's the hard drive?" he growled through clenched teeth. His facial muscles twitched with barely restrained rage.

Jack lifted his chin up high to give Scar a good reach with the blade. He knew they were going to kill him and there was no point in causing himself more pain or agony than they were going to intentionally inflict. He was tired of being teased by Hell. He was ready to go.

"It's in the clock," he told Scar.

"Not that one, Asshole!" Scar pushed the blade into Jack's throat, intending a killing blow, but Ox's hand caught Scar by the wrist and stopped the knife just as it penetrated.

"Louie, you can't kill him yet." Ox spoke calmly, as though to a child, and held Scar's shaking hand tight as he tried to reason with him.

"Idiots!" growled the mortician. "Nothing but a couple of idiots! If you can't do this right then get the fuck out of here!"

Scar's lips curled with hate, frustration, and anger as he pulled his arm out of Ox's grasp and turned on the mortician. "I'm sick of you telling me what to do!" He swung at the mortician's face with the knife, but Ox easily caught Scar's wrist again.

"Calm down, Louie," Ox continued to try to sooth Scar, but his own voice reflected his growing anxiety. "We just need to find out what he did with that hard drive then you can kill him. Just calm down a little. Please." He held Scar's wrist out and above Scar's head making him look like a child being tortured by an older brother.

"Fuck you!" Scar screamed at him, flailing futilely in the Ox's grip. "Fuck all of you! I'm sick of being told what to do!"

"Asshole," muttered the mortician and turned to walk away. Scar squirmed wildly, dangling from Ox's arm like a piñata.

"You gotta calm down, Louie. This temper is what got you in this mess in the first place. We talked about this. I promised you I would help you stay in control. You need to get control right now, Louie." Ox's voice was growing desperate.

Scar screamed in rage and tried to kick Ox in the groin. Ox stepped back, avoiding the foot but setting Scar down in the process. That gave Scar just enough leeway to reach into his boot and pull out a second knife, which he slammed up into Ox's arm.

Ox let go and Scar dropped to the ground, whirling on the mortician, both knives at the ready. The mortician was already at a drawer pulling out a pistol before Scar could even leap. Two shots rang out deafeningly in the closed room. Ox was hit and blood splattered across Jack's vision.

Scar flew through the air, landing on the mortician, knives pummeling at the figure below him. More shots rang out, but all Jack could see was Ox stumbling drunkenly backwards towards him. Ox lurched once and then fell back on top of Jack. The chair crumpled under the weight of the two men.

THIRTY-SEVEN

Jack slowly came to, his old friend, pain, greeting him with the familiar throbbing welcome. It took him a moment to get his bearings, but the splintered chair underneath him and the loose ropes around his aching wrists reminded him where he was.

A distant sobbing came to his ears and he quietly moved to look around, wincing at the renewed pain in his ribs. When he put his hand to the floor, more pain attacked. He stopped and looked at the hand that had been stabbed. It made him feel nauseous and faint to see it, so he stopped looking and did his best to pretend he had never noticed it.

Ox was leaning heavily on one of the gurneys with a cardboard casket on it and slowly pushing it towards the furnace. He was crying and muttering under his breath incoherently about trying to protect someone. Blood was everywhere.

Jack looked around and spotted one of Scar's knives on the floor not too far away. He was silently working his way towards it when Ox collapsed to the floor.

Jack grabbed for the knife, but his fingers wouldn't close around the pommel. He used his other hand, and picked up the knife awkwardly. Standing slowly, he went towards Ox.

Ox had been gut-shot. Crumpled in a heap at the foot of the gurney, he was sobbing, mumbling he was sorry and still weakly trying to push the cardboard casket into the furnace with one hand. Scar's bloody body had been laid out in the casket with his arms crossed. It looked like he had been shot in the face.

Jack looked around for the mortician, but then noticed the thing burning in the furnace. The smell made him retch.

Ox startled at the sound. His head snapped up and his fist, shaking wildly, came up with the gun. It was pointed nowhere near

Jack. He was growing weak and was unable to do much more.

"You need medical attention," Jack said hoarsely. "I'll call for help for you, but you need to toss the gun so I know you won't shoot me."

Ox thought about it for a few long seconds. He stared into Jack's eyes, searching, trying to decide what to do. Then he tossed the gun. His throw was weak and it only went a foot or so.

Jack went over and kicked the gun away, sending it spinning off under a metal rack.

The man gasped weakly. "Kill me quick." His breath was short and pained. Tears streamed down his cheeks.

Jack shook his head. "One murder was enough for me. Where's the phone? I'll call for help."

Ox sobbed and pointed weakly. "Louie is dead." He told Jack with pleading eyes and sobbed some more. "I tried. I tried to protect him ..." He continued to sob while Jack went looking for the phone.

"I know you guys wanted to kill me, but I don't know why." Jack found a cordless phone lying next to a computer on the desk. "I don't know anything about a hard drive," he continued to talk as he tried the phone and found it couldn't connect with its base.

"Where's the base? It doesn't work." Jack had to go prod Ox for an answer. The man pitifully raised his eyes to Jack's face and reached up for the phone, shaking his head dazedly. "It doesn't work. Do you know where the base is? Do you have a cell phone?" Jack asked.

The man's breathing was becoming more ragged. He just shook his head and went back to crying about Louie.

"Why do you think I have a hard drive? What's on it?" Jack asked as he searched for the base to plug the phone into. "Why did you kill my uncle?" Anger and tears began growing in Jack's voice as the man refused to answer. Jack considered getting the gun and threatening the man, but knew it would do no good. The man was already dying, Jack couldn't hurt him anymore than he already was, and threats wouldn't make any difference.

He finally found the base and sat the phone into it, then picked it up and got a dial tone. "I don't know where we are. You need to tell them." He dialed 911 and handed it to Ox.

"You? You really gonna help me?" Ox huffed breathlessly in surprise, taking the phone from Jack.

"It's the right thing to do." Jack had tasted vengeance already, and it was bitter. He didn't like it. "I've always been big on doing the right thing."

Ox gasped into the phone, breathily telling the operator he had been shot and giving his location. The tears continued to roll down his cheeks as he hung up the phone in spite of the operator's protests.

"Sorry," he gasped at Jack through painful sobs. "So sorry about … family." He shook his head tiredly. "Not right. Not right." His face twisted as pain or emotion momentarily overcame him. "They wanted you all dead to get … Gardner's Patch." He gasped and squeezed his eyes tight. "So sorry. Not right. Were gonna kill you anyway, but then … hard drive. They … moved up the hit on your family because you had it. It-It can put them in jail … forever." He wheezed and put his other hand over his wound, holding in the pain.

"Can't believe you would help me …" Ox tried to smile gratefully at Jack, but his face was only a grimace. "Get out of here. I-I can tell them you … dead … already in fire …" A horrible burbling sound came from his belly under his hands; his eyes went distant and his mouth fell slack.

Jack felt helpless, unable to do anything. "Hey!" Jack shook the big man's shoulder. "You gotta stay awake until they get here!"

The man rolled his eyes wildly, fighting to come back to consciousness. "Gotta help Louie!" he gasped. His eyes pleaded with Jack as he lost touch with reality. "Louie!"

Sirens suddenly appeared in Jack's awareness, close enough he must not have been hearing them approach.

"Hurry, Louie …" Ox pushed Jack away. "You can't let them catch you again …" He wheezed and closed his eyes.

Jack grabbed the spy clock off the desk and ran.

THIRTY-EIGHT

The lake was smooth as glass, flawlessly reflecting the sunlit mountains, blue sky, and two wispy streaks of clouds. Marveling that such a large body of water could stand so still, even for a moment, Jack watched as a white snowy egret flew low across the water, gliding silently above its mirror twin before pulling up and landing on an old dock post with two billowing flaps of its wings.

He was sitting on an old park bench at the end of an overgrown trail. A makeshift walking stick he had broken off a dead log leaned against his knee. There was no beach here to speak of, just a rocky bank. He suspected that was why the trail was in disuse.

He had washed the blood out of his clothes in the sink at the Rainbow City Park public facilities. Expecting screams of panic as soon as he set foot near the kids' playground, which was next to the toilets, he was surprised no one took notice of him. When he came back out soaking wet but clean, he looked around a bit more carefully and spotted the vagrants and junkies that haunted the edges of the park. He had not really stuck out at all.

Now he was waiting for night to fall, so that any of the 'police' who had been following him these last few weeks would have a hard time recognizing him if they spotted him. He hadn't yet figured out how he was going to get back home, back to Colorado, but he had finally figured out that was where he needed to go.

He needed to find Alfonso 'Sancho' Robles—the kid Bogie had given the little pink backpack to on the day his family had been murdered. It was the backpack that he could see so clearly in his dreams, but had not noticed when Bogie had brought it into the halfway house. That was not unusual. The inmates were experts at sleight of hand, pick pocketing, and misdirection. They all practiced

223

it all the time.

That was how they snuck stuff in and out of jail. Even though they had little need to use it at the halfway house, they did anyway. Out of habit or sense of accomplishment, Jack didn't know. They were almost free to come and go at will at the halfway house; there shouldn't have been any need to sneak something in or out. But they had. Bogie had.

He had passed off the backpack to Sancho, who had promptly disappeared with it. *That was what the police had searched so hard for after they killed Bogie. After killing Jamie and Wendy. And Chuck. And Little John.* They had killed anyone who may have had any knowledge of it. They had killed everyone except the one person who had it; Alfonso, who insisted on being called Sancho. They had framed him for the massacre and put him on the most wanted list so they could find that backpack.

Now, after all this time, Jack finally knew what must have been in it. A hard drive.

Jack put his face in his hands. Ox had said they were going to kill his family anyway. So they could take the land. They had been eliminating anyone who might have had actual legal claims to the property the pot farm and the casino had been built on.

It hadn't been as random as it seemed. His family had been marked for death and Bogie had just accidentally moved up the timetable.

Why had Bogie stolen a hard drive from these people? Did he know what was on it? How did he get it? Had he known my family was marked for death? Was that why he came to me that day?

Jack tried hard to remember Bogie's file. It was forever ago that Jack had been at the halfway house, but he always tried to learn as much about each inmate as possible. There were so many things to read between the lines in the files. Things you weren't allowed to say about an inmate because they could be interpreted as speculation or conjecture and then called prejudices, not necessarily racial. They could be used against you, or even to free an inmate, if they ever came to light.

By the third or fourth time someone was caught going through a woman's underwear drawer looking for 'jewelry', even though they had skipped the purses and wallets, it was pretty obvious you had a sex offender on your hands. But the charges would never reveal that, so you couldn't write it in their file. Nevertheless, if you knew where to look and how to read it, the case manager's notes on the inmate's conversations or plea agreement might reveal it all.

Part of Jack's job at the halfway house had been to determine if they were willing to accept an inmate, if they were too high risk or not. So he had studied every file in detail, reading between the lines and evaluating the risks. As a result, he knew most of the inmates better than their case managers had.

Jack stretched his sore legs out and leaned back against the bench, wincing as he put pressure on his ribs. He readjusted, trying to get comfortable and looked up at the blue sky. He wondered if Bogie had intended to blackmail these people somehow.

Bogie had been proud of the degree he had earned in janitorial services. He had all but taken over the cleaning of the halfway house while he had been in it, and the staff had sorely missed him when he was released on parole. The degree may seem laughable to some people, but it was a good foothold out of a life of crime, unless you had sticky fingers.

Jack closed his eyes and enjoyed the warm sun on his face. A new job could easily have gotten Bogie access to a hard drive. Looking into where he was working at the time of his murder might show where the drive had come from.

But where to find Sancho and the hard drive? He rubbed his eyes wearily. Sleep threatened to overtake him in this peaceful stretch of lakefront.

First, he had to figure out how to get back to Colorado.

THIRTY-NINE

The blinking red light was very small and hardly noticeable, but it suddenly seemed bright in the dark night when it finally caught Jack's attention. It came from the back of the spy clock. He was walking along the side of the highway, making his way back towards Toni's with a vague notion of getting her to help him when he noticed the light flashing.

He had been staying as far off the highway as he could and holding still anytime a car went by, hoping to avoid being noticed. A flashing red light could ruin that pretty quick. Fumbling at the back of the clock he finally found what he thought was the off switch. He flipped it, but the light continued to blink. He held the back of the clock up to his face and tried to read the raised lettering next to the light. It was hard to make out in the dark with the red light blinking in his eyes. When he put his thumb over the light and reflected it onto the lettering, he was finally able to make it out. The hard drive was full.

If the hard drive just now reached full, he realized, *it had been recording all this time.* Being motion activated, it should have been recording anytime someone was in front of it. There was no telling what was on it now, depending on how long that light had been blinking.

There might be information to help free Archer. It could have captured the murder of Sheriff Rambo by the assassin. Ox, Scar, and the mortician attacking one another. The mortician's phone calls, conversations with Scar and Ox when Jack had been unconscious; there might be a lot to learn from it.

He still needed to find Sancho and the other hard drive, though. This one would still have gaps in information, and might not lead him to whoever was responsible for all of this.

He leaned on the rough end of his makeshift cane and wished he had his old one back as he dug the batteries out of the clock.

227

When the red light finally went out, he relaxed a little. He hadn't realized just how anxious he was about not being spotted.

He rethought his decision to go see Toni for help. She didn't need the stress of worrying if they were going to come after her, or of even knowing he was alive. If Ox had lived long enough, and if he was as good as his word, he may have reported that Jack was dead, and it might easily be assumed his body had gone into the incinerator ahead of the mortician's.

Jack had thought being dead would make it easier for him to travel unnoticed. Without a car or money, that wasn't turning out to be the case. He couldn't bring himself to steal someone's car, and if he went back for his own they would realize he wasn't dead. And no money meant no bus.

He wished he knew where Archer's house was, it had already been ransacked and most likely no one would go there for any reason anytime soon, but he had never been there. He wouldn't feel too bad stealing from Sheriff Rambo, but, again, he didn't know where he lived, either.

He considered calling Leif and asking for help, but he was still concerned there had been a leak of information there, even if Leif refused to admit it. Bill Addison might help, but Jack didn't have any reason to trust him.

For all he knew, Bill Addison had been the one to sic Rambo on him when he told Bill about the spy clock.

He sighed heavily and continued onward down the highway for lack of a better direction to go, grateful he at least had clothes and shoes. His stomach growled and he began rethinking visiting Toni.

"So where you headed?" The trucker was not what Jack had expected. It was hard to tell with him sitting in the cab of the semi, but Jack was sure he was five foot nothing and a buck twenty at most. He was neatly dressed in slacks and a collared shirt and groomed immaculately.

"Colorado," Jack answered, trying not to make too much or too little eye contact. He glanced down at the clock he had shoved in a plastic grocery bag he had pulled from a trashcan. He hoped it made him look less demented than he had walking around with a clock.

"You're in luck. I'm going all the way to Cheyenne. That'll get you pretty close." The man flashed a quick grin that looked nervous only because he was such a small man. "You havin' a bad spell?"

Jack nodded. "Got rolled. Small town sheriff didn't give a shit about me." It was pretty close to the truth.

The trucker nodded out the window. "Seen it before. Hope not to see it again. You got anyone can help you?"

Jack shook his head.

"No family?"

"They died. Just me now."

The trucker nodded some more and stared at the oncoming lights. "Have you thought about accepting Christ into your life?"

"Joe told me to come here." Jack looked the heavy lady in the eye and realized he needed to be more demure. He looked down at the ground and shuffled his feet nervously.

"That Joe," she *tsked* the truck driver. "He sure is one for picking up the hard luck cases. You know he donates almost twenty thousand dollars a year to our foundation?" She waved Jack to come inside the homeless shelter. "Not that I don't think it is wonderful," she continued. Jack realized she wasn't really talking to him or expecting him to listen anymore, "but one of these days he's gonna get hisself killed picking up strays like this."

Jack got off the bus at the Denver station. It wasn't as bad as he had thought it would be, cleaner than he expected, but still not great. He couldn't complain. It had taken him two weeks of odd jobs in Cheyenne to earn enough money for the bus ticket. Work had been hard to come by. The homeless shelter had been full, but not of the drunks and druggies he was used to. It had been full of families; people out of work, out of money, and out of their houses.

He had spent a long time feeling the world was a dark cold

place that had it out for him, but he had never been without a home before. He had seen it slowly breaking these people. It didn't take long for him to stop feeling sorry for himself.

Once the workers at the shelter had realized he wasn't a bum on a binge, they were quick to help any way they could. When this was over, Jack kept telling himself, he was going to pay them back, as well as Joe the truck driver, and anyone else he could help.

He took a deep breath and thought about heading for Leif's office. He didn't know how he was going to contact Leif yet, but he had to find some way to do it without giving himself away to whomever had leaked information out of the lawyer's office. It would wait.

Finding out where Bogie had worked would have to wait, too. He had no way of looking into that without revealing himself, and right now he needed to stay hidden.

He went into the bathroom and found a stall where he could change. He took off his clothes and put on some old ones he had acquired from the shelter. He shoved the nicer ones into an old rucksack and wrapped them around the clock. Stepping out, he looked at himself in the mirror.

His hair was the shaggiest it had been since he had finally gotten out of the hospital bed forever ago. He hadn't shaved and was developing a pretty scraggly beard. He looked the part of a bum.

One last touch, he thought as he unwrapped the bandage from his hand. The scars left on his hand from Scar's knife were ugly, red in some places, purple in others. It had been infected, hot, and painful, by the time he had arrived at the homeless shelter. Fortunately, emergency rooms are required to treat anyone who walks through their doors. Unfortunately, he had had a hard time getting follow up treatment and more antibiotics, but that was behind him now.

He wrapped the bandage around the other hand, adding the illusion of even more things wrong. Leaning heavily on his newly acquired thirty-year-old steel-gray cane, he set out to find Sancho.

FORTY

Jack was almost ready to give up. He had staked out the neighborhood for almost three weeks, sleeping under the bridge with the other transients, collecting aluminum cans, pretending not to notice when someone stole something, ignoring drug deals and bum bashings.

He worried constantly about his clock and the information on it, but he never found a place he felt was safe to leave it. He never put the rucksack down. He even slept with it. Sometimes he wondered if this was what it was like to be crazy.

He knew this was the right neighborhood. Not just because of what he remembered from the file. He was sure he remembered; it had been the last thing he had done at the halfway house. He had seriously been considering letting Sancho go home for his mom's Christmas party that night, but had decided against it. Not only because it was a serious bend in the rules, but because it had been this neighborhood in particular. It was not a good one.

Even if his memory had been shaky, the cops that came by every couple of days and offered money for information on Sancho would have confirmed it. After watching how the cops always kept an eye on a particular house when they were around, Jack was pretty sure he had figured out which one belonged to Sancho's mother.

Tonight was the second night in a row for the cold rain. Even on a hot August night, the Colorado rain was cold. The first kiss of cool air was always welcome, but when the nickel sized drops fell, everyone went under cover. Everyone except Jack, who huddled miserably under a plastic poncho made from a trash bag. He stayed where he could watch the house.

Sometimes he went numb and couldn't feel the cold water

anymore, other times it was all he could feel. Every now and then he dreamed his wife had her arms around him, keeping him warm. Sometimes he argued with Archer about keeping the bird. He missed the raven. He hated Gray for having shot it. He was glad he had shot the assassin.

Cold water dripped down the back of his neck, and he woke up again even though his eyes had never been closed. He was fading off into imaginary conversations more and more often. It scared him. He wiped rain out of his eyes and finally decided he was done trying to find Sancho. He had to be. He couldn't take it anymore. It was time to figure out how to approach Leif without giving himself away.

Why? Why did he care if he gave himself away now? He had used up all this time trying to find Sancho, without fear of someone trying to find him, only to be miserable. He had been living on the edge of society, starving, freezing, and in constant danger of unexpected attack from random unfortunates around him—all for nothing. He weighed less now than he had when he had gotten out of the hospital. His body was weak, his soul was tired, and he was afraid he was losing his mind. He scratched at his leg. He was pretty sure he had scabies, too.

It was time to turn in his spy clock and try to get Archer out of prison. It was past time. His first priority should have been to get her out and then prove who framed her.

Guilt hurt his heart. He had thought of her often during the last two months. He had wondered how she had taken the news of his death. He had wondered if everyone really thought he was dead. A quick trip to the library to look up the news for Rainbow County had only shown that Rainbow County was almost too backwards to be mentioned on the internet.

He huddled, cold and shivering, under his trash bag and imagined Archer huddled in a cold cell. Thoughts of her flirting with him had warmed him inside more than once, even when he hadn't been hallucinating. Had they done the same for her? Not if she thought he was dead.

A movement caught Jack's eye. If he hadn't been staring right at it, he wouldn't have seen it. On the side of the house, a dark shape broke away from the silhouettes of a trashcan and a pile of broken pallets and junk. The dark blob hardly had to cross two feet before it passed through what appeared to be a dog door in the fence and vanished into a neighbor's fenced yard.

Jack was on his feet and trying to run before he realized it. It had to be Sancho. The trash bag tangled with his cane and slowed him, but he hobbled on, running wide, away from the house and around the corner. He hoped he had guessed correctly and that Sancho would come out on the other side of the block.

He cut around the edge of the wooden privacy fence as fast as he could and ran headfirst into another darkened figure. Pain lanced through his bad knee and his barely healed ribs, making him gasp for air as he tumbled and fell, splashing into the gutter flowing with runoff.

"Fuck!" the figure hissed at him. "Watch where you're going, man!" The man paused to look at the wretch in the gutter. "At least you got a fucking bath." He turned and started away.

"Sancho!" Jack called as best he could. The pain and cold water stole most of his breath.

"Oh, shit!" Sancho broke into a run, getting away now that he had been exposed.

"Wait! It's me! It's Jack Tabor!" Water from the gutter went up Jack's nose and he choked and sputtered, unable to call out anymore. He rolled over and out of the water, grateful he had put his spy clock in sealed plastic bags dug out of the trash. He choked and coughed, trying to get the water out of his lungs.

Finally he was able to breathe again and he grabbed his cane out of the cold water and worked his way to his feet.

He was done. It was time to quit. Sancho wouldn't be back here for a long time now that someone knew he had been here. He slowly limped back towards the bridge he had been living under to wait for the sun to come up. It was time to give the clock to Leif and see what happened.

A hand touched the dirty hoody pulled over his face and Jack came up with a knife. Weeks out here had taught him to sleep light. He was fast, but the other was faster. Jack's hand was caught and the barrel of a pistol pressed hard against his nose.

He let go of the knife and his hoody was forcefully pulled back off his head.

"Sonofabitch! It is you!" Sancho looked down into the face of a world weary vagrant with wide eyed-surprise.

"Hey Alfonso, how've you been?" Jack's smile was weak, but genuine.

"It's Sancho."

"I know. Every cop in the city has asked me if I knew where you were."

"You went through all of this just to turn me in?" Sancho's eyes hardened and the gun came back up.

"Right. I'm living like this because the cops are my friends and I want to help them catch you." He coughed up more water.

"What you want with me then, huh?" The gun stayed where it had been, pointing at Jack's chest.

"Did Bogie give you a hard drive before they killed him?"

"Yeah, but I ditched it. I don't need no hard drive. Especially a hot one I didn't steal."

Jack closed his eyes and hung his head.

"Why?"

"Because it could have let you and me safely walk the streets again."

FORTY-ONE

"$ee? I told you my moms would fix you up."

"And I appreciate it, too. It's been a long time since I had a hot shower and decent food."

"Alfonso tells me you waited outside our house for three weeks to find him?" Mrs. Robles was a very polite and proper woman who had been a very gracious hostess in a strange situation.

Jack nodded, "Yes ma'am." She couldn't have been much older than Jack, but he owed her the respect.

"And it wasn't to get revenge?"

"Moms! I told you, he's the one with the lawyer that proved I didn't do it!"

"I know your son didn't do it. I was there."

Mrs. Robles blushed. "I-I know. I just worry so much about Alfonso." She broke into tears. "I am so sorry about your family. I felt so horrible when they said he did it." She choked on her words. Sancho handed her tissues as she tried not to blubber. "I knew he didn't. I mean—just the thought that my baby might have done something like that!" She blew her nose loudly. "And I met your wife. She counseled my oldest. And she was good, too. Actually cared! Not just there for the money like those other ..." She blew her nose again.

Jack turned back to Sancho. "So you really think you can get that hard drive back?"

"Yeah. I gave to a friend of mine who's a real geek. I wanted to know if anything was on it, but he said it was encrypted. I know he's still got it. If there's any chance it had stolen credit card numbers on it, he's still trying to crack it."

"Alfonso!"

"Sorry, Moms."

Jack followed Sancho, imitating the way he stuck to the shadows in the night. He thought he should have felt silly as he went along with the skulking, but after weeks of begging for food and looking in dumpsters, his dignity was completely unaware of the slight. Besides, Sancho was worried that there were people in the neighborhood who would be only too happy to turn him in for the reward. Sancho's friend lived only a couple of blocks away, in a house that looked like all of the rest; iron bars on the doors and windows, peeling paint, dead lawn. He followed Sancho around to the back of the house and in through a basement window that lifted like a flap.

The inside of the house wasn't any nicer than the outside, which was at odds with all of the expensive electronic equipment set up everywhere. Two teenagers were playing a 3D video game on a giant flat screen television, the glasses making them look like children pretending to be cool. Two more giant televisions were in the same room, side by side with the first, one playing ESPN and the other a music video. Video game systems and components were scattered carelessly across the floor along with empty chip bags and aluminum cans. It looked like an opium den for video addicts.

"Man! You can't be comin' in here! You too hot! You gonna get me busted!" At seven feet tall and with muscles on top of muscles the man who came at them nearly cowed Jack, another feeling he hadn't experienced for a long time.

"Oh, no you didn't!" The man stopped and pointed at Jack. "You did not bring him into my house!" He reached out with a long arm and smacked Sancho upside the head. "What's wrong with you?"

Jack recognized the man. He didn't know him, but he had signed in as a visitor at the halfway house a few times. Jack thought he must have been recognized, but remembered his appearance at the man's next words.

"Now every bum in the world is gonna be trying to crawl in my window! What were you thinking! Oh, wait! I know! You weren't!" He tried to smack Sancho again, but missed this time and turned his attention to Jack.

"Hold on, Moe!" Sancho quickly stepped between them. "This is Mr. Tabor." When it didn't register he continued, "The guy whose family I *didn't* kill. He's the one that lived."

Moe had shuffled Jack and Sancho into what he called his 'geekdom sanctum sanctorum' and shut the door behind them. The room was a small bedroom filled with pieces of scavenged electronics and humming servers surrounding a modest desk with four computer monitors on it, each doing something different. Moe reached up to the top shelf and grabbed a small silver box.

"I don't know what you're gonna do with it." Moe handed the drive to Jack.

Jack turned it over in his hands. It was hard to believe this little silver box was the center of so much trouble. "I'm going to find out what's on it and see if I can use it to find the people who killed my family."

"How do you plan to find out what's on it? It's encrypted." Moe asked.

Jack looked up at him. "Can't we just break the encryption and read the files?"

Moe smiled sadly. "If you used all the computers in the world, you might break the encryption in twenty years, if you got lucky. You need to have the key to unlock it."

"Can't we just pick the lock? Or break it?" Sancho asked and then ducked as Moe's huge hand passed through the air where his head had been.

"Dumbass. Key code. A number with twenty-five zeroes behind it. Or more." Moe scowled at Sancho.

"Then how do they …?" Jack started to ask, but didn't even really have the knowledge for the words.

"That's just TV magic. They can't. You have to get someone to cough up the key. Or steal it. If you can find it. That's why I didn't do anything with it. If it had just been the simple encryption that came with the computer, I'd have done it a long time ago, but this … You'll probably have to figure out who was using it and hack their computer. Put a key logger on it and steal the passwords."

Moe shrugged.

Jack looked at the drive despondently. He had been so sure it would solve all of his problems, but it was worthless.

Moe watched the emotions play across Jack's face as the meaning of the exchange sunk in for Sancho.

"Shit! Man." Sancho sulked out the door leaving Jack and Moe alone.

After a long moment, Moe spoke up again. "Any chance you know who might have the key?"

Jack shook his head. The assassin had said he knew it, but he was dead.

"Where did it come from?" Moe asked. "Maybe you could find someone who knows."

Jack shook his head again. He had no idea where Bogie had gotten it. "My best guess is from somewhere Bogie was working, but I don't know anything about that."

Moe rubbed the top of his head absently and thought out loud. "This happened last year? And Bogie had gone legit? Supposedly."

"Yeah. Supposedly."

"If he was legit, then there is a W-2 tax form with his employer on it. Get me his Social Security Number and I'll find the form."

Jack looked up at Moe. "Thank you."

FORTY-TWO

Jack and Sancho, who begrudgingly agreed to stick with being called Alfonso, at least for the time being, walked boldly into Leif's office wearing their new Sunday bests. Neither of them had clothes that had looked remotely respectable in Mrs. Robles' opinion, so she had come back from the local hospice store with new suits for them both. She had given them both haircuts and made them shave, then she had fawned over how good they both looked. Jack had blushed.

A pretty, blonde receptionist greeted them with a wide toothy smile that was cold and professional. "Hello. May I help you?"

Sancho shifted nervously. His tie was bothering him. He hadn't worn one since Sunday School over a decade ago. Jack smiled at the woman with a grim satisfaction in his eyes.

"I'm Jack Tabor. I'm here to see Leif."

Jack thought he caught a hint of surprise in the woman's eyes. Perhaps she knew who he was and thought he was dead.

"Mr. Postumaus is not available right now. Would you like to schedule an appointment?" Her professional veneer was thin and Jack could see through it easily. "We'll wait."

"But Mr. Postumaus …" She tried to deter him, but Jack had already ignored her and moved to sit down. A tick of a smile pulled at the corner of Sancho's mouth. He enjoyed watching people get shut down like that.

"Can I use your cell phone?" Jack asked as Sancho sat next to him awkwardly, catching himself in the middle of flopping onto the plush armchair and trying to turn it into a dignified seating.

"Sure." Sancho fumbled with the inside pocket of his blazer and retrieved it.

"Sir? Sir?" The receptionist was frowning hard, at a loss for what to do about Jack's insolence. Sancho grinned at her, obviously enjoying her discomfort.

Jack dialed the phone and held it to his ear. He spoke a moment later. "It's me, Jack." He paused, listening then grinned wryly. "In your waiting room waiting for your secretary to get off her ass and tell you I'm here."

"My God! Jack! I thought you were dead! Look at you! You're skinnier than the day we met! Where have you been? What have you—" Leif shut himself up and waved his hand at the chairs in his office. "Please. Sit and explain."

"Leif, this is Alfonso Robles. He needs a good lawyer." Jack introduced Sancho and sat down. Sancho and Leif shook hands briefly before sitting.

Jack hefted the slightly worn briefcase he had borrowed from Moe and sat it on the desk. He looked at it for a moment then glanced up at Leif.

"Before I start, I would like to thank you." He told the lawyer sincerely. "The bullet-proof handbag you gave me was, literally, a life saver, many times over. I would not be here today if it wasn't for that bag. It saved Archer, too." He set his face in a melancholy smile. "Thank you."

Leif nodded, not sure what to say.

"Can I ask how Archer is?" Jack inquired.

"As good as we could hope for. The wind went out of her sails when she heard you were dead. She seemed to lose interest in fighting the charges against her."

"Hopefully Bill Addison is still working on that?"

Leif nodded again. "Yeah, but they're stalling him, delaying court times and appointments: anything to make it harder for him."

Sancho silently watched the men talk. He had learned most, if not all, of Jack's story during the last couple of weeks and he knew Jack was worried about the Game Warden.

Jack frowned and opened the briefcase. He was sorry Archer had thought him dead. He was sorrier she was still in custody. He pulled the spy clock out of the briefcase and sat it on Leif's desk. The glass front was cracked. It was battered and worse for wear after so long at Jack's side in the old rucksack.

"We can use this to get her out." He told Leif.

"Are you sure? What's on it?"

"Oddly enough ..." Jack started to answer and then stopped. He looked at Sancho and back at Leif. "Are you accepting him as a client? We kind of need the whole attorney-client privilege thing right about now."

Leif looked at Sancho. "Are you the same Alfonso Robles who is on the most wanted list for shooting Jack's family and escaping from the halfway house?"

Sancho nodded silently.

"And do you want my help?"

"Yes sir."

"I'll take the case."

"I don't got no money. Sir." Sancho swallowed hard.

"I'll take care of you." Leif smiled. "And I need you to start practicing now. It's 'I don't have any money.' I'm going to need you looking and talking like a college boy if we ever end up on the stand, do you understand?"

"Yes. Sir." Sancho acknowledged trying to articulate his words more clearly.

Jack smiled at Sancho. "I told you my lawyer would take care of you." He turned his attention back to the briefcase and pulled out the hard drive and sat it on the desk.

"This is what the cops want so badly." He told Leif. "This is why everyone was chasing Sancho, uh Alfonso ..." He glanced over and Sancho grinned at him. "And it's why I left a lot of dead bodies behind me in California."

Leif raised an eyebrow. "You really did kill all those men? I mean, they said you did, but I didn't ..."

"No." Jack shook his head. "Just one. I only killed one of them." He swallowed hard. He didn't like thinking about it. He didn't like admitting he was a murderer.

"What's on it?" Leif startled Jack out of distant thoughts.

"Well that's another story. You see, the hard drive is encrypted, and without the key ..."

"Without the key, it's useless." Leif looked disappointed.

"Useless to you maybe, but it's worth a lot of money to me." The three men looked up to find the receptionist pointing a gun at them.

"Molly?" Leif stammered dumbfounded.

"Told you there was a leak in your office," Jack said out of the side of his mouth.

"But she wasn't working here then! She's Eric's fiancée, for God's sake!" Leif's eyes widened. "You came on to Eric just to get into this office? How could you!" Leif started to stand in indignation but Molly pointed the gun right at his nose.

"Money, of course. Now hand me those, like a good boy, and nobody gets hurt." The gun was on Sancho now, and he carefully picked up the clock and the hard drive. "Put them back in the briefcase and then hand it to me."

Sancho's eyes flicked nervously from the gun to the other men, but he did as he was told.

Molly grinned. "I can't believe you just walked in here like this. I have been debating for weeks if I should give up and leave." The three men watched Molly back out of the room, keeping them covered with the gun. "I think you should have realized by now, I intend to disappear, Leif. I hope you also realize that since I already have that plan in place, shooting anyone who follows me is on my list of things that are definitely doable."

As soon as Molly was out of the front door, Leif was on his feet, cussing furiously. He started to pick up the phone, but didn't know who to call, then he started to follow after Molly but Jack caught him by the arm.

"Let her go. It's not worth dying over," Jack told him.

Leif tried to reply but he was too stunned, too furious. Jack reached into his pocket and pulled out a little note and handed it to Leif. Leif frowned and looked at it. *Are you 100% sure this room is not bugged?*

Leif looked back at Jack and sadly shook his head.

FORTY-THREE

Y ou know, I hate to say I told you so ..." Jack began.

"Then don't." Leif shook his head as they walked down the sidewalk. "I can't believe it! I just can't!"

Leif turned to look at Sancho. "I am so sorry. I am so sorry we lost the evidence you needed to exonerate you."

Sancho's smile tugged at the corner of his mouth again. "Don't be, man. It all went according to plan. A little scarier than I expected, but, shit! What a rush! Woo!" Sancho whooped and took a hop step.

"Don't give us away, Sancho." Jack muttered. "We don't know if anyone is still watching."

"Right. Sorry." Sancho smoothed his tie and put his hands in his pockets.

"What plan?" Leif glared at Jack.

"The one that leads us to the bad guys," Jack answered nonchalantly. "Don't worry. We've got copies of both drives. And we already decrypted it. We know who most of the bad guys are, except those who got involved after the hard drive was stolen. Like Molly. Oh, and those hard drives she just took? They both have GPS locaters in them. Everywhere she goes is being tracked and recorded right now. We'll find her and whoever she is trying to get the drives back to. Not to mention, that clock does a good job of recording things, even when it's being carried around. If we recover it before it gets destroyed or erased, we'll get the face of anyone who looks at it as well as anything they say." Jack grinned at Leif, obviously pleased with himself.

Leif led them to a hole-in-the-wall Chinese restaurant with loud ambient noise, and they took a table in the back to talk.

"How did you know about Molly?" Leif asked after the hostess left them.

"I guessed. She was your only change in staff anywhere near the right time to leak information." Jack answered while Sancho pulled off his tie in relief.

"But she wasn't working there! She was dating Eric!"

"Who's Eric?" Sancho asked.

"My partner. He's engaged to her."

"I'd break it off if I was him," Sancho advised sagely.

"Yeah." Jack agreed. "She started dating him not too long after you took me on as a client. It's on her social networking page."

"Okay! Okay!" Leif threw his hands up. "What do we do now?"

"Now that the leak from your office is gone, I was hoping you could work on getting Archer released. Then we'll take down the Governor."

"The Governor?" Leif stared at Jack. "Are you serious?"

Jack nodded. "You told me you had been tracking some of this pretty high up."

Leif hesitated before responding. "Most of our leads dried up and went away. I guess Molly kind of explains that …"

"Well," Sancho jumped in, "we got lots of leads. And names. We gonna be namin' names and kickin' ass!"

Jack grinned at Leif. "When we decrypted the drive we found bank accounts, names, dates … Hell, we found receipts! It's like these people were running a legitimate business! They are growing and selling marijuana to half of the 'legal' marijuana dispensaries in the country, and they have dozens of law enforcement officials and officers in their pockets, not to mention a few politicians."

"And the Governor is named in there?" Leif asked again, leaning forward nervously.

"Not just Colorado's either," Sancho assured him.

"Shit!" Leif began to look shaky. "Something like this could cause us a lot of problems!"

"More than you know." Jack raised his eyebrows at Leif.

"How's that?"

"We didn't tell you how we got the encryption key, yet."

Sancho leaned forward, eyes wide. "You can't tell him that!"

"Attorney-client privilege. He won't tell." Jack reassured Sancho.

"Won't tell what?" Leif demanded.

"We broke into the Governor's office to get the encryption

key." Jack whispered across the table to Leif.

Leif's jaw dropped, but the waiter showed up to take orders before he could say anything.

Sancho looked at Jack inquiringly.

"Order away." Jack told him.

Leif was still speechless.

"He's broke, and I'm dead." Jack reminded Leif, who finally remembered to close his mouth. "We'll pay you back in publicity. You wanted the trial of a lifetime when you picked me up pro bono, remember? Well, you got it."

Leif bobbled his head, overwhelmed with everything. "I sure did." He waited for the waiter to leave and hissed. "If you broke into the Governor's office, none of that evidence will be admissible!"

"Why?" Jack asked. "It's not like we did an illegal search and seizure."

"No, it was more of a breaking and entering!" laughed Sancho. "But we didn't break anything, honest!"

Jack shook his head. "All we did was plant a key logger on all the computers in the office and wait until we got the encryption key. They never even bothered to change passwords when the drive was stolen. Hell, they were using the government computers!"

"That's still not legal!".

"Yeah. But they're never going to know who did it. At noon tomorrow, all of the information on both of those drives is going public on the internet. There won't be any way of saying who leaked it or posted it. It will just be part of the public domain, and then we can clear our names and get Archer out of jail." Jack smiled, pleased with himself. "And then we go after the sons of bitches who did all of this."

FORTY-FOUR

Jack was waiting when they released Archer. She walked out slow and dignified, wearing the uniform she had been in when they arrested her, minus the badge and weapons. She would get those back soon enough. She had never looked more beautiful, he thought as she proudly held her head high and was cleared through the security doors.

As she approached him, he felt tears start to burn in his eyes and he realized there had been times he had completely lost hope this moment would ever come. She stopped a few feet short of where he was standing with Leif, Toni, and Bill Addison. She met their eyes, but even as his own vision blurred, he could see the shine of welling tears in her eyes.

Then her arms where around him and her face was buried in his neck. He felt hot tears on his neck as she sobbed once and whispered, "I thought I would never see you again."

His own eyes blurred with tears as he held her tight. "I didn't think so either."

They stood like that for a long time before Archer whispered "I thought you were dead, you son of a bitch. You waited just long enough for me to think maybe I love you, and then you went and died on me!"

Jack sobbed a little and laughed a little, the tears streaming down his cheeks now. "I think I love you, too." He had dreamed of a moment like this for months now, not daring to hope it could ever happen.

Archer sighed raggedly, he could feel tension flowing out of her body and she whispered, "If you ever do that to me again, I'll shoot you in the dick."

Someone behind Archer cleared their throat and she reluctantly pulled herself away from him, wiping her tears away as she did. She looked at him and grinned, reaching up to wipe the tears off his cheeks as well.

"Thank you." She turned to Bill Addison and gave him a hug. "Thank you for never giving up on me. And thank you." Leif got his turn before she turned to Toni. "And you. I'd like to adopt you as my mother. Are you available?"

Toni blushed and broke into tears, the only emotions Jack had ever seen her express that weren't gruff. The two women embraced. "Anything for you, Green Cheeks!"

Jack, Archer, and Toni sat on the outdoor patio exchanging stories and catching up. Toni chained smoked and had gotten tired of going back in for more alcohol, so she had just brought out a couple bottles of wine for Archer and a bottle of whiskey for Jack and herself. Yogi, the raven, hopped back and forth along the rail, tipping its head forward and back, begging for food.

Toni had found the bird 'winged', as she described it, and hopping around the house when she had gone to check on Jack after hearing rumors he had killed Sheriff Rambo. She had brought it back with her and nursed it to health.

As the sun went down, Jack learned Toni had been a continual visitor at the jail, bringing Archer anything and everything she could possibly need. He hadn't known that Archer, like himself, no longer had any family. Well, almost. She had a couple of cousins on the East coast she barely knew.

Then they pressed him for his story. He took a deep breath and started at the beginning, with the murder of his wife and child. He told them how there had been a file on the drive showing Bogie had owed almost forty thousand dollars for 'product' he had 'distributed'. He speculated Bogie had learned of the plan to kill Jack's family and had hoped to get help and use the hard drive for blackmail.

He roughed through the parts they knew after arriving in Rainbow county, and then he told them how the shootout had really been a massacre on the part of the assassin. His eyes fell to his drink as he admitted to shooting the assassin in the back.

"You did what you had to do. No one could ask or expect anything more or less of you." Archer's hand on his shoulder was a comforting source of strength he had never imagined could exist. He smiled warmly at her and continued his story.

Toni frowned after hearing about how he had lived trying to find Sancho. "You actually ate out of dumpsters? You sick bastard! Do you have any idea the kind of stuff that gets thrown in those?"

Jack laughed. "Better than you do!" He gazed across the highway to the trailer park as he talked about living under the bridge. He mentally renewed his vow to pay back the people who had helped him. Yogi finally got bold and jumped onto the table, only to be shooed off by Toni.

As Jack told how Moe had learned Bogie had been working for the janitorial service contracted with taking care of the Governor's offices, and how he and Sancho had snuck in to plant key loggers on the computers, Archer's face became hard enough he had to stop and ask what was wrong.

She shook her head slowly. "I know …" She started but had to stop and gather her thoughts. "I know you did what you had to do, but that is such a serious felony. It could even be twisted into treason. I can't stand the thought I might lose you again because you did that."

Jack nodded quietly and looked away from Archer's gaze. Toni decided to have another cigarette.

"These people destroyed my life." Jack hesitated. "Twice. They took my wife and daughter away from me—and then they took you away from me. They tried to kill me so many times I've lost count. I take full responsibility for my actions, and if anyone ever presses charges for murdering that assassin or for breaking into the governor's office, I will face up to them and explain my side of the story. But they made me do it. They backed me into a corner and forced me to keep fighting. They made me a murderer, and once that happened…" He shook his head. "Well, that was the point of no return for me. I hate myself for admitting this, but I would do anything to stop these people, to make them pay for what they have done to me. To you. God knows what else they have done. Maybe the files from the hard drive will reveal even more murders, more lies and corruption than even what we know of. They had to be stopped." He looked at his drink again then decided to slug it down.

"I still don't get it. Why would so many people go through so much effort to sell marijuana? I mean, hell, they were selling to dispensaries, right?" Toni muttered as she crushed her smoke and started playing with the near empty pack it had come from.

"I think I get it." Archer twirled the wine in her glass in the last vestiges of the sunset, throwing light patterns across the table. "I don't know that I could have ever guessed it before, but looking back on some of the strange ways Rambo and his guys treated me, some of the things they said. I always thought it was because I was a woman, or an outsider maybe, but I think they maybe tested the waters to see if I was interested, and then shut me out when I didn't bite."

"Nice fishing analogy, Warden." Jack said drolly.

Archer wrinkled her nose at him and continued. "Rainbow County is damn near broke, in more ways than one. They were slowly dying before the recession. I bet some people got together a long time ago to figure out what to do about it and came up with this idea. It's not a bad one either, if you think it through. And if they would have tried to stay legal ..."

"What do you mean?" Jack gave in and allowed Toni to refill his glass.

"California legalized medical marijuana a long time ago, and tried to legalize it for personal use, too. It's probably only a matter of time until they do. Meanwhile, other states have approved medical use too. You know all that marijuana has to come from somewhere, and Rainbow County is a perfect place, climate-wise, to grow it. In fact, your uncle's place, your place," she nodded at Jack, "would be the perfect place to set up the world's biggest legal pot farm."

"I see where you're going with this." Toni mumbled as she spoke around the new cigarette in her mouth she was lighting. "They were planning for the future and trying to get a foothold in the market early, maybe a monopoly, even."

"But aren't there already legal pot farms?" Jack asked. "Where the legal dispensaries get their stuff legally?"

"They only *kind of* get it legally," Archer answered. "I looked into it a few years back, when I was trying to figure out who I was supposed to arrest and who I wasn't, and it gave me a headache. Once they have plants, they can grow their own and they can dispense it. But, and this is a big 'but', I couldn't get an answer on how they legally obtain a starter crop. Once they have it, not only do they have to account for every plant they grow and every ounce they sell, but there are these weird limits about how much they can have, how much they can sell. In some places they just act like a pharmacy, but in others, well, they don't get new customers per se, they take on the role of a care provider, a care-giver who administers the drug, and it's not like they can go down to the pharmacy and say 'hey, I ran out of laxatives, order me some more'. They don't really have a supplier, other than a contract with some little pot farmer somewhere who is praying he doesn't get raided by the Feds who don't recognize his marijuana as legal. And then the pot farmers' have the same problems. How do you get started? How much can you grow? They've got to account for every single plant, too. It's a damned mess."

Jack nodded as he thought out loud. "I can see how business boomed so well for them once they got started. And I think you're right. I think they were taking the long view and planning on a whole legal corporation in the future. That would explain why there is a hard drive full of every detail of everything to do with their business. Someday, when it was legal, they were going to go legit."

"Old man Gardner was a huge part of this county," Archer contemplated. "I bet there was more to his death than trying to acquire his land. I bet he knew about it or was in on it from the beginning."

Jack nodded his head. "I wondered how they would have been able to do all of that work on his land without him knowing. I mean, it's a big place and all, but a pipe into the lake? All of those small water tanks and pipes everywhere—it's not like two guys with shovels could have done all of that."

"Was there anything about him on the hard drive? Any evidence he was in on it?" Archer asked.

"I don't think so, not specifically, other than the stuff about the land for the casino being annexed. But there are a lot of files on there. People are still sorting them out, but my guess is, if he was a problem and they cut him out, they wouldn't keep any records of that."

They sat in silence for a while watching the pink clouds go by. Jack sipped his drink and finally looked over at Toni. "I've gotta ask. Why do you call her Green Cheeks?"

Toni guffawed and Archer slapped at Jack's arm. "That's none of your business!" Archer told him, blushing even in the pale pink light of the sunset.

"When I first met her ..." Toni started.

"Don't you dare!" Archer insisted, but Toni ignored her and kept talking.

"She was making an arrest on the lake and fell in. She came out looking like a soaked kitten." Toni held a bony finger up and waved it at Jack. "Don't think she didn't keep her cool though, I've never seen anyone cooler under pressure than she is. She handcuffed those idiots to that pole right over there," she pointed to the one closest to the front entrance, "and came in and asked to use my bathroom to change."

Archer rolled her eyes and then covered her face with her hand.

"I went in to make sure she was all right." Toni leaned over conspiratorially. "I was worried she was having a breakdown and didn't want those two idiots to know." She sat back up with a smirk on her face. "I caught her with her pants down, literally. And her ass was greener than a new mowed lawn." Toni snickered at the memory.

"They were new pants. I hadn't had a chance to wash them yet." Archer sighed and gave Jack a look of resignation.

Jack started to say something and thought better of it. He almost said something else, but stifled that too. He tried really hard to keep a straight face but only managed a weird smirk. Archer pursed her lips and shook her head at him.

The silence seemed to bother the raven. It took that moment to get on the table again and call out "Jack! Jack!"

All three of them exchanged glances and giggled at the bird. The alcohol was taking effect.

Jack, thankful for the segue, raised his glass and toasted the bird. "Thank you for saving my life."

Archer raised her glass to the bird and toasted, "Thank you for convincing me Jack was a harmless gimp and that it would be all right to fall for him."

Toni snorted a laugh and raised her glass to the bird. "Thank you for being here so these two could eat crow after being so sure I was wrong they would like each other!"

EPILOGUE

So how does it feel to be the proud new owner of a casino?" Archer asked as she replaced the finalized settlement papers in the envelope.

"You tell me, it's half yours."

Archer shook her head and smiled dazzlingly. "Not yet. Not until you say 'I do'."

"I do."

Archer laughed and gave Jack a quick peck on the cheek. He made her feel girlish, and she kind of liked it.

"You know, you still haven't signed the prenuptial agreement Billy sent over," she admonished him with a finger as she headed back towards the living room.

"I don't want to." Jack called after her. "If I can't share it all with you, I'd rather just give it to you anyway." He stuck the envelope in his filing cabinet and followed her.

He caught Archer staring at the photo on the mantle. It was of Jack, Jamie, and Wendy, taken in their Christmas best the week before they died. Archer, determined to make sure Jack found peace in his soul, insisted that he put it up on the mantle so that he would never feel like he had put them aside.

"I wish I could have known them," she whispered as she heard him walk up. "The millions of dollars doesn't make up for any of it."

"No, it doesn't."

She reached down and caught his hand, feeling awkward about having him because they were dead, yet selfishly glad she had him. He squeezed her hand reassuringly. They had been through this conversation before, more than once. Archer was determined to be the best wife she could without dealing any blows to his memories.

She sniffed trying not to cry again. She was the toughest, strongest woman he had ever met, but when it came to him and his now-dead wife and daughter, she cried at the drop of a hat. It gave him all the more reason to love her.

He gently pulled on her arm until she followed him outside. Leading her to a bench, he sat her down and joined her with his arm around her. They sat quietly looking out at the lake and listening to the grebes squawk until Yogi flew down and landed at their feet. The raven strutted back and forth in front of them calling Jack's name and making strange crackling sounds.

"Do you regret it?" She asked him.

He raised an eyebrow at her.

"Staying in Rainbow County, after all that happened here," she explained.

"It's where you are, and where you are is where I want to be. Besides, you're a Warden through and through, I couldn't have asked you to give that up. I wouldn't have wanted to." He gave her a quick kiss on the cheek and continued. "We couldn't come here and look at the lake. We couldn't go to Toni's and eat shit on a shingle."

"But you won the lawsuit, and now you're a highfalutin millionaire owner of a casino."

"You know I don't …"

"I know." And she did. He resented the idea that the settlement could make up for his losses. In spite of the fact the casino had been illegally built on his uncle's land, he still didn't feel like it should be his. A lot of the local people had put a lot into it, legally. They shouldn't have lost out the way they had.

"And …?" she added when nothing else was forthcoming from him.

"And what?"

"And you wouldn't have been here in Rainbow County helping so many pick up the pieces of their lives after the real estate bubble popped. Helping them find homes, jobs, food …"

Jack laughed. "I get it! I get it!"

"Well, do you regret it?"

He hesitated for a moment. "A little, I guess. Life would have been a lot simpler if I could have just swept you off your feet and gone to hide in Antarctica."

"You'd have been bored."

"Maybe."

"And it would have been cold there. Why Antarctica?"

Jack laughed. They both became instant celebrities when their story had hit the news. There was nowhere they could have gone that they wouldn't have been recognized and they knew it.

"So we would have an excuse to snuggle all the time." He grinned at her and she snuggled closer.

"I don't need an excuse."

The waves lapped at the shoreline rhythmically as they enjoyed each other's company. The breeze from the water smelled slightly fishy, but it was refreshingly cool.

Archer sat up and looked Jack in the eyes. "Have you decided yet?"

He shook his head. "It's a stressful decision. I already have so many irons in the fire with the …"

"Yeah, yeah," she interrupted him, "we all know you are Rainbow County's generous benefactor. Why not make it official? You're already doing the job, you might as well take the position and wear the name tag."

"I don't know. County Commissioner sounds so intimidating."

"Well, you are an intimidating man, when you want to be."

He laughed. They both knew that wasn't true. "I guess I'm worried about the pressure and the stress."

"You can handle the pressure," she ran a fingertip up his forearm suggestively, "and I can help with the stress …"

He kissed her on the forehead, and they went back to watching the waves for a while.

"You know what I need?" Jack asked her.

"A swift kick in the ass?"

"That too, but I was thinking I could really go for another glass of our house wine."

"Mmmm!" Archer sat up and smiled at the idea. Miguel's son had turned out to be an excellent winemaker.

AUTHOR'S NOTE

Rainbow County is a fictional amalgamation of various areas in Northern California and really should not be considered any place in particular, although some areas were based on actual places. There are no Loquait Indians, there is no Loquait Rancheria. I chose to fictionalize rather than risk misrepresenting actual people.

Yes, some corvids can talk. Or at least mimic like a parrot. Terry the talking raven is the most famous current example, and videos of him can be found on the internet easily.

Yes, a council of crows really exists. It is a myth-like old wives' tale, and no one can say what is actually occurring in the 'council', but it has been reported many times by many witness. I confidently claim they exist, as I have witnessed one. My personal experience is recounted on my website at http://samknight.com/?p=344 in the du jour Brain Know? section, under Council of Crows.

I apologize if anyone was offended by Toni's reaction to, and opinion of the Rainbow County Festival, it too is a fictional amalgamation of actual festivals, as is her opinion.

Game Warden Archer Durante is a completely fictional representation of the fine men and women who truly are Game Wardens. I apologize for anything about her character that would reflect poorly upon the Wardens. Theirs is a truly remarkable and difficult labor of love.

Overworked and underpaid, the California Game Wardens are so much more than the person who checks your fishing license. There are only around 200 Game Wardens for the entire state of California, less than any other state per capita, responsible for the policing of all of California, including the coasts and waterways. According to the California Department of Fish and Game website, approximately 2 million fishing licenses are issued each year. That is one Warden for every 10,000 fishermen. That seems like maybe a reasonable number. Maybe. If each Warden checked 25 fishermen every day to see if everything was in order, they would manage to check almost 2 million people. That's seems like a reasonable way to look at it, bureaucratically. Until you realize that was just fishing licenses obtained legally. How many fishermen didn't bother to get a license, let alone how many of those of those 2 million are not fishing in a legally prescribed manner?

Well, you may say to yourself, there aren't that many people who fish illegally. 200 Wardens can handle that. Sure. Maybe. If that was all they did. The job responsibilities of the California Game Warden are mind bending, and being added to every year. Not only are they responsible for policing the legal hunting and fishing of wildlife, they also deal with pot farmers/drug runners, illegal border crossing/homeland security, smuggling, pollution, destruction of lands, search and rescue, and on and on. Not to mention little things like commercial fishing.

California Fish and Game issues over 150 types of licenses. The California Game Warden's job is nothing like what you may have thought when you had your hunting or fishing license checked. It can be one of the most dangerous and harrowing jobs out there, and they are severely under-budgeted and underpaid. The average Warden is paid about 60% (sometimes less) than other law enforcement officers. For more information, most of it eye-opening and unbelievable, I recommend checking out the following web site of the California Fish and Game Wardens Association. (It wouldn't hurt to support them, should you so feel moved to do so) www.californiafishandgamewardens.com

Also, a quick search for the California Fish and Game Warden Expose will find a 2007 report on the Wardens that is astonishing in not only what it reports, but in that it was largely ignored.

A documentary film entitled *Endangered Species: California Fish and Game Wardens* by James Swan is a good quick summation of the Wardens and what they are facing.

And finally, a retired Warden by the name of Terry Hodges has written four books of true stories of the Game Wardens. These stories, being true, are entertaining, enlightening, and astonishing. You can find him at: www.gamewarden.net

ABOUT THE AUTHOR

Photo by Stacey Vowel

A Colorado native, Sam Knight spent ten years in California's wine country before returning to the Rockies. When asked if he misses California he gets a wistful look in his eyes and replies he misses the green mountains in the winter, but he is glad to be back home.

Sam has written two novels and is currently at work on two more. He has three children's books to his credit, which he illustrated as well as wrote, and he has had stories published in half a dozen anthologies and a few magazines, not to mention websites.

He has appeared on many panels, both as participant and moderator, on a wide variety of subjects at his local Colorado Conventions. Sam has recently been branching out to other states, including Nebraska, New Mexico and Utah. Having been a speaking guest at both Denver Comic Con and Salt Lake City Comic Con, he claims to have faced his fears of speaking in public, and won.

Currently, Sam is also on the E-book Team at WordFire Press, making sure we all get access to the back catalogs of greats like Kevin J. Anderson and Frank Herbert.

His grandfather and mother are both readers and Sam says his own passion started when he pressed his grandfather to find out what was so interesting. His grandfather handed him a book and Sam has been an avid reader ever since. He claims to have finished the Hobbit and the Lord of the Rings trilogy in fourth grade and says he can still remember the look, feel, and smell of some of those early books. (He has been spotted sniffing books as he ruffles the pages, and he refuses to buy an e-reader.)

When asked why he would want to become a writer, Sam recounts a time when he was in fifth grade. Illness stuck him in bed for two weeks with only books for companions. (This was a bit before video game phone implants were in common use.) He burned through the Xanth trilogy (back before it expanded into thirty some books), the Riddle of Stars trilogy, a couple of John Carter of Mars books, and several Pip and Flinx novels, relishing the moments when he would become so engrossed he would forget the ills of the physical. A thought floated through his mind at that time, about being able to return the favor to the authors who were providing so much to him. That thought never left, and now he sincerely hopes anyone picking up one his stories can find something they were looking for.

While doing research for a Western novel, Sam was not surprised to find out that, once upon a time, half of his family had been on the wrong side of the law. It stands to reason that when your great-great-grandfather was a marshal in Cripple Creek, Colorado, someone in the family had to be a horse thief. Sam was, however, surprised to find the family name had originally been McKnight and that the thieves had taken the 'Mc' part of the name with them. (Or the lawmen let them have it to distance themselves from that side of the family.) Having served a stint *working* in a correctional facility, he has wondered if being a lawman runs in the blood. His great grandfather upheld the law in Mooreland, OK, as well as Springfield and Florence CO, among other places, with his grandfather occasionally deputized to assist.

Drop in and see what he is up to at SamKnight.com. If you have something you want to say, leave a comment, or contact him at Sam@SamKnight.com.

ALSO BY SAM KNIGHT

In the light of day, it is easy to chalk it all up to nightmares, to say it doesn't exist, it wasn't real. But what do you do when the nightmares begin to happen while you are awake?

What if you don't believe in auras, but now you can see them? What if you don't believe in ghosts and demons, but now they have become a part of your world?

How long can you pretend it's not real? Until you see a ghost? Until something attacks you in your sleep?

How about when it takes your wife?

Made in the USA
San Bernardino, CA
15 January 2014